WHISPERS THE BLOOD

DANIELLE RENINO

Cover design by ebooklaunch.com

ISBN: 979-8-9865241-0-8 (paperback); 979-8-9865241-1-5 (ebook)

For you

CONTENTS

BEFORE

The first time I died, I was too young to remember it. According to my brother, Victor, it happened gently. A muted thud, a surge of red across the whites of my eyes, and I was gone. He split me from navel to clavicle and sifted through the space between my ribs until he found a way to bring me back again. To him, my death is poetry.

"I wrapped my hand around your heart, Silvie," he reminds me every chance he gets. "I held it as it went still inside your chest. No one will ever get closer to you than that."

It's equal parts a declaration of love and a threat. Typical of Victor. He's all sharp edges and intense emotion. I should consider myself lucky that he's such a talented surgeon, that he cared enough to save me, but the thought of my insides unspooling and him wading through the wreckage keeps me up at night.

I wish I could say that dying has gotten easier, but I'll never get used to it.

This time, I regain consciousness with my teeth clenched and a low buzz droning in my ears. My body lies splayed on a table, the metal cold against my skin. I keep my eyes shut tight and do my best to ignore how my lungs hang limp inside my chest, even though they burn, even though there's a fuzziness in my head that makes it difficult to concentrate on anything else.

Victor has a list of non-negotiables when it comes to resurrection. Don't open your eyes too soon, don't take a breath until you absolutely need to, and never think about where you go when you're gone. That's a sure way to lose your mind.

I used to keep the non-negotiables written on my palm in the hope that having the words so close would make the process easier somehow. It never did. I haven't died in a few months, but this hurt is familiar and all consuming. It's almost enough to drown out the other, more unsettling parts of the revival process.

The fly inside my mouth, for example.

It skitters along the back of my throat and settles on my tongue, tasting like vinegar. Same as last time. My ears pop and there's a wet sound, like someone shucking an oyster. Same as last time. The only thing that's not the same is how I got here. I had wanted to test something, which, judging by my current spot on the table, didn't go as planned. But Nora says it's important for me to push the boundaries with Victor whenever possible.

"Won't he get mad at me?" I asked one afternoon while we sat on the back porch, Nora's white coat freckled with blood. She'd only been helping Victor with his latest project for about a month, but she draped her legs over mine like we were old friends. While I didn't hate the closeness, I wasn't exactly sure how to handle it either, partially because being near Nora triggered a needle-like pain in my temple, and partially because I'd never really been around anyone aside from Victor—yet alone someone my own age. I sat with my spine rigid, worried that if I so much as breathed the wrong way, she'd pull back.

"Nora," I said, my voice barely above a whisper, "I don't want to make him mad."

She smirked. "That's kind of the point of pushing boundaries, Sil, to see how far you can take things before the other person snaps."

I've taken things too far this time. Usually, I would focus on the electric whirl of the specimen fridge or the lazy click of the ceiling fan as I drift back to life, but all I can hear is Victor. Victor wheeling over the cart, Victor cursing under his breath, Victor slamming his fist down against the table.

"Why do you keep doing this to me, Silvie?" His fingers sweep a lock of hair back from my cheek and trace a line to my jaw. Plastic gloves make his touch feel alien, and I shudder as his hand reaches my throat. He doesn't do anything at first, and I think that maybe he's in a forgiving mood, but then he presses down. Hard. Tears prick the corners of my eyes and my lungs hitch, but he clamps his free hand over my mouth.

"Don't you dare take a breath," he hisses. "It's not time yet."

We stay like this for a long while. My eyes shut tight, Victor's hand clamped over my mouth, and the fly frenzying against my gums. My lungs burn, and the pressure in my chest is almost unbearable. Finally, when it's clear that I'm not going to breathe, he pulls away and I can hear him laying out the instruments: needle, tourniquet, little glass vial. The unholy trinity. Dying isn't the worst part. The worst part is coming back... and everything that happens after. The fly trills against my teeth as if to agree.

According to Victor, the fly is my mind's way of dealing with the trauma, an imaginary courier whose sole purpose is to bring me back to the land of the living. It tastes real though. Sour. Sickening. I'm not sure how much longer I can take it.

"Okay, let's start the process," Victor says, and I relax a little. If he hasn't brought it up by now, then he doesn't know how I died this time. He's just pissed that he had to bring me back again.

I lift my eyelids, and the room slips into focus. It's long and rectangular; its gray walls lined with metal shelves which are stocked with various medical instruments. Bone saws, sample tubes, and scalpels are all meticulously labeled and arranged. Cuts of light tumble in through a small window to the left of the table, and my hand drifts toward it, but Victor catches me by the wrist. I stare up at him. His mouth is set in a hard line, his green eyes flat and emotionless. Something is very wrong. His dark hair, which he usually keeps perfectly slicked back, hangs in greasy tendrils over his forehead, and his shirt is wrinkled. He only neglects his appearance when he's angry.

"I know what you did." His fingers dig in deeper, and I wince. "Did you think I was fucking around when I said that you can't skip the pills?"

My pills are small and square, the color of snow. Victor usually watches me take them. He makes sure that I drink a whole glass of water and really swallow them, no hiding them beneath my tongue, but he's been distracted lately. Part of me has always wondered if the pills are necessary, so I figured I would test it. Clearly, it was a mistake. Clearly, without them I'll die.

"Lesson learned," I want to tell him. "It won't happen again."

But I can't open my mouth yet, so I lie motionless as he glares down at me. He grabs my jaw roughly and jerks my head to the side so that I face the cart next to the table. It takes me a moment to settle on what sits there, but a little thrill goes through me when I do. My pillow torn open. My stash of medication bleeding out in a spill of dirty white.

I'm starting to get a taste for small acts of rebellion. I crave them in ways that I never used to before. The medication in my pillowcase. The annotations in my paperback books. Lists of things that Victor would balk at if he ever read. My conversations with Nora. I shudder to think of what he'd do if he knew how much time we spend together—or the things she tells me.

There's an itch beneath my skin, a hum, a pull. These things I've started to do, these things that are uncharacteristic of me, actually make me feel more like myself. But how do I tell my brother that when I know how he'd react?

I wonder if it's normal to love someone and still be so afraid of them.

"This isn't like you," Victor says, releasing me. "You're usually well behaved."

He moves clinically through the rest of the resurrection process. My blood warms, and I lift my hand in front of my face, the bruised tips of my fingers regaining some of their normal color. The burning in my lungs is almost unbearable, but I don't dare take a breath until he tells me to—even though he should have given me the okay by now.

I stare up at him pleadingly and he stares back, his eyes hollow disks. "You can't do this anymore. You need to be good."

My body goes slack as I realize that this is my punishment for stashing the pills. He's going to keep me like this until I pass out, or worse, die again.

Or you could take a breath without his permission. I reject the idea as soon as it crosses my mind, but my lips part a fraction of an inch as there's a sudden, stabbing pain in my temple—same as when Nora's around. *Take a breath. It's your body.*

True, but it's only mine because of Victor. And he's right, I can't keep doing this.

Even though I want to.

Oh dear, I really want to.

"I hate this as much as you do." Victor's eyes soften as he leans in and runs a gloved finger along the side of my cheek. His touch lingers there for a few moments, achingly gentle. He eases me into a sitting position and pulls me against his chest, his heartbeat steady as a metronome. Even though my insides are screaming, there's comfort in the way he holds me. It reminds me that he cares.

"You're the most important thing in my life," he whispers, petting my hair. "I can't lose you."

Guilt churns my insides. Because he loves me. He loves me, and he keeps me alive, and it's my own fault that I died this time. Still, as his hand clamps down on the back of my neck, I can't stop thinking about the pull beneath my skin, the thoughts that don't feel like mine, and all the ways that I've been changing. I'm going to chase down this ache. I'll slice it out, I'll set it free. And the fact that he doesn't know makes it that much more dangerous, that much more enticing. He hasn't seen me misbehave yet.

Victor grips me a little too tightly, but I refuse to flinch.

"Okay, Silvie," he says. "Go ahead and take a breath."

1

I press my palm against the scar on my chest, the deep purple mirroring the bruised skin of a plum. I always wear dresses with low collars so that it has room to breathe.

Which is what you should do right now, I remind myself. *Breathe.*

I can't let Nora see how anxious I am, or she won't help me sneak out again and I'll never cross another item off my list.

It's more than a list. It's my obsession. Ten things meant to distract from the terror of my anatomy, the parts of myself that I can't explain. The blood that's darker than black one day and bright as a crime scene the next. The wine-colored liquid that sometimes leaks from my nose and dries to the consistency of a soft-boiled egg. Whether they're side effects from my long string of resurrections or something else entirely, I can't be sure, but they hold a special kind of horror all the same.

"Let me guess, brother dearest found out that you're not where you're supposed to be and he's losing his shit." Nora pulls her trowel from the dirt and stands, brushing off the knees of her jeans. Damp, dark earth clings to the fabric, layered over spilled paint, turpentine, and a bloodstain the size of a thimble. She won't admit that it's a bloodstain, but I can tell. Nora always carries a switchblade in her pocket, and she's known for being twitchy.

I press my palm deeper into my scar. It's my anchor, the only thing that keeps me level when the ocean in my mind begins to swell. My other hand stays clamped around her cell phone.

"Silvie," Nora says when I fail to answer. "You look like you're gonna puke. That was Victor, wasn't it?"

I shake my head and hand her the phone. "It wasn't anyone. I can't get it to turn on."

"I'm not surprised. Stupid thing's been acting up since we entered the woods."

The late November wind shrieks through the pines, and Nora pulls her scarf up over her nose. The only things that are visible are her wide eyes and a lock of golden hair poking out from under her knit hat.

Nora and I look so much alike we could be sisters. We have the same curly hair and gray eyes. We could be identical twins if it wasn't for the way she keeps her hair cropped short and always wears bright colored turtlenecks.

She's a sunrise masquerading as a teenage girl.

I'm a storm cloud.

Nora's been acting as Victor's pseudo lab assistant for over a year now, but I still can't figure out why he hired her. She cares more about painting than lab work, and the tension between them is palpable. It's the sharp scent of an oncoming storm—the electricity in the air before a lightning strike. Victor's brow creases every time I mention Nora. Probably because she's glued to my side when she isn't helping him with his project... and because she agreed to help me get out of the house.

The last time Nora tried to sneak me out we barely made it to a drive thru three streets over before Victor called demanding that she return me. This time we made it three states. From there, we took four side roads and hiked for a little over a mile to reach the backyard of an abandoned Victorian mansion. The building's property line only stretches back a few acres and includes the plot of grass we're standing on and an overgrown cluster of apple trees in the far corner. It's a large yard, but compared to the monstrosity in front of us, it's a postage stamp.

My scalp prickles as I look up at the Victorian. The right side has almost completely caved in, and there's a gaping hole in the roof, a mess of charred boards and fragments of shingles kicked up around it. A cracked spine of a building. Massive chunks of paint flake off in the wind, and loose bits drift down like wisps of overcooked skin to where we stand. Pieces keep getting caught in my hair, and I pick them out using the tips of my fingers, imagining that they're blow flies or silverfish. Somehow that makes it less disturbing.

Nora's been talking about the Victorian for weeks, but she didn't mention digging until we pulled up to the mouth of the hiking trail. Half a dozen holes dot the left side of the yard. Several hours' worth of shallow graves, and still nothing. No hidden treasure. No explanation.

"Let me try your phone again. It's not like Victor to go so long without calling." I hold out my hand, but she shakes her head.

"My phone's dead. Besides, I'm not going to willingly put you in contact with that psychopath." She spits out the last word and my face stings as if she's slapped me.

"What do I need to say to convince you that he's not a bad person?" I pull my hand back and grab the handle of my shovel, a massive digger with a splintering wooden handle.

"It's not what *you* need to say, it's what *he* needs to do." She prods at the dirt with the heel of her boot. "He needs to stop being such an abusive dick."

"He's not abusive." It's the same argument, different script.

We've been fighting about my home life for months, but it's gotten worse over the last few weeks—built up like a hunk of phlegm in the back of my throat, or the nose drippings that Victor insists are a natural part of my condition. Thick and sick, and impossible to breathe through.

"He put a padlock on your bedroom door, Silvie."

I flinch. "Yeah, but that's not... he watched me die..." My fingers trace the outline of my surgical scar.

"You had a near death experience. It's not the same thing. Besides it was like, twelve years ago. He needs to get over it."

Except the last time I died was in August. Nora doesn't know the extent of my unique biology or how many times Victor has brought me back from the dead. We're not supposed to keep secrets from each other, but it would sicken her to know how much my body has been through, and I can't stand the thought of her looking at me differently or treating me like I'm damaged. Not to mention what she would say about Victor. The stress of keeping the secret is nothing compared to the stress of having to explain.

"It's been eight years," I say, the truth sitting like a stone at the back of my throat. "And it's hard for him. He sacrificed his twenties to take care of me." Our thirteen-year age difference is only one of the reasons why Victor and I don't exactly connect.

"Whatever. You freak out the way you did last time, and it's back to brother dearest and that glorified cell you call a room."

I nod even though I'm not sure how to admit that I'm already regretting my decision to leave home—even if it's only for a few hours. Victor's not going to be happy when I get back, and a messed-up part of me misses the safety of my routine.

Awake at seven in the morning, in bed by ten. Math and science lessons at the dining room table. Blood tests every three weeks to make sure that I'm getting better—or at the very least not getting worse.

"Shouldn't we go to a doctor for this?" I asked Victor about two years ago, the first time he tightened the tourniquet around my arm.

"I am a doctor."

"You're a surgeon."

His upper lip twitched. "Semantics."

My body stiffened as I waited for him to retaliate, but he just gave the tourniquet a final tug and set to work prepping the needle. "I brought you back from the dead, and you don't think I'm qualified to draw a few vials of blood? Do you know how ridiculous that sounds?"

"I didn't mean—"

"We'll talk about it later. Now make a fist."

I balled my fingers into my palm. He sunk the needle in.

End of discussion.

Until Nora. Until the headaches, and the hum beneath my skin. There's still a dull pulsing in my temple when I'm around her, but most of the time it's soft enough to ignore. I'm more concerned about the pressure that's been building behind my ears since we got to the Victorian. They need to pop in the worst way, and there's a fullness at the front of my skull that's blistering on the verge of a migraine.

Nora bends to adjust her duffel bag, which lays on its side in the yellowed grass, what looks like an oversized stuffed animal bulging at its center. She nudges it away from the edge of a hole and onto a more level patch of land.

"Promise that you don't have a body in that thing." I nod toward the duffel. No matter how many times I ask, she won't tell me what's inside. Goosebumps break out along my arms every time I look at it, and I half expect something to rip from the depths of the nylon. "I draw the line at helping you cover up a murder."

"You think I'm capable of killing someone? Really?" I can't tell if she's amused or annoyed.

"Well, you're not denying it..." My mind wanders to the bloodstain on her pants, and the switchblade in her pocket.

"No body, I swear."

"Okay, but how much longer do we need to dig? I feel like an undertaker." There's dirt smeared across the front of my dress and stuck under my fingernails.

"Until we find what we're looking for."

"I don't know what we're looking for," I remind her, propping myself up against the handle of my shovel. At five-foot-one, I'm barely a head taller than the thing. Nora insisted that I use the larger shovel, that the wide blade makes it easier to break through the top layer of soil, but I still find myself eyeing her trowel with envy.

"You will when you see it. Just promise that you won't scream."

I release the shovel so that it falls to the ground with a thump. "Why would I scream?"

She laughs. "Come on, I know how you are. And in case you forgot, this little field trip was your idea, so perk up."

"I wanted to cross a few items off my list, not dig holes for half the day. I don't understand why you won't tell me what we're looking for."

"Because I can't. Once we find it, I have a small errand to run, and then we can do whatever you want to. Okay?"

"Sure." I ignore the sharp pains that grip my stomach, the worry that makes it difficult to breathe.

Nora drops her trowel at the base of the hole and wraps an arm around my shoulder. "Look, I appreciate you coming out here with me. I couldn't do this alone, and you're the only one I could ask to help me dig. After all, we're sisters. Closer than sisters."

She yanks off her glove and raises her palm in front of my face, showing off the white scar that runs down its center. It's the product of fifteen minutes spent carving at ourselves with the dull end of a paper clip, finished off with a pocketknife and a promise. At least that's what Nora claims—I don't remember it happening. Our twin wounds are the only proof.

When it comes to my friendship with Nora, there are a lot of gaps in my memory. Sometimes she'll reference things we've done together—movies we watched, jokes we made—and it's like there's a blank space where the moment should be. More likely than not, it's a side effect of my resurrections, but I haven't gotten up the courage to ask Victor about it. Maybe I don't want to know the answer.

I turn and press my scarred palm to Nora's.

"A year down, forever to go," I say, even though it feels like I've known her all my life.

"Forever to go," she echoes, lacing her fingers through mine.

The moment our hands knot together, there's a loud pop behind my ears and my body spasms. My vision blurs as two more pops, like fireworks, sound off before fizzling to white noise. I stumble, lightheaded.

Nora grabs me under the arms, holding me steady.

I look up to find her head tilted to the side. She seems more fascinated than concerned. I can't tell if she's entertained by my quirks or only keeps me around so that she'll have a front row seat when I finally self-destruct.

"I'm fine." The pressure drains and the fizzle sputters out. "It was just a headache or something."

I step back, but she leans in, her nose inches from mine. Up close, she looks even more like me and when she speaks there's a hunger in her words that chills me to my core. "We don't keep secrets from each other, Silvie. Tell me what you saw."

"I didn't see anything," I insist, my heart hammering against my ribs. "My ears popped, that's all."

An expression that I can't quite read flashes across her eyes, and she backs off immediately. "Oh, well I'm glad you're okay."

The sudden shift in her tone is enough to give me whiplash.

I'm not sure if I am okay, but I don't want to risk setting her off again. While the initial sound has receded, there's still a slight whine inside my head—like a tuning fork set to a high frequency. Staring at the Victorian seems to make it worse, so I turn to face the tree line. The sun melts through the pines, sticky shades of gold falling across the holes we've dug. It's later than I thought, and I watch as the gold of the sunset gives way to red. The sky gushes color like an open wound.

"That red is way too bloody," I say, barely able to hear myself over the tuning fork inside my head.

"You're way too morbid," Nora replies lightly. "It's gorgeous. Like you."

"You're only saying that because we look alike."

"You seriously think I'm that vain?" She reaches into her coat pocket and pulls out a small sketchbook. She plucks a piece of charcoal from behind her ear and flips to a random page.

"Come on, pose for me," she says with a dramatic flick of the wrist. "Look off into the sunset."

"Shouldn't you be digging?" I cross my arms, sticking my hands into the crooks of my armpits. "This was your idea."

"No, this was *your* idea, remember? You're the one who wanted to get out of the house." The charcoal glides over the paper in fluid, exaggerated sweeps. Nora's hand goes and goes and goes. She flits around me like an insect, turning her sketchbook to the left and to the right while the sunset casts shadows across her face and dyes her clothes crimson. Then she pauses to sweep a strand of my hair behind my ear.

"Stop." I swat her hand away. "Since when do you sketch?"

"Concept drawings are the bones of any good painting." The charcoal continues to glide over the page, but her eyes remain focused on me.

"You're not even drawing anything, let me see." I reach for

the sketchbook, but she extends her arm over one of the holes, and lets it go. It hits the ground with a dull thud.

"Whoops," she says with a shrug.

"Why would you—" The whine inside my head explodes into a higher pitch so loud, so all-consuming that it knocks the air out of my lungs. Spots dance in front of my eyes, and my knees go weak, but I force myself to stay upright. I refuse to collapse. Not here. Not in front of Nora.

"Sil, are you okay?" She reaches for me, but the edge of my vision sparks and her voice blends with the screeching inside my head. My body twists. My mind twists with it. Toward the Victorian.

Nora's fingers graze the back of my neck, and it feels like a scream. I recoil, locking eyes with the uppermost row of windows. Electricity pulses through me and I run to the building, on some awakened instinct.

All I can see is the Victorian.

All I can hear is what's inside my head.

The pull is back beneath my skin, stronger than anything I've felt before, and I let it guide me as the whine is overtaken by radio static. The static bounces around between my ears, like someone is flipping from station to station, and even though Nora keeps calling for me, I can't make out what she's saying. I don't want to. My feet keep moving. Closer and closer, around the edge of the building and across the yard until I'm directly in front of the Victorian.

Up close it's less revolting. There's a sadness in it that I didn't recognize before, and I reach my arms out, as if I could hold it up, as if I could be the one to save it.

The static bursts sending a flood of words through me. *Blood. Mother. Fire. Scar. Fire. Fire. FIRE.* Again and again, faster and faster, louder and louder. A merry-go-round of noise. Words with color and texture. Words with hands and teeth.

They tear into me, and I shrink against them as the Victorian looms larger and larger, the sky dripping red.

I throw my head back, aching to howl, to hiss, to shriek. There's so much energy coursing through my body that I don't know what to do with it all. The words come faster, the sky grows redder, and at my core, I know this isn't me. In this moment, I'm more than myself. The realization sends a shudder through me, and I surrender to the pull, the electricity, allowing it to swallow me whole.

Then the static cuts to silence and I'm left gasping for air. There's empty space where the words used to be. Nothing but empty space and the Victorian. Nora catches up to me and I press my hand against my scar. I try keep myself anchored, but it's so quiet now. So quiet inside my head.

I'm not complete. Not anymore.

"What the hell was that?" Nora asks, her eyes wide.

The Victorian was calling me, and I was trying to answer. My fingers drag along the edges of my scar. "Do you ever feel like you're not yourself?"

She looks at me for a long time, her brow furrowed. "In what way?"

"Sometimes when I think things, it doesn't feel like I'm the one doing the thinking. That's what happened... there were thoughts, but they weren't mine."

"What kind of thoughts?" she asks and my cheeks burn. I hate the way she's looking at me, like I'm broken.

"The word fire over and over again."

She opens and closes her mouth a few times, then presses her own hand against her chest, and we stand side by side, mirror images of one another.

"Did you cut yourself while you were digging?" she asks, and the question is so strange that I almost laugh.

I shake my head. "No, why?"

She lowers her hand and frowns slightly. "Nothing. Are you feeling better now at least?"

"I'm fine, but there's something wrong with this place."

Something splinters behind her eyes. She looks sad and determined at the same time, a cocktail of emotions twisting across her face. She drops her duffel bag in front of the door and grabs me by the shoulder—like she's searching for a lifeline. "You're right, there is something wrong with this place. It's on the verge of collapse. Which is why we're going to stay out here just long enough to finish digging, and then get the hell away from this house and not look back."

"It's almost dark, how much longer do you expect us to—" Suddenly, I'm struck by how late it is, and how far we are from home. The fire in my head snuffs out, the strangeness of what just happened dulls. All I can think about is Victor. He's probably already waiting for me in the living room with his arms crossed and his journal laid out on the coffee table, the well-worn pages open to the entry about the first time I died. He'll read it out loud when I get home as a reprimand. A warning.

My thoughts are a swirling undertow. Dark, and deep, and dangerous. I open my mouth but all that comes out is series of shallow gasps. I can't get air into my lungs.

One mile back to the car. Four hours back to the house. Victor sitting at home, hands clasped tightly in his lap. The clock on the living room wall. The padlock on my bedroom door. Victor. Nora's phone isn't working. But if I can get to... if I can contact... and then... and then...

Nora rubs small circles down my back and stifles a sigh.

"Hey, it's okay. Breathe," she says. "Take a deep breath, everything's okay."

It's our ritual for when things get to be too much for me, and normally it would be enough to drain the tension and stop my body from shaking. But not this time. Nothing will erase the fact that it's her fault we're here in the first place.

"Breathe," she repeats, and the wind howls through the pines.

The cold plunges me deeper into the riptide. *If I gasp for air, if I try to breathe, my lungs will fill with salt water. And then, and then—*

"Silvie." Nora's hand clamps down on my wrist. "Breathe."

The wind lets out another shriek and she digs her nails in, causing me to wince. Her grip is so much like Victor's. It's enough to jolt me from the riptide, and I pry her fingers from my skin.

My breathing steadies. "I'm sorry. We've just been away from home too long. I got upset thinking about what Victor's going to do when we get back."

"There's a difference between being upset and being *upset* though, Sil." Nora pulls off her hat and shakes out her hair, before stuffing it into her jacket pocket. "It's my own fault. I know how you are. You've got enough to deal with at home. You don't need me dragging you all over creation, not with what brother dearest puts you through."

"Victor doesn't..." I turn toward the forest, the pine needles shining green against the dripping sky. The red melts to a deep, blush coated orange. "He loves me."

"He sure has a funny way of showing it."

Ground up citrus bleeds through the hemlocks, pulpy and dangerous, as the last traces of static filter through my ears... like it was never there to begin with. Like the electricity beneath my skin was never there. Like the thoughts weren't either and I'm slowly losing my mind. "I think there's something wrong with me."

Nora's expression softens and she pulls me in for a quick hug. "You're fine." She squeezes once before releasing me and turning to face the front door, a large oak thing with an oversized brass knob. "What do you say we go inside?"

"Inside?" My pulse radiates through my forehead and my

body burns despite the chill in the air. "What happened to getting out of here and not looking back?"

"I didn't realize how late it was. We can't hike back in the dark."

"Victor will literally kill me if I don't make it home tonight."

The wind screams again as if to agree.

"He's already going to kill you for sneaking out with me, what's a few more hours? You ran full force across the yard and up these steps, and you're really telling me you don't want to know what's inside?"

I hate to admit it, but she's right. The pull may have softened, but I still find myself drawn to the building. I reach out and turn the knob so that the door swings open. A jaw, unhinged.

Nora slips her hand into mine, and we step over the threshold together, our fingers laced.

Early evening bruises the walls on either side of the door and a spiral staircase sits directly in front of us, dark red carpet running up each step. Hallways stretch back behind the staircase and extend on either side of the main door, cavernous and aching. The far ends are cloaked in velvety darkness with shades of blue, and purple, and burgundy straining through the black.

My body goes rigid.

I recognize it. I recognize the interior.

2

The inside of the Victorian is ripped straight from my nightmares. Last night I was trapped in an endless web of hallways, and stairways, and windowless rooms, images that built to a crescendo inside my head. Pulses of color, of cold, of this place—this exact place. Even the air has the same burnt smell, something reminiscent of charred meat.

Nora pulls her hand from mine. "Wow, it hasn't changed at all."

"You've been here before?" I thought that she had read about it somewhere, found an obscure article about buried treasure or a buried body, and became obsessed.

"Of course," she says, like it's the most obvious thing in the world. "How else would I know about the thing in the yard? I'm the one who buried it."

A chill runs down my spine. "Shouldn't you know *where* you buried it then? Shouldn't we have found it right away? How come I recognize this place? Does that mean I've been here too?"

Nora's expression darkens, and she closes the door behind

us, effectively shutting out the wind and fading light. "What do you mean you recognize it?"

"It looks like..." It doesn't *look* like anything. It *is* my nightmare in harsh living color. I pinch my wrist, half convinced that I'm asleep, that this whole thing is some sort of panic induced hallucination. But I don't wake up, and the room remains the same.

My eyes dart around the foyer, and I take inventory of all the things that are the same. The same dark rooms. The same high ceilings. The same luxurious carpeting and brass picture frames on the walls... but there's no way I could have been here before. There's no way I could know what it looks like. I barely left my house before I met Nora, and this place is hours away—Victor would never take me this far from home.

"What does it look like?" Nora asks, watching me expectantly.

My eyes continue to dart around the entryway, and it snaps into place all at once. My heartbeat slows, and relief floods over me. I'm so happy I could cry.

"It reminds me of the painting you gave me for my birthday. I had a nightmare about it, set in a house like this one."

She frowns slightly, but her voice remains light and teasing. "Nice to know my art made an impression."

"You have to admit that your stuff is creepy."

Nora's paintings are still frames from fever dreams. Swing sets engulfed in flames, a children's choir floating over a snowy hill. Bright, acidic colors. The jewel tones swirling through the darkness here may be off palette, but the subject matter is on par with some of her more disturbing works.

"Yeah, well they say paint what you know."

"Does that mean your paintings are based off this—" I stop short as a long string of wine-colored liquid leaks from Nora's left nostril. "Nora, your nose."

The liquid trails to her upper lip, and she raises a hand to her face, cursing as her fingers come away red.

"Damn it." She pulls a tissue from her pocket. It's spotted with dark stains, each one layered over the next. A bloodied watercolor painting. She blots at her nostril. "It's like I'm allergic to this place, I swear."

The color, deep and familiar, is enough to curdle my insides. I want to scream; I want to grab her by the shoulders and demand to know why she's bleeding the way I do—dark, and thick, and not quite right. But there's a gummed up feeling in my throat, and all I can manage is, "I get nosebleeds like that too sometimes."

She stuffs the tissue back into her pocket and makes a noncommittal noise as she lifts her duffel bag.

"Do you get nosebleeds like that a lot?" I ask.

"No. Look, your little freak out in the yard, those 'thoughts that aren't your thoughts,' that was your adverse reaction to this place, the nosebleed was mine. It's not a big deal. Now come on and help me find a light switch." She stalks deeper into the foyer while I stay by the front door.

"What do you mean adverse reaction?" I ask. "And why would the electricity still work?"

I hurry after her and we wander the first floor; Nora pulling me along after her. She flicks on light after light as we walk, orbs of pale orange and fluorescent white, crystal chandeliers in awkwardly placed parlors.

The layout of the building doesn't make any sense. There are sitting areas deep within the home, halls the width of dining rooms. Every time I expect to make it to the end of the place, to one final hulking wall, there's another turn, another set of rooms. Another hallway.

If it wasn't for the dust coating the floors, I would swear someone still lived here. There are too many decadent, expensive things left behind: twinkling charms, jewelry boxes, ornately carved furniture. I keep waiting for a well-dressed lord or lady to come around the corner and greet Nora with a kiss on either cheek. But the house, labyrinthine and silent, offers no explanation for its treasures.

I run my free hand along the walls. There's a different type of paper in every hallway, with a different fabric accent. Velvet and foil and silk.

We turn left twice and head down a hallway that's wrapped in flowered paper which bubbles where the glue peels from the plaster. Faded roses parade down from the ceiling, tangled in thorns and stems and leaves. Color leaks out along the edges of the paper like it's taken water damage. The roses bleed.

Nora doesn't stop to notice what's around us. She barely pauses to turn on the lights. It's like she knows exactly where they are in each room.

Worse, I feel like I know where the lights are located, and where each hallway will spill into a sitting room. The house, equal parts familiar and strange, melds Nora's paintings with reality.

"Seriously," I say, as Nora drags me along after her, her grip on my wrist tightening. "Why does the electricity work?"

Nora doesn't answer, and the air thickens the farther we walk. It's musty and smells of boiled meat and sweat. Even the windows, although numerous, are comprised of thick panes which swirl and bubble like the wallpaper. There's no escape from the heaviness in the air. It's as if the collapsed roof is part of a different building altogether—there's no trace of fire damage on this side of the Victorian.

"The kitchen should be at the end of this hallway," Nora says. "I need to check something out, then we can settle in for the night."

"How do you know where the kitchen is? How can you tell where anything is? These hallways don't make any sense. And the electricity shouldn't work."

"I don't know where to start. I didn't think it would be like this when we got here. I thought this would be so much easier. I thought we would dig up what we came for a lot sooner and everything would make sense once you saw it... but that's not the case, and I'm not good at explaining."

She pauses and takes a deep breath before continuing. "Remember that there's no such thing as coincidence. It's not a coincidence that we're here and the lights still work. It's not a coincidence that you feel the way you do about this place."

"That it reminds me of your paintings?" My heart hammers against my ribs. "You're not making any sense."

"Nothing here makes sense. You'll need to get used to it since we're going to be staying the night, Sil. Stop trying to understand it and be glad it's not pitch black in here."

"Does this have to do with your parents? Was this your family's house or something?" I ask, hoping to reel her back in, to inject some normalcy into the conversation. It's a shot in the dark and she stiffens at their mention, but it does seem to ground her a bit.

"I don't have parents," she says, quickly—eyes trained straight ahead.

"I don't either," I offer lamely, struggling to keep pace with her. "My parents died too—I know what it's like."

"At least you have Victor. I don't have anyone at all. I'm completely alone."

I want to remind her that she constantly goes on and on about how I'd be better off without my brother, how toxic he is. I want to remind her that the two of us are practically family, that the scars on our palms prove that we share a bond deeper than sisterhood, but I bite my tongue. She wouldn't listen to me anyway.

We come to a wide doorway and Nora skids to a stop. She releases my wrist.

"Here it is," she says, a faint smile playing on her lips. "You know, I almost had a panic attack of my own back there. I thought it might be on the right side of the building and we'd be screwed. But the kitchen's to the left and unaffected by the collapse."

"That's lucky," I offer, unsure of what else to say.

"There's no such thing as luck, and there's no such thing as coincidence," she repeats, and I cringe. The words sound like something straight out of a fortune cookie. They're too hokey for Nora.

Oblivious to my discomfort, she focuses her full attention on the entrance to the kitchen.

The door sits off its hinges, propped up against the wall on the opposite side of the hallway. The kitchen itself is pitch black, and the only things that can be made out from our position are the first few black and white checkered tiles beyond the entrance.

"Wait here," she instructs, dropping her duffel bag at my feet.

"I'll come with you," I offer, but she shakes her head.

"I don't want you to freak out again."

"I won't, I can hold it together," I insist. "I'll freak out more if you leave me alone in this place."

"You won't be alone for long. Trust me and stay out here. You don't want to see—hell, I'm not even sure if it's still there..."

"Whatever it is, I'm going to see it when you turn on the light anyway."

"I'm not going to turn on the light," she says, disappearing into the thick darkness.

"Wait, what?" I poke my head into the kitchen, but sure enough the kitchen remains dark, and the only noise is the sound of her boots on the tile floor.

I frown.

She's messing with me again.

It seems over the top to keep the light off. Especially when she was so hell bent on keeping me calm before we got inside the Victorian. Unless this whole thing is some kind of test to see if I have what it takes to keep exploring with her, in which case I've already failed.

When I first told her about my list—the ten things that I wish I had the guts to do but couldn't imagine ever acting on—she laughed, probably because they were much less grand than what she would put on her bucket list. But eventually she agreed, and in the past few months her attempts to get me out from under Victor's thumb have gotten more and more aggressive, like she's working within some self-set timeline.

I nudge her duffel bag with my shoe. Whatever's inside sinks beneath my foot with the softness of a comforter, or maybe a sleeping bag. The thought sends ripples of unease through my body. A sleeping bag would be proof that Nora knew we wouldn't make it back tonight. I step away from the duffel and lean against the wall.

Resting my cheek against the flowered paper, I raise my hand to trace the outlines of the roses, tapping gently against each thorn as I fight the urge to unzip the bag.

Suddenly, the paper shifts beneath my cheek and I jump back.

In my nightmare, there were walls cloaked in snakeskin, walls that squirmed as if they lived, as if they breathed. And now the paper in this hallway shifts. It rises and falls as if there's life beneath the plaster.

I stand mesmerized, sickened.

Then the wall settles, like nothing happened. Everything is quiet and still.

"That wasn't real," I murmur. "That wasn't real, that wasn't real."

But the wall buckles again, and a larger ripple of movement disturbs the roses. This time it's accompanied by a hurried whisper—faint but growing in volume—and I can't help it: I lean in and press my ear against the wallpaper.

Words creep up from behind the plaster. I press my ear closer, my heart thrashing inside my chest with the hurried panic of a fly.

The words are soft and quick. The slicing of a knife through fabric. The creaking of an old chair.

"... no before, no forever, no afterward," a voice says, and my blood curdles.

There's someone inside the wall.

3

No before, no forever, no afterward. This isn't the first time I've heard it. It's a memory I can't quite reach. It's an echo of something I once knew. The hairs on my arms stand on end, and goosebumps cover every inch of my exposed skin. No before, no forever, no afterward. A script from a dream, a line from a poem, a song, or a slogan, or something my brother might have mentioned in passing as he brought me back from the dead.

Nora emerges from the kitchen and finds me standing in the center of the hallway, my hands trembling.

"There's someone inside the wall." The words barely escape past the riptide inside my head, the bite of sodium and raw, unfiltered fear coursing through me.

She stares at me the way people stare at a car wreck, with a mix of curiosity and revulsion. "It's an old house, Silvie. There are mice and rats and all kinds of things inside the walls."

"I said someone, not something."

"I know what you said." She bends to inspect the duffel bag. "You didn't look inside, did you?"

"Why? Is there a person in there too?" I snap, reaching for the bag. Nora kicks it behind her and catches me by the wrist.

"Relax," she says through gritted teeth. "You heard some mice crawling around or something. I get that you're anxious about spending the night here, but don't take it out on me."

I pull away. "You know how Victor gets; you know what's going to happen when I don't come home tonight."

"You need to take a deep breath."

"What's buried out there, Nora? Why did I hear a voice—a *human* voice—inside the wall... and why did it sound like me?" That's the part of all this that really makes my skin crawl. The voice may have been muffled, it may have been low, but it was mine. I know what my voice sounds like, and it was inside the wall.

"Silvie, you're spiraling. This place is abandoned." If she thought I was a car wreck before, I'm a six-car pileup now. "We're the only ones here."

I shake my head. "The wall's softer than it should be, and whatever's in there was kicking at the plaster so I put my ear against it and..."

Nora walks over the wall and lays her palm across the flowered paper.

"Can you feel it in there?" I ask. "It's like—it kind of buckles, that's how you know it's moving around."

She frowns. "I don't feel anything. Like I said, it's an old house. Stay away from the walls and try not to think about it too much."

I want to remind her of the constant undertow that rips through me, the deep darkness, and how her hands are the only things that can pull me back when I'm face down in the whirlpool. I want to say that she can't seriously expect me to not think about something when all I do is think. Think, and think, and think until the thoughts crystalize and drag me down into the salty sweep of indigo inside my mind.

"But it's me," I say instead, my voice so low that it's barely audible.

"I'm sorry." She comes over next to me and wraps her arm around my shoulders.

"You really didn't think we'd need to stay here tonight?" I ask, and the thought of the sleeping bag, comforter, whatever it is inside the duffel rolls around like a rock inside my head.

"Believe me when I say that I'd rather die." She raises her scarred palm to me again, and I reach for it. Her fingers lace through mine and her hand is warm. I grip it tightly.

"Your blood is in my veins, and my blood is in yours," Nora tells me. "I won't let anything hurt you."

She guides me across the main floor, flicking the light switches off as we move. Back in the entryway, she tests the front door to make sure it's shut tightly before guiding me up the staircase and into a thin purple hall. I'm on autopilot. My hand drifts lazily toward the wallpaper, but she swats it away.

"Don't even think about it," she warns. "There's nothing inside the walls."

"But if there was someone in there, do you think it would count?" I ask after a few moments of silence.

"Count for what?"

"Another thing off my list: a conversation with a stranger." It's one of only three items that remain out of the original ten. Most of the others involved disobeying Victor in some small, seemingly insignificant way: getting Nora to smuggle me sci-fi paperbacks, stashing my medicine in my pillowcase, sneaking out with Nora, sneaking into Victor's study, staying up past curfew. A conversation with a stranger is so much bigger than anything I've crossed off so far. Except what if it isn't a stranger, what if it really was my voice that I heard inside the wall? The possibility makes my head spin.

The farther we walk down the seemingly endless hall, the more I find myself scrolling through ideas for how to tear into the paper, how to dig through the plaster and find whatever lies beneath. It shouldn't matter how badly I wreck the place since the house is abandoned, and Nora never needs to know, but I promise myself that I'll find my way inside. I'll prove that I heard my voice.

No before, no forever, no afterward. I repeat the words again and again inside my head and try, without success, to figure out where I heard them before.

"You know how you incorporate poetry into your paintings sometimes?" I ask Nora as we turn down a navy-colored hall. The wallpaper shimmers with silver accents that flicker in the low light.

"There are maybe two paintings where I've done that," she says without looking back at me. "Why?"

"The words I heard downstairs sounded familiar." I'm careful not to mention the person in the wall. "I'm pretty sure that I've heard them before, and I think maybe they might be from a poem. Since you've been here before and painted this house, and since I recognized it from your paintings—"

"You're rambling. Let it go."

We stop at the end of the hall. There are two doors on either side, both coated in chipping white paint. Slivers of mint green bleed through the cracks. I frown. Victor insists that pastels are supposed to be calming, but they make me queasy. I had to beg him to repaint the resurrection room gray because every time I opened my eyes to pale blue I would vomit.

Nora points to the door on the left side. "I'll take this room, and you take the one across from it."

"We're not sleeping in the same place?" I ask, water rushing beneath my skin.

She adjusts the duffel bag and shifts her weight. "It'll be for like, less than twelve hours, I'm sure you can handle it. Besides I snore, and you'll want to get some rest if we're going to finish digging tomorrow."

My stomach tightens. "More digging? We're not going to leave first thing in the morning?"

"Not until I find what I came here for." Nora sighs and rubs her forehead with her thumb and middle finger. She makes it look painful. She makes it seem like it's such a burden that she has to dig again tomorrow. "I'm really sorry. I know this isn't fair. If we still don't find it tomorrow, we can leave, and I'll explain."

"Okay." The response is automatic, and for a moment I forget that Nora isn't Victor, that I'm allowed to say no. My cheeks burn and I curl my fingers into my scarred palm.

I should be so much better than this.

A two-letter word shouldn't make me feel like I'm drowning.

It takes me far too long to wade through all the dark thoughts, and by the time I decide on what to say and how to say it, it's too late. Nora's already disappearing into the room she claimed.

"Try to get some sleep, okay?" She pokes her head out around the threshold. "I'm a knock away, if you need me."

It isn't until the door swings shut that I realize she never told me what she was looking for in the kitchen—or if she found it.

I slip off my jacket and wander the perimeter of my bedroom for the night. Moonlight spills through two tall, skinny windows casting shadows across the floor. Freckles of dust and dirt coat the wooden beams. There's a large wardrobe, a standing mirror, a bed, and side table inside the room.

The comforter on the bed is the same pale lavender as the wallpaper, and almost identical to the one I have at home.

"At least I know why that seems familiar," I whisper, running my fingers over the patterned bedspread. Even without the comforter, the room has more in common with my room back home than I'd care to admit. The placement of the windows. The width of the floorboards. The heavy scent of lemon and clove in the air. It's all the same.

Only the walls are different—decorated, instead of bare. Stretched canvas paintings cover them like a second skin, each one roughly the size of a paperback book. From a distance, they're abstract, nothing more than globs of color, and texture—patterns that seem to blend with the paper behind them. The effect is dizzying, and I keep my gaze lowered to where the wall meets the floor.

The bottom corner of the wallpaper peels where it meets the molding. I kneel, gripping one of the loose pieces and tear upward, revealing smooth plaster underneath. The wallpaper only rips off a few inches, and I scrape at the plaster with my pinky nail, but don't get far. It isn't sharp enough, and all I manage to do is add to the layers of gunk burrowed beneath my nail. I wish I had one of Victor's scalpels.

If he were here, he'd treat this like surgery. He'd make sure to sterilize the subject, sedate it, slice it up in the most delicate of ways before stitching it back together again. I'd act as his observer. No need to get messy. He'd take the lead as he peeled apart the wall, and he'd do it with grace. My brother has always been good with a knife. I trace the length of my scar, not sure if the thought comforts or disturbs me.

I stand, picking bits of plaster from under my pinky, and circle the room. I test for weak spots, areas that bend inward when I press against them, like the wall downstairs.

There are two directly across from the far wall. One next to the standing mirror, and one next to the door. I press my ear against each spot and my heart beats a little bit harder with each dip in the paper. But I don't hear anything. No words. No movement.

I lean against the wall and draw in a shaky breath. "What am I doing? This isn't like me..."

If I didn't sneak out, Victor and I would be sitting in our

living room right now. I'd be drinking tea, and he'd be nursing a cocktail while he writes in his journal. He always sits in an overstuffed leather chair across from my usual spot on the couch. Most nights, he lets me read—always nonfiction, always some kind of educational text having to do with medicine or the history of surgical procedures. But I used one of his scalpels to slice the pages out of a volume on open surgery techniques and tucked a sci-fi paperback inside, *The Body Snatchers* by Jack Finney. I'm obsessed. It drives my imagination wild, and even though I'm only halfway through, I find myself scrutinizing my brother, trying to determine if I'd recognize it if he were replaced. If I didn't sneak out, I'd be engrossed in Miles and Becky's battle against the otherworldly invaders while Victor drinks himself into oblivion.

"Dirty martinis help me keep my mind off it," he'd say, swirling his glass, the two olives he always impales on a toothpick moving counterclockwise with the liquid.

"Off what?"

"What I'd do if I didn't have you," he'd respond without looking up from his journal, continuing to write with feverish haste while the clock on the wall counts down the hours until it's time for me to go to bed.

So much of my life is measured by routine, by lists, by non-negotiable rules.

Back home, I'm corralled from place to place. Locked in my room at night, brought down to the kitchen in the morning for breakfast—two eggs, sunny-side up with toast. Two pills and a tall glass of water, condensation dripping down the sides. Victor always leans against the counter and watches me eat, watches me take my pill, watches as I bring my empty plate over to the sink.

Being here without him, it's hard to know what to do. The pull beneath my skin has been chillingly silent since the incident in front of the Victorian, and without it, the only thing keeping me tethered to this place is the voice inside the wall, the promise that there's more to this building than brick and boards. There's a current coursing through it.

I step away from the wall and continue taking stock of the soft spots trying—without success—not to worry about how Victor's handling my absence.

The painting directly above the final soft spot catches my eye, and I stop in front of it. It's of a little girl on a swing set overlooking the backyard of the Victorian. She stands on a single plank swing, a glassy look in her eyes as she surveys the apple orchard.

The cluster of trees in the painting sits in the same position as real life, only they're well-tended and ripe with fruit. There's nothing wrong with the painting itself. The girl's arms are a little too long, and her eyes a little too empty, but there's nothing overly horrifying about it.

Still, it takes everything I have not to vomit.

I recognize the little girl in the painting.

She's me.

4

Nora painted it. It's obvious that she painted it. It's her palette of choice. It's her signature style. The composition, the thickness of the paint, the brush strokes—everything about the painting screams Nora. While the execution may be less refined than her most recent pieces, it's still her work.

I spin around looking from painting to painting, my heart beating itself to a pulp inside my chest. All of them are Nora originals. From a distance, they looked like nothing more than globs of color and texture, but up close, I find the narrative scenes buried in the paint. I should have seen it before. I should have noticed, but I was too focused on getting inside the wall.

The two on either side of the standing mirror are early incarnations of Nora's snowy choir series: clusters of children hover above bruise tinted snow, and icicles the size of baseball bats hang from the silhouettes of trees. The two opposite of the windows depict long, snake-like hallways the color of reptile scales. They're the same as the one she gave me for my birthday, the same as the serpentine walls from my nightmare.

And of course, there's the painting of me on the swing.

It's not just that the girl looks like me, she's wearing my

clothes. I trace the outline of the figure and feel the sticky wool of the sweater, the itch of the fabric against my skin.

My breath comes in short, shallow gasps, and I press my palm to the exposed portion of my scar, so roughly that my knuckles crack—but I can't steady myself. The room continues to spin, colors blurring, bleeding, bruising across the walls.

Nora's paintings stare down at me from every corner of the room, and I stand frozen for what seems like hours before I'm able to calm my breathing. Even then, the riptide continues to tear through me. The more I try to rationalize what I've found, the more I can feel the sweater against my skin—and the more I'm convinced that it's really me in the painting.

I pluck it from the wall and run my fingers over the canvas, my hands shaking.

Everything from before the first time I died has been walled away behind stained glass. Memories come in distorted shades of red and blue. Victor's face. Our front yard. Sunrises and sunsets. But this house and Nora's paintings, no matter how hard I try, I can't conjure up a memory—only fragments of nightmares, images pulled from paint. Enough to make it familiar, but not enough to explain why.

The painting is proof that I've been here before along with Nora, but that doesn't make any sense. We've only known each other for a year. We have no history beyond my brother's house.

My breath catches in my throat.

Unless we do.

Unless I can't remember because our history extends back before the first time I died.

I take off across the hall, and pound on Nora's door, striking the heavy oak with my fist. She opens it a crack. A small slice of her face comes into view, her eyes puffy and red as if she's been crying even though Nora never cries.

I hold out the painting. "You painted this."

She slips out of the room and shuts the door behind her,

and although she turns to face me, she won't look me in the eye.

She bows her head and focuses on the painting, shifting uncomfortably. "Look, Silvie..."

"You put me in a room full of your paintings and thought I wouldn't notice?" I say through gritted teeth, the irritation almost enough to drown out the slosh of salt water inside my head.

Nora takes the painting from me and runs her fingers over the canvas. It's the same motion I made, the same sweep of the hand from left to right. "I can't believe you took this down off the wall."

"It's me. I remember wearing that sweater, that exact sweater. It..." I wrack my brain. Images filter in, murky and muddled and broken. Thin slivers of a mirror. The bright red color that faded to pale pink after one too many washes. Victor pulling it over my head and loose threads getting caught in my open mouth.

"It's not you, Sil." She continues to run her fingers across the canvas.

"Yes, it is. I remember the sweater."

Nora takes a deep breath. "No, you don't. It's a painting of *me*, okay? Don't go off the deep end."

Heat rises to my cheeks. "I'm not going off the deep end. The girl in this painting is wearing my clothes!"

She hugs the painting to her chest. "We should talk about this."

"You should have told me about it before you stuck me in that room. We shouldn't be staying in separate rooms to begin with." I can't stop staring at her bloodshot eyes. I can't stop thinking about the wine-colored liquid that bled from her nose.

"I didn't know what room the paintings were in. I didn't even know they were still here. I never thought you'd see them."

"Because you didn't think we'd spend the night?" The soft squish of the duffel bag replays inside my head.

She nods and takes a step farther into the hallway. "I didn't think we'd come inside here at all. If you'd calm down for a second, I can explain."

I bite the inside of my cheek. No matter what she says, I still remember the sweater. I still remember the scratch of the wool against my skin.

We sit across from each other on the floor in the hallway. I press my back against the wall, keeping my spine straight, and my eyes locked with Nora's. She attempts to smile at me, but I glare until she shifts her gaze to the silver accents on the wallpaper behind my head.

The air in the hall is thick enough to cut, and I feel the weight of it everywhere—my hands, my skull, my chest. I'm acutely aware of the textured wallpaper and how it brushes against the base of my neck. I run my fingers over my scar and the waxy tissue keeps me anchored while the wall behind me stands still and undisturbed. No movement. No hurried whispers.

Nora rests her hand on a loose floorboard, and it sinks beneath her touch, rotten and molding.

"Well?" I ask, my voice clipped.

"I forgot that I even painted it." She nods to where the canvas lays face down between us. Her signature is scrawled across the bottom stretcher bar in thick magic marker. The letters bleed together. "I mean, I figured there might be some of my paintings in here, but it's been so long, I had no idea what they were of anymore or which rooms they were in. And that one..."

Her voice tapers off, and her words soak the space between us, adding to the heaviness in the air.

"It's a self-portrait," I prompt, eyes narrowed.

"Yeah. Back when I lived here, painting was the only thing

that kept me sane. It's not like I had a dozen willing subjects to choose from or anything, so I painted myself most of the time."

"You were here before this place was abandoned? You *lived* here?" When Nora said that she'd been here before I assumed that it was after it had already been left to rot. The thought of her burying something in the yard before this place slipped into a state of decay is nauseating, but the sheer volume of paintings in this place piques my curiosity. Nora cares about her art more than anything. Sometimes she'll paint over old canvases or put them in storage until she figures out what to do with them, but she would never abandon so many pieces. Something awful must have happened for her to leave an entire gallery behind.

"It was a long time ago, before the right side of the building burned down," Nora tells me. "I made a lot of the art in here, not just the paintings either. Some of the charcoal drawings on the first floor. There are also two murals, but I can't remember which rooms they're in. I don't remember a lot of things about this place, and what I do remember is hard to explain," Nora says, picking at the loose floorboard. She pauses for a moment, then speaks slowly, intentionally, as she continues—her eyes burning into mine. "I have all these gaps in my memory."

My scalp prickles. I was already starting to warm to her story, but this pulls me in completely. She knows how terrible my memory is. She knows how much it bothers me.

I close my eyes for a moment, and peer through the kaleidoscope of red and blue, the memories I can't quite reach. Victor's face. Pine needles. The sun beating down on a long dirt road.

The kaleidoscope shifts to more recent memories, though even they remain hazy. Math lessons. Grilled cheese sandwiches—with tomato and avocado. Victor's face. My pills. And somehow, even though it's my life, even though the days stretch on inside my memory—each one familiar, each one the same—I can't help but feel like it isn't me. It's a movie. It's fiction. I'm in each scene, but I'm not really there. A sharp pain blooms in my temple as I try to make sense of it all. Maybe something went wrong the last time I died; maybe something got knocked loose inside my skull and that's why I'm so messed up.

"This house is important to me even though it's painful to be here now," Nora says, pulling me back from the ocean of stained glass. "This was my home, my one safe place until the right side burned within an inch of collapsing, and I lost it all. I lost everyone I loved in the fire."

This is where her family died.

I glance down at my scarred palm. It's supposed to mean that we share blood, that we share everything. My stomach tightens as I look at it.

I think of all the time we've spent together. All the hours on the back porch, at the kitchen table, sitting cross-legged on my bed. All the times I kept her company in Victor's lab as she sorted and labeled blood samples. All the things she confided in me about. Her fear of commitment, how she only really feels comfortable when she's painting, and how she secretly hates her birthday. This is something she would have mentioned, if not the Victorian, if not all the details of what happened, then at the very least her loss. She would have told me, even if there was no way I could understand.

"I didn't know how to tell you," she says, as if she can read my mind. "I didn't want you to look at me differently. I didn't want you to treat me like I'm damaged."

My chest tightens because I understand. I've never told her how many times Victor's raised me from the dead because I don't want her to treat me like I'm broken. It's like something deep inside me cracks open and bleeds. We're so much alike it hurts.

Still, even though I want to believe her, there's something in the quick staccato of her voice that tells me she's not being completely honest. If she's the one who lived here, why do I remember the Victorian? It's more than just her paintings or my nightmare. It's the hum beneath my skin and the thoughts that tumbled through my head out in the yard. It's the room where I found the painting and how it's a warped reflection of my room back home.

It's my voice inside the wall.

"Your blood is in my veins, and my blood is in yours," I mumble, fingers curled into my scarred palm. "You can tell me anything."

Looking at her now, she does seem damaged, and I hate that I'm seeing her this way—her eyes red, her cheeks flushed from crying. I'm not sure why I didn't notice before but she's holding onto something very heavy, and she clearly doesn't trust me enough to lay some of that burden on me... that or there's another reason why she refuses to confide in me completely, and both possibilities are terrible in their own way.

I cross the hall to where she sits and sink to the ground next to her, leaning against the wall. My back sinks into the paper and the soft spot in the plaster writhes behind me. I stiffen at the movement.

"You." The word is light against my ear, barely more than a leak of air, but it's still there. It still sounds like me.

"Me," I whisper and Nora frowns.

Her switchblade sticks out of her pocket, and I can't help but think of the plaster still caught beneath my pinky nail. I inch closer, my hand resting near her thigh and the bloodstain on her jeans.

What's the difference between flesh and paper? I wonder. Peeling back the wallpaper can't be any different from skinning an animal. Whatever flows through the veins of this building leans against me feeling warm, organic, alive. I press my spine flush against the wall and the paper strains against the pressure.

"You're here," the voice—my voice—says, and I feel my pulse in my forehead. I feel it everywhere.

"I'm here," I whisper back, and Nora shoots me a concerned look.

The person inside the wall pulls back. She's swallowed into the depths of the Victorian and my heart pounds, filling the silence that she leaves behind.

"Do you think there's any way I could have been here before too?" I ask Nora. "Maybe we met when we were little, and that's why we were able to become friends so quickly. Maybe that's why Victor hired you in the first place, because we have history together, and he knew your family... or something."

"What are you saying?" She shifts slightly, and the knife pokes farther out of her pocket.

Down the hall, the wall bulges slightly and I trace the path that the person inside the wall walks as she sinks away from me. Not for long. I won't let her go for long...

"There's something about this place that pulls at me," I tell Nora. "Like what happened outside earlier. I've never experienced anything like that before, not to that extent. It felt like my whole body was pulsing, like there was this electricity beneath my skin. Only I didn't hate it, it didn't hurt. It felt like... I don't know, like it was meant for me. I guess that's why I'm so hung up on what I heard inside the wall. I keep thinking that it's me in there. I know it sounds crazy, but I meant what I said out on the front steps: I don't feel like myself."

Nora stares at me for a long time, a pained expression on her face, and when she finally responds, her words are spoken as if she's thought a thousand times about this conversation, as if she's reciting a script that she's spent damn near a year memorizing. "You're not inside the wall, Silvie. Look, nobody ever feels like themselves, not completely. Individuality is a lie that people invented to feel special, but there's nothing special about us: we're the same. And that's not a bad thing. If anyone was truly themselves then they'd never make any friends. You remember why we started hanging out? You only introduced yourself to me because we look so much alike."

"*You* introduced yourself to *me*."

"Does it really matter which one of us said hi first? We started talking because we have something in common. We're the same."

Me and Nora, the same? It's laughable.

She's a lightning strike, she's the eye of a storm. No fear and no hesitation.

Limited by nothing.

Controlled by nothing.

I'm so much less than she is, and I feel my inferiority like a physical ache in my side. I rake my fingers along my scar, as if I could dig inside myself and pull out the broken pieces.

"You're so much better than I am," I tell her. "I'm a mess."

She studies my face, her eyes shimmering on the verge of tears again. Nothing like the Nora that I know. She opens and closes her mouth as if she can't decide on what to say.

"I'm a mess too, Sil," she admits, finally, after a long stretch of silence.

I shake my head. It's impossible. It's a lie, and an obvious one at that. Either she thinks I'm stupid or so pathetic that I need her coddling.

"You see this?" she says, opening her mouth and pulling back her upper lip to expose her top row of teeth.

I frown. "Your teeth?"

"Yeah, my teeth. My chipped to shit front teeth, top and bottom row."

Sure enough, her top and bottom front teeth are angled slightly, the left sides shorter than the right, and jagged—cracked. I don't know how I've never noticed before. Nora's always seemed so perfect.

She pulls her hand back, her teeth disappearing behind her bow-shaped lips. "You know why they're so messed up?"

"Why?"

"Anxiety, Sil. It was really bad a few years back and I—well, there was a lot going on back then. Point is, I clench my jaw and grind my teeth when things get to be too much for me, and my teeth are all fucked up because of it."

"I don't even realize that I'm doing it sometimes," Nora continues. "But there are moments when my back teeth will ache for days on end. They'll hurt so badly because of how hard I clench my jaw. And there are times when little bits of my front teeth will chip when I'm eating. There will be this soft crunch and gritty taste—almost like sand—and suddenly I'm swallowing a little piece of my own tooth, and it's so freaking disgusting, Sil. It makes me feel helpless, like I have no control over my body..." she draws in a shaky breath.

Nora the summer wind.

Nora the brightly painted sunrise.

She feels the same way I do. She feels the same disconnect, the same separation from her own body, her own mind. Heat pulses down the back of my neck and my fingers hook against my breastbone. The waxy texture of my scar mirroring the silver accents in the wallpaper.

"It's like I have no control over anything, least of all myself." Her eyes burn into mine again, and her words sink in. A knife to flesh.

Who knew words could make you bleed?

"You want to know why I'm being such a psycho about digging?" She blinks and tears trace two perfect lines down her face. "There's a piece of myself buried out there, one of the only things left over from before the fire. You want to know why we're here? We're here so that I don't chip my teeth anymore. We're here so I don't clench my jaw. We're here because I'm tired of feeling tired all the time. Do you understand what it feels like to not be in control of your own damn body, to feel yourself slipping away a little bit more every single day of your life?"

I nod, blinking through my own tears. Victor said that he held my heart in his hand, he said that no one will ever get closer to me than that, but here Nora is, closing the gap. Here she is melting into me, until it's the two of us, a single unit against everything. I don't think I'll ever get closer to someone than I am to her in this moment.

She reaches out and pulls my hand away from my scar and hooks her fingers through mine. "I know you better than I know myself. We're the same. And that's all that matters, not the why or how, just that we're the same. I know that being here is weird, and scary, and fucked up, but I need you to trust me. Because I trust you, and I *need* you here with me. Please Silvie, I need you here with me."

She squeezes my hand twice before releasing it.

"I didn't realize you were struggling," I tell her.

What was I talking about before?

I'm disoriented. Everything's spinning.

"Don't be so hard on yourself. I hide it well," she says with a wink. She flicks the tears from her cheeks and just like that, she's back to her normal, bubbly self.

It's as if the last few minutes never happened, and suddenly I'm the one crying. I'm the one shaking and she's comforting me. Just like she always does.

My fingers rest lightly on the handle of her switchblade. No matter how hard I try to stay focused on the knife, I can't get her words out of my head. I can't stop thinking about how puffy her eyes were when I knocked on her door.

She asked for a separate room so that I wouldn't see her cry.

She grinds her teeth.

She gets anxious and afraid.

It's like I've caught a glimpse of the real Nora, the girl who hides behind her veil of carefully chosen words and brightly colored clothes.

There's a thunderhead inside of her that I never noticed before.

But still...

"What are you thinking about, Sil?" she asks.

I'm thinking about us. I'm thinking about how I want to believe her, but the pain in her voice is different from the pain in her eyes. I'm thinking about how she wouldn't have told me any of this if I hadn't found the painting.

But there's no way I can say it.

I keep hearing Victor's voice in the back of my head telling me not to ask questions, to stay quiet, to behave. I keep feeling his breath on the back of my neck, even though he's not here.

I held your heart as it went still inside your chest, he said. *No one will ever get closer to you than that.*

"Silvie?" Nora asks again. "What are you thinking about?"

"Just that I never noticed how badly chipped your teeth are," I say, and she laughs. She laughs like everything is all right. She laughs like she didn't just tell me...

Her family died.

She feels like she has no control over her own body.

She worries, and she lets the worry bury her. Same as me.

"They're really bad, huh?" Nora relaxes her posture and grins, her chipped teeth looking like small, sharpened knives.

I feel Victor's hand on my arm—even though he's not here. Warning me to keep myself in line. But I look at the patterned wallpaper and the voice in the wall repeats its poetry inside my head.

No before, no forever, no afterward.

You.

You're here.

Even as my chest aches, and my muscles tense, and every

inch of me begs to surrender to the dark swell of the undertow, a greater feeling takes hold.

Nora isn't going to explain my connection to this place, I'll have to figure it out on my own.

I snatch her switchblade in one swift motion and hide it in the folds of my skirt. My heart kicks against my ribs like a caged animal, but she doesn't notice. She can't hear my panic.

"I'm so relieved that I finally got to share all of that with you." She rises from the floor and smiles. "Now get some sleep. I'll see you in the morning."

"Sure." There's a sour taste in the back of my mouth, the taste of flies, of legs and wings beating relentlessly against my gums. I pull the switchblade out and run my fingers over the handle. I'm getting inside the wall tonight.

"Hey Sil," Nora says as she closes her door. "You're the most important person to me in the whole damn world."

The door slams, and I'm left sitting alone out in the hallway.

That wasn't a talk; it was a performance.

If she had really opened up to me, I wouldn't feel so gutted.

5

After Victor found the stash of medication inside my pillowcase, he started grinding my pills into a powder which he mixed into my drinks.

"You broke my trust, Silvie. You hurt me," he said one morning as he ground the pills down with a mortar and pestle. "But it's my own fault for being so lenient with you."

I sat stiffly at the kitchen table while he hunched over the mortar, digging his wrist into the crushing motion. The sound of stone against stone set my teeth on edge, and the way he looked at me as he pulverized my pills, the venom in his eyes, chilled me.

"You've always been so well behaved, I assumed that you didn't need discipline." He slammed the pestle into the bowl, and I flinched.

"I won't skip the pills again, Victor. I promise I'll be goo—"

"Or structure." He smashed the pestle down one last time, then dumped the powder into a glass of milk. "Shame on me for believing that you would be smart enough not to put yourself at risk."

He crossed the kitchen to where I sat and placed the glass in front of me before pressing against the back of my chair, his body framing mine, his breath hot against my neck. "Now drink."

The cup was nearly overflowing, and there was a scummy froth along the surface of the milk that churned my stomach. "Please, if you just give me the pills, I promise—"

He pressed in closer. "Drink."

"Victor, I swear I won't—"

"Drink!"

He slammed his fist down on the table and I drained the cup.

"Good girl," he whispered, tucking a strand of hair behind my ear. "You understand why I need to do this, don't you?"

I did. He and Nora were nearing the completion of their project, and he didn't have enough time to monitor me the way he used to. Between the pill hoarding and my most recent death, he couldn't risk leaving me to my own devices.

Which is why he had to grind up my medication.

And why he put a padlock on my bedroom door.

I actually don't mind the lock; it's comforting in a sick way. Victor rarely steps foot inside my room, and it's the only place I can read my sci-fi paperbacks without having to conceal them within hollowed out medical textbooks. Back home, when Victor shuts my door at night, the click of the lock is soothing. There's a certain safety in it that I miss when we're in the kitchen eating grilled cheese and tomato sandwiches or sitting together in the living room—Victor scribbling in his journals, while I sip my tea or read my secret copy of *The Body Snatchers.*

But I don't miss it now. I keep my door open a crack as I move the furniture away from the walls. If I linger on my conversation with Nora for too long, I'll spiral. And if I spiral, I'll drown inside the riptide. Especially after everything that happened today. Concentrating on finding whoever's inside the wall is the only thing that matters, and if I'm going to reach her, I need full access to the plaster.

Upon closer inspection, the room is just as strange as the rest of the Victorian.

None of the furniture matches. It's as if someone took pieces from all over the house and dropped them in the first place they could think of. The iron bed frame is like something out of a mental hospital. It already sits in the center of the room, and my jacket lays crumpled next to the headboard, looking strange in a way that everyday objects shouldn't.

There's a cheap plywood bedside table and a stainless-steel floor lamp. Both positioned in opposite corners of the room, facing away from each other. I bring them over next to the bed, and the lamp's chord is just long enough for me to plug in. The bulb flickers twice before dimming into a smoky gold.

My hand brushes against the bed frame and there's a soft pop behind my ears. It's chillingly similar to what happened in front of the Victorian, and I freeze, anticipating the blurred vision and static whine that's sure to follow. Instead, there's a slight pull beneath my skin, like the movement of a tide. It compels me toward the wall. And somehow, instinctually, I know that the bed needs to go against it.

Despite the heavy frame, I wrestle the bed beneath two of the soft spots in the wallpaper, leaving four deep gouges across the wooden floor. The boards are so dark they're almost black, and the scratches reveal pale wood underneath, like exposed bone. I half expect them to bleed.

I wonder if Nora has gotten her phone to work, and a dull pang shoots through my body at the thought of Victor calling again and again without an answer.

There's nothing I can do about that now, I remind myself, and turn to the large oak wardrobe that's pushed against the far wall. Too heavy to move, it looks like something that could be found at a retail furniture chain, too modern for how long the house seems to have been abandoned, at least twenty years newer than the other furniture. Cherry finish. Easily worth more than what Victor spends on groceries each month.

The standing mirror is the focal point of the room. It has round edges and sits within an enormous wooden frame. The frame is dark—the same deep chocolate color as the floorboards—and looks twice as old. Carvings of mythical creatures dance around its borders, people with painted grins and animal legs. It drips a type of old-world decadence that inspires curiosity. And fear. It's more like an unsettling movie prop than a real-life piece of furniture.

The bed now sits directly across from the mirror, and I lay sprawled out across the comforter, catching my breath. I hold Nora's switchblade above my head, pop it in and out of its holster and wait for my pulse to steady.

The Victorian sighs around me. Windowpanes strain against the wind, floorboards groan. Each bulb and board shivers silently through the dark. Somewhere, on the opposite end of the house, the hole in the roof yawns against the sky, allowing the house to breathe.

I roll onto my side and examine my reflection. My face is dirty from digging. My clothes are a mess, and my hair is greasy. This afternoon feels like it happened last week. I wish I could summon the same feeling of resolve I had out in the hallway, but now I'm not so sure if slicing away at the wall is the best way to move forward.

Back home, I carved tallies into the portion of wall behind my headboard—long, thin scratches that look too much like prison bars. Whether it was due to boredom, or an innate, deeply buried need to destroy, I can't be sure. But cutting into my room back home is easy; it's less alive than the Victorian.

I sit up and turn to the wall. Knees tucked beneath me, I test the dips in the paper until I find an area that sags. It's slightly damp beneath my fingertips, and I cringe as I rest the sharp tip of the knife against it and press my forehead against the wall.

"Are you there?" I ask, my voice barely above a whisper. I close my eyes and press my forehead deeper into the spot. It sinks in like the skin of an overripe peach. My hands tremble, and I wait for the voice.

"Can you hear me?" I ask the wall, the knife still poised to pierce its lavender wrappings.

I keep my eyes closed. The dark under my eyelids is different from the dark inside this house. It has fingers and a human voice. My voice. Through the dark...

I can't stop thinking about Nora's anxiety, the death of her family, and everything else she never told me. It's too much to take.

There's a piece of myself buried out there.

Why not tell me that from the beginning? *We're going to my old house. I buried something in the yard before the house burned down, and I want it back. It's the only thing I have left of my family.*

It should have been that simple to explain.

Then again, cutting into the wall should be simple too. But I think of Victor, the way the corner of his mouth twitches when I so much as move the wrong way, and I can't bring myself to slice into the paper. I try to recreate the feeling I had out in the hallway, I try to smother his voice until it fades to static, but I can't. Even though he's miles away, he's still so loud inside my head.

"What's wrong with me," I murmur.

Victor can't see what I'm doing. It's not like I can disappoint him or make him angry. But I break out in a cold sweat anyway. It's psychosomatic. An ache. Worse than an ache—an emptiness.

I hold back. I punish myself because he isn't here, because I shouldn't be away from him like this. I shouldn't feel *relieved* that I'm away from him. But the relief is there, beneath the worry, rotting me from the inside. It blooms in the spaces between my ribs and coats my heart like mold.

The worst part is that none of this should matter. Not when there's a person in the wall, and I know that I've been inside this house before but can't remember why. Not when Nora refuses to explain. It shouldn't matter what Victor thinks.

He's not going to find me here.

He doesn't even know where I am.

My eyes snap open.

He's not here.

My chest constricts.

He doesn't know where I am. He can't find me.

And then...

What if I don't go back home?

The knife slips out of my hand and falls against the comforter with a muted thud. I stare blankly at the wallpaper. Up close, the lilacs blur. They look bruised.

I turn from the wall to face my reflection. The dirt on my cheeks, the greasy tangle of my hair, even the way my hands shake seems different. Less hopeless. And for a moment, I forget all the reasons why I shouldn't stay here. I forget that Victor loves me and that I can't leave him. I forget that there's a hole in the roof and it's only a matter of time before this building decays around me. That I don't have my pills with me, and without my pills I'll die.

All I can think of are the reasons why I should, why I could, stay.

Even though I'd be alone.

There's someone in the walls. If I stay, I won't be alone, I remind myself. *Maybe I could convince Nora to stay too. I've been to the Victorian before; my body remembers this place; it shouldn't be scary.*

And Victor...

No.

Tears sting the corners of my eyes.

Victor loves me.

He loves me and I can't leave him.

I can't turn my back on our routine—our life. Our morning cups of tea. Our math and science lessons. Our lunches. The smell of melted cheddar cheese and bacon, and the lazy way the sun falls through the windows over the kitchen sink. How soft the light looks even though it burns.

Victor loves me.

I can't leave him when he works so hard to keep my broken biology in check, even with all the vials of blood and the way his fingers press into my skin a little too deeply when he tightens the tourniquet.

"It wouldn't hurt, if you held still," he said the last time he drew my blood. I couldn't help but wince when he stuck the needle in.

"I hate this," I said once he was finished, and I held a cotton ball to the small, red entry mark.

"You think I enjoy it?" He heaved a sigh and peeled his glove off with a loud snap before moving the vial into a worn leather case—filing it away with the others. "It's a lot of work to keep you well. Caring for you takes a lot out of me. It's exhausting."

I lowered my head and stared at my feet, curling my toes into the slate tiles. "I'm sorry. I don't mean to make things difficult for you."

His fingers tightened around my wrist. "Then learn to sit still."

He loves—

Something slides across the surface of the mirror.

A shadow or a person. It's only there for a second before it vanishes.

My brow furrows.

"Nora?" I ask, even though there's no way it could be her. There's no way it could be human.

Another flicker. Another shadow slips across the glass, as quickly as before. And just as quickly, it's gone.

I slide off the bed and approach the mirror. My reflection echoes my footsteps. I tilt my head to the left, then to the right. I blink and my reflection blinks back at me. I see myself inside its eyes, layers and layers of glass separating us.

"I thought the only thing I had to worry about was the person in the wall, but there's something in there too, isn't there?" I say to my reflection and remind myself to take deep evenly spaced breaths. I remind myself to resist the undertow. Push against the current. Stay calm.

I lay my hand against the glass so that my reflection's palm presses against mine. It's strange to see so much of myself all at once.

Victor doesn't keep mirrors in the house if he can help it. I've only ever known the arch of my eyebrow, the bend of my elbow reflected in a side mirror, a compact, a storefront window. Severed at the waist, at the torso, at the clavicle. Cut apart. Bisected by the corners of buildings, or the rounded edges of utensils. I've never seen myself this close, this complete. Not without a seam or a slice down my center.

My fingers dance across the glass. I trace circles, triangles, and squares into its surface. Tiny sparks of warmth zap around my fingertips. Bursts of electricity. Like there's a jolt of lightning ringing out from inside me, like the glass is reacting to my skin.

My hand.

My touch.

My anxiety.

Same as the hum beneath my skin when I was digging with Nora earlier. Same as the pull I felt when moving the bed. Only different somehow, more cautious—almost tender.

Then a shock pulses out from the mirror and into my

fingertips, and my eyes stretch as wide as they can go. Something rushes through me, up my arm. An electric current filling my veins, chilling the highways of my skin. There are barely more than three seconds of trauma, but something's pulled from the core of my body, and something rushes in to replace it.

It leaves my fingers and toes feeling fuzzy. I pull my hand away from the mirror, and even though I expect to find my fingers burned, they look fine. A little red. A little swollen, but okay.

I take a breath and wade through the water inside my mind. Avoid the deep end. Avoid the dark.

It's late, and I haven't eaten since lunchtime. It's late, and I'm tired, and I'm seeing things that aren't there. Except they are there, and suddenly every piece of furniture in the room looks menacing, and I watch them as if they might move, or call out to me, or do whatever the mirror did—burn me, shock me, scar me.

"No before, no forever, no afterward," I whisper, as if the words have the power to draw the person in the wall to me or summon whatever hides within the mirror. But nothing happens.

I sigh and turn from the glass, make my way back to bed before flicking the switchblade into the handle, laying it down next to my pillow.

Victor loves me. I know he loves me. But I've decided I'm not going home tomorrow. I might not go home at all.

I rest my hand against the wall and beneath my fingers, in my last coherent moment before I fall asleep, something moves.

A young woman stands at the edge of a lake, her face obscured by a mess of wavy black hair. The sun drips below the tree line, moments away from setting. The sky isn't quite red yet—it's still speckled with

orange, like the pulp of a citrus fruit—but it will be red soon. Sunsets are always the same here.

There's a child standing next to the young woman. She wears her blonde hair in long, thin braids. It resembles spider's silk, fine and patchy in places. She seems so much older than she looks, already balding, her body already soft with decay. Her face bleeds into the sky.

It's yellow, and orange, and red.

Everything except for her braids is out of focus.

"I hate it when the sun sets this way. It is too violent," the child says, pulling at the hem of the woman's skirt. Her skin is slightly gray, her fingernails completely black. She speaks in a jerky staccato that seems to emphasize her unease. "It frightens me, Mother."

The woman, Mother, takes her hand, squeezing gently. "It's okay. I'm here."

The sunset shifts. The water turns red, and everything blurs around the edges even more.

"Your hand is cold," the child says.

"So is yours."

"I do not think I will ever be warm again. Not after what happened..."

Mother bends down, so her face is level with the child's though it remains hidden behind her hair. She considers her words carefully before speaking.

"I want to ask you about what happened. Is that all right?" she asks, her voice grave.

The child hesitates, twisting the hem of her skirt.

"You can tell me anything," Mother assures her. "It's important that you feel comfortable around me."

"I do feel comfortable around you!"

"Good. Now, I understand that what happened was traumatic. I understand that what happened might make you wonder about certain things." She pauses for a moment. "You know what kind of things I'm talking about, don't you?"

The child squirms, clearly uncomfortable. "Yes."

"I'm going to ask you a question and it's very important that you answer honestly."

The child nods again. "I will."

Mother takes a deep breath, as if preparing herself for the child's answer and what it will mean... for both of them.

"Do you know what you are?" she asks.

The child slips completely out of focus, her braids disappearing into the skyline. She hesitates for a moment, but eventually nods. It's a small nod, barely enough to constitute an answer. "I also know that I am not what you wanted. I try my best, but I am broken..."

Mother heaves a sigh and shakes her head. "I'm sorry. I never wanted you to find out, especially not like this."

The sky melts around them, and citrus streaks down from the stars. The child huddles against Mother's shoulder.

"You know that I love you, right?" Mother asks.

"Of course. And I love you."

"But you know what you are. And you know what they expect me to do now."

The child nods solemnly, burying her face deeper into the fabric of Mother's dress.

"Look at me," Mother says, and even though it takes some coaxing, the child eventually pulls back, and Mother takes one of her braids between her fingers, worrying the fine hair.

"You're the only thing I've ever wanted," she says. "You're the only thing I'll ever love in this world." With that, she releases the braid and wraps her hands around the child's neck, spinning her around.

Mother pulls a knife from the folds of her skirt, the short blade glinting red in the fading light and before the child has a chance to react, Mother plunges it into her chest.

She stabs, and stabs, and stabs.

She cries while she does it, she tries to look into the child's eyes, tries to convey how truly sorry she is, but it's impossible to see past the color.

It's so hard to focus. Past the red, and red, and red.

The water is so dark that it's impossible to tell where it ends, and the blood begins.

"I'll tell you what you are. You're—"

6

I wake with a start. Cold sweat plasters my dress against my back, and my hair lays damp and tangled across my cheek. It takes me a second to realize that I'm not at home, that the room isn't mine. The colors, the shapes of the furniture are similar, but they aren't mine.

The sunrise filters through the windows in vivid shades of orange and red. It's too much like the nightmare, and the nightmare is unlike anything I've dreamt before. None of Nora's paintings come close to the attack I witnessed. The violence of it, the vicious smear of blood and sky.

I watch the sunrise for a few moments until the color is eclipsed by clouds though muted light still shines through, the telltale brightness of a coming storm.

Do you know what you are?

I shiver. "It'll be okay, you had a shitty dream that's all."

Nora's family burned to death in this house.

I press my palm into my scar. "You'll be okay."

No wonder I had a nightmare though.

Nora's family died here.

Her paintings stare down at me, globs of abstract color, and texture, and terror. The one of the little girl on the swing remains out in the hall, and—still shaken from the nightmare—I consider pulling the others down to join it. There's comfort in the square of discoloration where Nora's self-portrait used to hang. It's pale and worn down. I trace the outline of the paper, feeling the soft sink of the plaster. My finger pokes right through it and my pulse quickens. There's power in destruction, I realize. There's power in me.

When I came back to life this time, I promised myself that things would be different. *I* would be different. Embrace my hunger for rebellion, chase down the ache inside my veins. But there's still so much push and pull inside my head, it's difficult to truly change.

Still, I owe it to myself to try.

I pull Nora's knife out from under my pillow and poke at the soft spot behind the bed, tearing into the hole I made. After testing the strength of the wall, I thrust the knife into the plaster as hard as I can and rip the paper from the center of the spot. It's like unwrapping a present. As I work, pieces fall away where the glue has melted from the plaster and the paper has bubbled. Other spots are stubborn, and the colored bits tear away while the underside of the paper continues to cling. It's like a hangnail that won't tear cleanly, it leaves wreckage in its wake.

I make my way around the room, remove Nora's paintings, and continue slicing at the wall. One, two, three strikes of the knife. I press my hands in, attempt to hollow out what I can, but beneath the flimsy paper, the walls here are sturdy, even where they bend. It's useless.

Slamming my palm against the plaster, I bite down on my lip until I taste blood. I'm trying so hard to be strong, to be brave, to be more than what I am, and it's still not enough.

I drop the knife before making my way to the center of the

room, suddenly uncomfortable, wishing I could crawl out of my skin.

I unzip my dress, letting it crumple to the floor, and examine myself in the mirror, pushing my greasy hair out of my face. I rub the dirt until it's faded, and my cheeks are red and puffy. I only need to step back three places to see my whole reflection.

It's exciting to see my scar without straining, without looking down at it. Straight on it's less grotesque. Despite the circumstances that brought me here, despite the voice in the wall, and the vicious nightmare, I can't help but think of my list. A conversation with a stranger, and how close I am to speaking with someone who might be able to explain why this house seems so familiar.

"I'm getting better," I tell my reflection: bony, scarred. At first, the sight of my body provides comfort. It reminds me of the things I've survived and what I have to show for the scar on my chest, but after a while my flesh breaks out in goosebumps, and I shiver. I reach down to pick up my dress, but recoil against the scent. Layers of dirt and sweat make it smell like a landfill—the salty stench of fear overpowering the softness of the lace.

I wander over to the wardrobe, thinking again of my list. One of the last three items: make a daring fashion choice. I always imagined it would be a skintight black dress, or leather pants... but still...

My pulse pounds through my forehead. I already slept in someone else's bed; I can't wear another person's clothing.

For all I know, the wardrobe could be empty, but assuming there are clothes inside, clothes that I could wear...

A shudder runs through me. But this me is different, this me is meant to transform.

I open the door and find six dresses hung up on the left side of the otherwise empty wardrobe. I leaf through them. The labels appear to be handmade, crudely sewn, and stuck into the collar of the dresses, almost like an afterthought. Each label has a number written on it in thick magic marker—seventeen, sixteen, fifteen, all the way down to twelve. A red velvet ribbon sits tied at the top of each hanger, and each size—my size—is marked in ink, same as the numbers.

Why are they my size?

The colors here are the same as your room back home too, I remind myself, but that isn't entirely true. The bedspread is similar, that's it. Maybe that's where the creeping, familiar feeling comes from. Rooms and decorations that are almost, but not quite, identical.

I lay three of the dresses out on the bed and take inventory before settling on the one with a plain black skirt and a white blouse sewn into it, the one with seventeen written on the label. It's perfect. The collar is low enough for a half of an inch of my scar to sit exposed. It's as if the dress were tailored for that exact purpose, for the scar to have the room it needs to breathe. The thought crackles across my skin, igniting as much fear as it does wonder.

I ditch my ruined tights, run my fingers through my hair, and after some consideration, tie it back using one of the ribbons.

Standing in front of the mirror, the outfit doesn't look half bad. The blouse is slightly yellowed, but it's almost impossible to tell. It fits me perfectly, and despite the aged appearance, the fabric smells sweet, like ripe apricots.

The smell reminds me of when Victor and I would sit out on our front porch in the summer and the warmth would settle under my skin. The scent of apricots mixing with freshly cut grass. The whirl of lawnmower blades our own private symphony.

I pick up the two other dresses and place them back inside

the wardrobe before slipping the switchblade into my pocket and piling my old clothes at the foot of the bed.

I wander back to the mirror. I step up close to the glass and hover my hand an inch from its surface, thinking of the shadow and the static I felt last night when I touched it. The tips of my fingers no longer tingle, and the glass doesn't appear different in any way—still, I can't help but wonder...

If I touch it again, will I feel the same thing? Is there really an electric current swimming beneath the glass?

My hand hovers over it for a long time before I finally pull it back.

I notice it to the right of the mirror, level with my eye.

There's a hole torn into the wallpaper, the size of a quarter. Like someone inside stuck their fingers through, like someone is trying to get out.

There are three layers to the wall: wallpaper, plaster, wooden planks. Skin on top of flesh, on top of hollow bone.

I trace the edges of the shredded paper. Beyond the tear, the plaster has cracked and fallen away, and the planks beneath it bend inward as if pulled by unseen fingers. Proof that whoever lives inside is real—capable of prying, and scraping, and trying to free themselves. I press my fingers to my scarred chest and focus on my breathing, eyes locked on the hole in the wall.

No matter how hard I squint or how close I press my eye to the hole, I can't see anything. I suck air in between my teeth, and remind myself to stay calm, to keep my pulse steady.

"No before, no forever, no afterward," I whisper to the torn wallpaper, the hole, and whoever hides inside. "I'm here. Now come find me."

I scoop Nora's switchblade off the floor, slice around the edges of the hole, and pull at the corners of the paper. It flakes off easily, like a sunburn, and my pulse quickens. As I tear at the plaster, the hole grows to the size of a small fist, and I tuck the knife into my skirt pocket. I reach inside. Cool, damp air washes over my skin. I push my hand in as deep as it will go, up to the wrist then the elbow, despite the waves of unease that wash over me.

At first, nothing happens. I curl my fingers into the dark and rest my cheek against the wallpaper, waiting for words to bubble up from the abyss.

I rake my fingers through the damp air, the scar down the center of my palm stretched outward, as if it might shed light on whoever lurks within the passageway. There's so much empty space, no insulation, no cobwebs—just space. Endless, aching. It doesn't make any sense. I press my arm deeper and deeper, past my elbow and all the way to the crook of my armpit. Nothing but space.

My fingers cramp and my shoulder aches from being twisted against the wall and suddenly all this feels insane. Even if the person in the wall was here last night, even if she tried to tear through the plaster, she didn't make it into the room, and the chances that she's still around are slim. She could be back in the kitchen wall or any number of places within the Victorian.

I heave a sigh and begin to pull my arm from the wall when a hand reaches out and curls around my own.

Thin fingers, frail as spider legs, lace through mine and I let out a cry.

"Shhhh, do not be afraid," the person inside the wall says, her breath light as a spring breeze against my fingertips. She still sounds exactly like me. "I am a friend."

She's not human—not completely. The texture of her skin is wrong, the length of her bones, the lack of fingernails... I stay pressed up against the wall, eyes locked on the carved frame—the mythical creatures etched into the side the standing mirror. My blood pulses in my ears, and it's difficult to stand still, to breathe, to do anything without feeling like I'm going to collapse into myself.

The person within the plaster speaks.

"No before, no forever, no afterward," she says again, her voice—my voice—soft and garbled.

"What does that mean?"

"It means that you have finally come home." She traces her fingers along the backs of my knuckles, and my breath catches in my throat. "After all this time, I am not alone."

Home? Does she think that I'm Nora? I want the words to be meant for me so badly that it hurts. I want this to be where I belong, as if that's all it will take to stop feeling like my skin isn't mine, like my body isn't mine, like none of this is me.

"You're confusing me with someone else," I say quietly.

"No. You have come home."

The Victorian is my home as well as Nora's?

When I think of home, I think of a ranch-style house on a hill. I think of grilled cheese sandwiches, and sci-fi paperbacks. Old cookbooks. Victor.

Vials of blood.

Little white pills.

The kaleidoscope inside my mind twists, and I wade through the red and blue. Through Victor's study, and past his leather-bound journals. There's something there, something deeper. Something closer to home, but just out of reach.

"Why do you sound like me?" I ask.

She chuckles and the sound is like a bell ringing. "*You* sound like *me*."

My skin prickles and I nearly choke on my response. "I want to ask what you mean, but I don't know if I can handle the answer."

"You were always the brave one, the strong one. You can handle anything."

A pang rings out inside my chest. The kaleidoscope shifts again. Home. Victor calling for me from the living room. Victor grinding up my medication and sprinkling it over my food like seasoning—watching as I clear my plate. The bitter taste that follows.

"You're confusing me with Nora." I resist the urge to tighten my grip on her hand. It feels too much like a corn husk. Bits of skin flake into my palm, and I worry that it will crumble if I squeeze too hard.

The person in the wall mutters under her breath, and I rest my head against the plaster, my neck stiff from staying in one position for so long.

"What did you say?" I ask. "I can't hear you."

"I said that I have been waiting for this for a long time." The more she speaks, the more I notice the strange cadence of her voice. There's a slight delay, a hesitation, as if it takes her a great deal of effort to string the words together.

My pulse screams in my ears, loud as a train horn, and the longer I stare at the mirror's frame, the more the creatures' legs seem to twitch within the wood.

"It has been over two years since everyone has been home," the person in the wall continues. She gently presses against each of my knuckles, as if she thinks I might disappear if she stops touching me. "Over two years of silence. I was not sure if I could handle any more silence. I was waiting for so long."

"You've been inside the wall for two years?" I ask, the word *everyone* echoing inside my head, making me dizzy.

"Nearly three. I did not think anyone would come back. Not her, not you. After what happened, I am surprised that she is able to walk down these halls again. I can barely squeeze through the walls without remembering everything and how much it hurt."

"She... you mean Nora?" I ask, my free hand pressed so hard against my surgical scar that the joint in my wrist strains beneath the pressure. I think of Nora's eyes, so red from crying.

She shifts behind the plaster. "I do not know anyone named Nora."

"The girl I came here with, the one who lived here before, her name is Nora. But after the fire her family died and..." That was a lie, wasn't it? A lie or a half-truth. Ice water floods my veins. I drag my fingers across the scar on my chest as her fingers continue to explore my skin. I keep my hand perfectly still, terrified that if I so much as breathe the wrong way her hand will snap off in mine.

She sighs again. "I am trying to find the words to explain. I have not spoken to anyone in a very long time."

I focus on the carvings in the frame, the hoofed feet and furry haunches. The legs that stretch around the edges of the mirror, as if dancing or preparing to dive inside the glass.

My pulse hums beneath my skin. "Why don't you come out here? We can talk face to face. I have trouble finding my words sometimes too, and it might help if there wasn't something so solid between us."

There's a sharp intake of air. She shuffles her feet, and a series of faint scratches sound from behind the plaster. "I cannot leave the wall. I cannot go outside."

Relief and disappointment, each one potent enough to kill, wash over me in equal doses. I won't have to face her. I can't face her.

"I have thought about getting out, but I have been in here for so long," she continues, voice wavering—sounding farther away, more buried, than before. "I am different... and I am not sure what you would think of me. It is dark back here, but at least I am safe. It is enough to have you back home—I am not alone—and that can be enough for me. I have planned this conversation in my head so many times, but now I do not know where to begin. I know I am not making much sense."

"I could come in," I suggest, my skin prickling at the thought. Deep down I know that I could never get up the nerve.

"You could come in," she agrees. "To the basement labs. But

the door is locked, and I am not sure which room it opens to on the first floor."

"Labs?" The hairs on my arms bristle. "What kind of labs? What do you mean there are labs in the basement?"

The person inside the wall draws in another shaky breath but remains silent.

I think of Victor. I think of his special workshop in our basement back home, where he runs my blood through machines that whirl and sputter. His secret place where he keeps his bookshelves, his journals, his reminders of my many deaths. Locked away downstairs, aging like wine.

The kaleidoscope behind my eyes shifts in shades of red and blue. Victor stretching plastic gloves over his hands, a bright snap, baby powder in the air. Needles in skin. Blood in vials. So much blood.

"What do you mean there are labs in the basement?" I ask again.

"How do you tell someone something that will destroy them?" There's compassion in her voice, sadness. Raw, flaking emotion.

We stand quietly with our hands clasped together for several minutes, and the only sound is the frantic drumming of my heartbeat. The carvings in the mirror's frame seem to flicker.

"Whatever you have to say won't destroy me," I whisper to the paper, my eyes clouded with tears. I can't stop shaking. "I think it would fix me."

Fingers trace the scar down the center of my palm. "Silvie..."

"Yes," I say, my voice cracking. "Yes, it's me, it's Silvie."

"No," the person says, letting out the word in a long, snaking wail. "You are not Silvie. Poor thing, you have no idea..." She pulls her hand from mine and floorboards creak behind the plaster, her body shifts back into the passageway. "You have no idea what you are."

A gust of wind erupts as they sink back into the wall, and tears stream down my cheeks. My free hand remains pressed against my scar, the side of my face flush with the wall.

"Wait!" I cry, choking on the words. "Who are you?"

Then, quietly, "Who am I?"

I tug my hand from the plaster, the rough edges of the wall scratching into my wrist. Flakes of skin kick up around it in a lopsided circle and it appears mangled in the dim light.

Silence fills the room, broken only by the occasional rattling of a windowpane. The hole in the wall glares out at me.

You poor thing, you have no idea...

... what you are...

I can't steady my breathing. The words are almost identical to what the woman in my nightmare said before she killed the little girl.

How old was the child in my dream? Eight? Nine?

The same age I was the first time I died...

There are *labs* in the basement.

I sink to my knees, my vision tunneling until the scratches in the floorboards are the only things I can focus on with any clarity. Everything else goes dark around the edges, and I sit halfway between reality and a nightmare.

The red of the sunset, the cornhusk skin of the person in the wall—it all bleeds together inside my head, and my breath comes in short, shallow gasps.

"But the nightmare wasn't mine," I whisper. "It's a coincidence that the person in the wall said those things."

Didn't Nora tell me that there's no such thing as coincidence?

Even though it was a coincidence that we met in the first place. It was a coincidence that Victor ran into her... where did he say they ran into each other again? The post office? The supermarket? He kept me away from her for the longest time. I wasn't allowed into the places she worked, but by coincidence we both happened to be out in the yard at the same time one day.

It was a coincidence that I'd been watching her for weeks when she finally noticed me—her eyes wide as she declared me her long-lost twin, surprised that we looked so similar.

"Please," I said. "Victor doesn't like me talking to people I don't know."

"It's okay, Silvie," she said, wrapping her arms around me. "We'll get to know each other soon. We're gonna be close, I can tell."

Only now I can't remember if I ever told her my name.

Now I'm not sure if any of it was a coincidence or if she was biding her time until she could get me alone.

It's as if she knew when to approach me and what to do once we spoke.

And if she knew, then we were never really strangers.

I push the thought from my mind and concentrate instead on the rise and fall of my chest, the beating of my heart, the rattling of the windowpanes.

Slowly, the room shifts back into focus. A fine sheen of sweat has broken out across my forehead, and I dab at it with the corner of my skirt.

My head aches.

I crave fresh air, and make my way to the window.

I poise myself to lift the heavy pane but freeze when I look through the glass to the yard below. Outside, there's a blizzard so thick that I can't see more than a few inches from the glass.

~

"Nora!" I pound my fist against her door again and again, painfully aware of the redness that surrounds my wrist like a cuff. "Nora, wake up!"

Panic. Ripe, raspberry panic. My blood feels thick as jam. It's sweet, and sick, and gummed up inside my veins. I thought I was ready for this. I was so sure that I could be strong enough.

You were always the brave one, the strong one.

I wish.

I run my hand along the velvet ribbon in my hair, and the texture calms me down a little. The softness of it. The strangeness of it. I steady myself and wait, but Nora doesn't come to the door. I need to tell her about the person in the wall. I need to get her to believe me.

"Nora, please. I… I spoke with the person in the wall… she's real." And there's a blizzard outside, we're not making it home today.

You have finally come home.

"You need to tell me the truth. Because I know that what you told me earlier isn't all of it, and I *have* been here before, and I'm not going anywhere, or helping you with anything, until you explain this to me."

It takes everything I have not to accuse her of orchestrating this whole thing from the moment we met. Somehow, everything—from the first time I saw her to the first time we spoke—has led us to this house, to these halls. And then there's Victor's role in it. Victor who brought her into our home; Victor who hates her so much but not enough to keep her away from me. I don't have anything to back it up, just a feeling—an uneasiness that refuses to fade.

"It's snowing so much that I can't even see the holes that we dug yesterday," I add. "Seriously Nora, open the door."

There's still no response.

My stomach grumbles. I haven't eaten anything since

yesterday afternoon, and I can't tell if I'm lightheaded from hunger or panic.

Waves of heat flash up into my forehead.

It would be a mistake to stay in this house. We'll starve in here. We'll resort to eating strips of wallpaper. We'll have to rip the stuffing from the furniture and chew until our gums bleed, until we chew the house down to its bones and then—

No.

I sever the thought. Amputate it. Get it as far away from myself as I can. I need to stay calm and focus on one thing at a time. We'll never make it out of here if I let myself spiral down into the undertow, and I'll never get better if I let the thoughts pull me into the brine. I'll never find out how I'm connected to this place.

I move my hand from the ribbon to the door.

"I'm coming in," I say quietly and turn the knob.

"Nora?" I ask as the door swings open, but the room is empty. She's not here.

I bite through the inside of my cheek and the metallic taste of blood spreads across my tongue. I take cautious steps into the room and let the door swing shut behind me.

The room is almost identical to the one I'm staying in, except there are no paintings on the walls and her mirror is covered by a thin white sheet. I peak beneath it and sure enough, the frame is covered in the same carvings as the one in my room.

Nora's bed sits in the center of the room, the same as mine before I moved it. The comforter—a pale blue version of mine—is still tucked into the mattress, and it doesn't look like she slept here at all. But her duffel bag sits on top of the bed.

I stop gnawing at my cheek and approach the duffel. Before I make it to the bed, the wardrobe catches my eye. The doors are open a crack and I move to where it stands and peer inside. The same six dresses hang on the left-hand side. They're arranged in the same order. Same cut, same style, same colors. The sheer pink one that looks like a glorified nightgown, the burgundy dress with the sequins, and the one that I'm wearing.

I push through the clothes and pull out the dress that I put on, but the number written on the tag is different, and I let out a small sigh. The room's not a mirror image after all, it's just filled with similar stuff.

I wander the perimeter, pressing my hands to the paper. I heave a sigh. The walls don't have the same soft spots as the ones in my room either.

Now, back to the duffel.

I sit down on the edge of Nora's bed, the bag within arm's reach of where I am.

I inch my way closer to it, run my fingers along the zipper.

Nora and I are best friends. The scar down the center of my palm proves that we're blood sisters. Even if she never tells me the truth about her history here, even if our coincidental meeting was anything but, we're still connected. And I have a right to know what she brought here, and why she's hiding it.

I grab a hold of the zipper and pull.

The duffel bag bursts open to reveal a pale pink comforter. I run my hand over the top and feel the outline of something solid within the blankets.

I reach into the bag and unfold the comforter to reveal the lid of a jar. I grip both sides of the jar and hoist it from the mess of pink bedding. It's heavier than I anticipated, but still easy enough to lift. I move carefully in case it's fragile and cast nervous glances at the door. If Nora walks in on me, it'll take a lot to convince her that I didn't come in here to snoop.

It's her own fault for wandering off to a different part of the house. For all I know, she could have left immediately after she was sure that I had settled in for the night. She could have spent the night in the kitchen or out in the yard digging more of her damn holes.

I pull the jar from the comforter and place it on the bed next to the duffel bag.

It takes me a moment to process what's inside it, to accept that what I'm looking at is really there.

My eyes dart from the jar to the door, to the sheet-covered mirror. Around and around the room. This can't be real.

This is sick.

This is...

I tug the jar closer to me, the whirlpool inside my mind swirling with salt and foam and an inky, endless dark. I rest the jar in my lap and stare down at it in horror.

There's a heart inside.

7

Tension.

Tightness.

The feeling of lungs and ribs, and all the meaty pieces of myself, being far too big for my body.

My insides strain against my skin. They bruise it.

And my heart.

Oh, my heart.

Kick, kick, kicking against my chest. Ripping at my scar. Making it worse. Making it hurt more.

I struggle to breathe.

I struggle.

To think.

Feel.

Hear anything but the sound of the blood rushing through my body, and in the back of my head I know...

... I know that I'm drowning from the inside.

It's in a jar. It's in a jar. It's in a jar.

Again. And again. And again. The rush of the water—

No, I remind myself as I gasp, and my vision tunnels. *I need to breathe.*

Through the madness...

Through the madness there are five things. Five things I can see.

One, the sheet over the mirror. Two, the wardrobe. Three, the closed door, and four, the peeling white paint.

The heart in the jar. There isn't any formaldehyde or vinegar or other pickling juice inside the jar, only a heart. I stare at it and—

No.

My stomach heaves. I can't look at the heart.

The bedspread. I focus on the bedspread.

I focus on...

Four things I can hear.

One, the storm outside. Two, the sounds of the house settling, old floorboards and thin walls. Three, the sound of my breathing. I suck air in and let it out again. I listen carefully so I can hear it, really hear it.

A buzzing radiates from the jar. The sound calls to me same as the whine I heard outside the Victorian, only this time it sings. It sings and it's so much stronger than before. It buries itself inside my ears and screams for me to reach out and wrap my hands around the heart. My fingers twitch toward the lid and—

No. I turn my attention from it. I focus on the room.

I am here.

I can see it.

Hear it.

I'm okay.

I breathe in. Breathe in the musty smell of the bedspread. The smell of my sweat and the sweet apricot scent of the clothes that I'm wearing.

I run my tongue along the backs of my teeth. Rough and sour. Like the fly that trills inside my mouth each time I resurrect. My teeth haven't been brushed in what feels like years.

Then there's the taste of sweat that's settled across my upper lip. Salty, sharp.

My fingers twitch.

The heart is still here, in the jar to my right.

They aren't supposed to stay red after they're taken out, but the heart is very, very red. It's red like last night's sunset and this morning's sunrise, red like the sunset from my nightmare. Red like the little girl's blood. It's the bright sting of a fresh cut.

I breathe in through my nose and out through my mouth. Again and again. My pulse settles, but my chest is still sore.

The heart in the jar is terrible and beautiful, and I can't stop looking at it.

I lift it in front of my face, my nose inches from the glass. I see myself, the wall behind me, and the heart reflected double across the surface of my eyes.

I run my fingers around the lid of the jar.

A heart.

I'm still raw from the shock of it. I'm still flayed apart and bleeding inside, but I tread water and keep my head above the frothy pull of the undertow.

Aside from a few scabs of blood along the bottom of the jar and around its edges, the heart sits alone.

I press it against my scarred chest and listen. The strange vibration is still coming from the glass. The soft melodic buzz.

"What are you trying to tell me?" I ask, my voice strained, and I wrap myself tightly around the jar. The humming is low and desperate, and I wrack my brain to think of where Nora could have possibly found the thing.

The buzzing intensifies, and I shift uncomfortably. It's all I can do not to drop the jar and cover my ears. A feeling like the pull of a current rushes through me. Like blood and water and plasma. The buzzing trembles in every vein, in every artery. My body spasms from the shock of it.

The sound is all encompassing. It fills me until I'm bloated, ready to burst. It fills the room until the air is so thick that I find myself sucking in huge uneven gasps, which leave me lightheaded.

My fingers twitch again.

Five, four, three, two, one.

Five, four, three, two—

I still need one.

One thing I can touch, feel. Really feel.

The heart in the jar.

Despite the soreness. The massacre. The aftermath of my panic attack.

The melodic buzzing keeps getting louder and louder. It calls for me, and I answer it.

I give the lid a twist and reach my hand inside, resting two fingers on top of the organ.

The noise stops.

It's so silent that all I can hear is the wind through the pines outside and the snow as it falls in sheets.

The heart is warmer than I expected it to be, and soft, and rubbery. I lean my whole hand down across it. Dribbles of blood sweat out through its flesh, still warm, still sticky, and the blood inches its way between my fingers.

I pull my hand away, and clutch it to my chest, my palm stained red.

The heart trembles. It starts, and stops, and starts again until it moves rhythmically.

It's beating.

Because of me.

I revived it with my touch, and the rush of power is unlike anything. It dizzies me. For the first time, I understand how Victor must feel when he brings me back from the dead.

It's like I'm drunk on the rush.

In awe of it.

I pull the jar closer, marveling at the way the organ rises and falls. The hum is back beneath my skin, chewing at me from the inside, and as I lift the jar level with my face, the first word the heart speaks sounds like a wheeze.

8

It's so soft, so garbled, that I almost write it off as the house straining against the storm, or my own mouth making sick, wet noises.

Then it repeats itself. Louder. Clearer. Very distinctly not the house. Or me. Or anything that I've ever heard before.

"*Silvie.*" My name squishes through my head, as if spoken through a mouthful of damp soil. There's no external voice, and I would mistake it for my own thoughts if it didn't sound so different from me. While it's distinctly feminine, there's a maturity to it, a confidence that inspires as much envy as it does fear.

The jar sits cradled in my lap, my hands pressed against either side of the glass. A bright red smear coats the center of my scarred palm, and with the lid back in place, the blood on my hand offers the only evidence that any of this is real. It sticks to the side of the jar like a melted lollipop.

It's still warm.

"*I can't hear your thoughts, so you're going to have to speak up,*" the heart says. "*Though hopefully we'll be able to communicate more effectively as our bond grows stronger.*"

I move my clean hand so that it lays flat against my surgical scar.

My mind spins through everything that's happened since Nora and I entered the house. My voice in the wall. Melodic buzzing. The heart beneath my palm. Blood between my fingers. And now, another voice.

I did this.

The Victorian called to me. My own voice called to me. The heart called out too. I answered the call with my touch, and now—

"Silvie," the heart cries out inside my head again, its voice growing less muddled with each new word. *"Speak up. I'm starting to worry that our bond is even weaker than I suspected."*

I shove the jar to the end of the bed. It teeters on the edge of the mattress, a gentle nudge away from falling to the floor.

"I know what you must be thinking: that I can't talk because hearts can't talk. But I'm not a heart, not really. And I've been waiting for you for a very long time."

No, it *is* a heart. It's obviously a heart. Despite the redness of it, the vicious coloring that looks so much more like an artist's interpretation than an actual human organ, it must be a heart.

What else could it be?

I ball my fingers around my scarred palm and pretend that I can feel Nora's hand in mine. I pretend that the warm squish of blood, the tacky coagulation, is nothing more than her fingers lacing through my own. She's here telling me to breathe. It will be okay, just breathe.

Even though this is all her fault. Even though she's hidden so much from me. Even though she's a murderer. Or worse. Grave robber, organ harvester. My mind spins through countless explanations, but none of them make me feel any better about the heart.

"Why won't you talk to me?" it asks.

"Because we aren't talking. At least you're not really talking.

I have pills that I'm supposed to take daily, and I haven't taken them since I got here, so you're probably a hallucination." Even though nothing like this happened the last time I skipped my medicine, and it took almost two months before skipping it killed me.

"White pills?"

"How do you know what color they are?" I pull Nora's switchblade out of my pocket and point it toward the heart, which pulses softly, unaware of the knife. My hand shakes and I can't bring myself to unscrew the lid a second time. I'm not sure I could stop myself from touching it again. Even now, there's a pull beneath my skin, a current tugging me toward the heart.

"I know a lot of things," it says. *"I'm not the first object to awaken beneath your touch, am I? It's the design of this place. A certain hand, a certain touch, for certain things. Your pills weren't keeping you well, sweet Silvie. They were preparing you for me."*

"What do you know about my medication?"

"I could ask you the same question."

A chill runs down my spine. I know that Victor keeps it locked in the cabinet above our bathroom sink, and he's the only one who's allowed to handle it, portion it out, crush it up and feed it to me. I know that I dread the moments when my throat seizes up and it doesn't matter how hard I try; I can't seem to choke the pills down—even when they're laced through my food or drink.

Ever since I stuffed two months of meds in my pillowcase and died for the first time in years, I've believed Victor when he told me that they were keeping me alive. But truthfully, I don't know anything about my medication, only that I have no control over what goes into my own body.

I pop the knife back into its handle and drop it onto the comforter.

"Judging by your silence, I've struck a chord." The heart burps out a large blood bubble, which splatters against the side of the

jar with a wet pop. *"But the pills are irrelevant now that we're together, Silvie. You're the only thing that matters. You don't know how important you are."*

I uncurl my fist and stare down at my bright red palm.

Victor tells me all the time how much trouble I am. Even when he compliments me, it's only in relation to how well I can sit still when he draws my blood or how quickly I can down my pills.

I'm efficient, well behaved—not important.

Nora claims that I mean the world to her, but her declarations of love are always punctured with quips about how difficult it is to plan around my anxiety. How it's the one thing she doesn't like about me. She smooths my hair, rubs circles into my back, all the while keeping her touch light as if pressing too hard would shatter me.

I'm fragile, breakable—not important.

"You don't know anything about me," I tell the heart. *I* don't know anything about me.

"I know that you were born in early March. Your favorite color is blue. Your favorite season is spring. You think that you died when you were a child. Should I continue?"

I inch closer to the jar, my pulse radiating through my forehead.

"I know you."

Yes, it knows me. And it's saying that the first time I died... my one true thing...

Water floods my lungs.

My list, my fears, my friendship with Nora. Everything leads back to my death, and the idea that I can get better. The idea that I can outrun the scar that bisects my chest and wear it more like a badge of honor than a brand. And the heart is saying—

"What do you mean I *think* I died? You can't say something like that and not explain."

"You died, but not when you were a little girl. You died when you were seventeen."

"Well yeah, I've died a few times since I was little. And the last time was entirely my fault, I skipped my meds and—"

"No, Silvie. You never died when you were a child. You died, for the first and only time when you were seventeen."

The water swells.

Salt and panic surge beneath my skin.

I cover my ears as if that's enough to block out the words, to relieve the weight of what it's told me.

I shake my head. "I don't believe you. I'm seventeen now... and I'm not... I'm not dead."

"You're not dead in the same way that I'm not really a heart." Even with my ears covered, its voice leaks through, and I drop my hands in defeat. Of course, covering my ears wouldn't make a difference: its voice is inside my mind.

"You need to be careful. If you keep pulling information in like you have, you'll bloat like a tick. Once you open the floodgates, they'll be impossible to close—but I'll help you. I'll help you filter what you allow in, I'll help make these things easier to handle as you pull more and more information into that tiny body of yours."

"I don't understand." I think the heart already knows how confusing this is for me. I think it's speaking in riddles on purpose, because that gives it the power to steer the conversation. It reminds me of how Victor locks away my medication and controls the dosage, controls the times that it's administered, controls everything. It reminds me of Nora, the way she orchestrates every conversation we have and knows exactly which buttons to press in order to shred me from the inside.

"There's no way for you to understand, not the way you are now. Touch me again," the heart instructs. *"Even better, bite into me—drink my blood—strengthen our bond. I can help ease your burden as you become what you are meant to be."*

Drink.

Its.

Blood.

The taste of iron. Rust. Old metal left out in the rain.

I look down at the knife, at my red palm, at the flowered pattern in the bedspread—the bloom of the colors, the creeping sickness of it.

My stomach clenches.

I *want* to touch it again. I want to taste it. Bite, suck, let the juices run down my chin and down my throat, and drink the life inside it. But I can't let it dangle answers in front of my nose and force me to perform like a wind-up toy.

Drink my blood, strengthen our bond. It's a command, not a suggestion. It's the same tone of voice Victor uses when he tells me to take my pills.

Good girl, you got them down on the first try.

Good girl, you let me medicate you.

You let me. You let me. You let me.

As if the only thing I'm good for is doing what I'm told. As if I'm so weak that even something without eyes can see how compliant I am.

A quiet rage billows up from the pit of my stomach. It burns my lungs like smoke.

I return the knife to my pocket and lift the jar so that it's level with my face. The water in my head drains.

I think of Victor and of all the things I felt but refused to acknowledge. The trauma etched into my chest, the trauma etched into the walls of my room back home—parallel lines carved into the paper behind my headboard, so much like prison bars.

The hurt.

The pain.

The unfairness of it all.

I tilt the jar slightly, my reflection a faint ghost across the surface of the glass. "I'm not touching you again, and I'm definitely not drinking your blood."

The heart gurgles, a small froth of bubbles pouring from it. *"We'll see."*

I put down the jar and pace across the room. Outside, the storm rattles the windowpanes and it's as if the house is screaming.

Even if the heart can offer me answers, it's just another thing looking to control me. Because that's who I am. I let other people lead, I let them decide.

But Victor isn't here right now, Nora's disappeared, and the heart is trapped inside its jar. And maybe for once...

"I can pull the answers I need from the mirror. I don't need you." I approach the white sheet covering the mirror and tug it off with a quick flick of my wrist. I can only assume that it's the same as the one in my room. It certainly looks the same. Carnival creatures stare at me from the carved frame. Their contorted bodies curve around the smooth pane of glass, as if they're dancing or attempting to run. "The last time I touched it, I had a dream that felt more like a memory. Maybe if I touch it again, it'll give me something else."

"I wouldn't recommend doing that."

I hover my fingers above the glass, tracing the contours of my face in the mirror. My reflection's eyes look like they belong to someone who has seen too much, who knows too much, who's spilling over with secrets until they're crushed beneath the weight of them.

I wonder how it can look so full when I feel so empty.

The kaleidoscope inside my head shifts as I hover my hand above the mirror. Victor smiles at me in shades of scarlet. My nightmare bleeds bright blue and the little girl by the water dies again and again, the knife moving in and out of her stomach in a quick staccato that's so loud I can almost hear it through the silence.

But I stay anchored. I'm the one in control. For once in my life, I'm the one in control.

"I'm sorry." The heart expels a wet sigh and rolls up close to the glass. *"I can see that I made a bad first impression. I've been waiting for this for a long time and being with you is overwhelming. I clearly didn't handle this well. What do I need to do to make you feel comfortable with me, Silvie? It's important that you feel comfortable around me."*

My body stiffens.

It's important that you feel comfortable around me.

"You could explain why you're so insistent on me drinking your blood for one thing," I snap at it.

"You've barely come to terms with the fact that you can hear me, how do you expect me to explain without sending you into a panic?"

I tap my nail against the mirror and static zips up my finger. "Use your words."

"There are no words that can describe what you're asking me to explain."

"Then I'll settle for pictures." I slam my hand down against the mirror. Electricity travels up my arm. Sharp and acidic.

My eyes roll up into my head and I see—

Mother standing over a metal table. The table is lit by a single bare lightbulb, and it's dotted with blood, puddles so thick that the centers are still tacky—not fully dried yet—even though the blood is old.

A tall man in a white jacket places a hand on her shoulder, his face obscured by shadows.

"You shouldn't have killed her yourself," he says, his voice deep and gruff. "You should have consulted with the board the moment you realized that something was wrong. We could have observed her for a few days before termination. We could have dissected the body and figured out what happened—learned from your mistake."

Mother shakes her head and uses a long, pointed nail to pick at the edge of one of the pools. The red of her nail polish matches the red of the scab. "The board's the one that told me to get rid of her, and even if I brought her in for observation, it wouldn't have made a difference."

"You can't blame yourself, Layla."

"Dr. Mathis," she corrects, although there's no venom in her voice. The words trickle out like spittle.

"You can't blame yourself, Dr. Mathis," the man repeats.

"Why not?" she says darkly. "It's my fault that it got to this point. I didn't notice the warning signs. I was too caught up in what it felt like to have her here."

"What did you do with the body?" the man asks but Mother—Layla—shakes her head again.

She pulls her hand back from the table. "I knew something was wrong the moment she woke up, there shouldn't have been this much blood."

Tears stream down her face.

The man sighs. "I don't understand why you're so torn up about it. You know it wasn't really Silvie."

The wallpaper to the left of the mirror buckles, and I pull my hand back, the tips of my fingers burning.

You know it wasn't really Silvie.

I stumble away from the mirror as the pain in my fingertips intensifies, and my reflection watches me from within the glass, its eyes so much sadder than my own.

"*What did you see?*" the heart asks from its place on the bed.

A shade of the truth.

"Not enough." I poise my hand above the mirror, readying myself to try again despite the blistering pain that radiates up my hand and into my wrist.

"Do not touch it again." My voice comes in muffled through the plaster.

I drop my hand to my side and turn to face the wallpaper. I scan it for any rips, or tears, or holes but the wall appears intact —there's no way she can see into the room.

"How do you know what I'm doing?" I ask.

"It is what I would do," the person in the wall responds, her voice thin as a gust of wind. "You did not get your answers, so you mean to pull more information from the glass, but you do not know—"

"What I am," I say, cutting her off. "That's what I'm trying to figure out."

"The mirror will not help you understand. It will only confuse you."

Different voice, same story. I'm not allowed to be in control because it would be too much for me to handle and it's like Victor says—

I only do it to protect you, Silvie.

Like the heart was trying to convince me—

There's no way for you to understand.

I ball my fingers into my palm. "I'm already confused. And it's not like you've done anything to help clear things up."

She sighs. "I do not mean to confuse you, but I do not know how to explain."

Which is exactly what the heart said. Why am I not surprised?

"Then figure it out." I press my ear against the flowered paper and slam my hand against the wall. "No before, no forever, no afterward. Come out here and tell me what it means. Tell me what's wrong with me."

She shifts behind the paper. "I cannot leave the wall."

"Just because you're afraid to do something, doesn't mean you can't do it," I snap, even though I know that's not the case. For the longest time I couldn't do things either, couldn't disobey my brother, couldn't ask questions—all because of fear.

Before we entered the house, when I was in the throes of the undertow, Nora told me that there was a difference between being upset and being *upset*. She might as well have called me crazy. And I just did the same thing to the person inside the wall, the person speaking with my voice.

I inhale sharply and try again. "I know what it's like to feel like you can't do things because of what's going on inside your head. But please, try."

She claws at the other side of the plaster, the scraping sounds slow and mournful. "All I ever wanted was to see you. I have lived in these walls and in the labs almost my entire life. Kept separate from you. All I ever wanted was for you to embrace me, and for us to be together. But Silvie, the last time I was outside of this wall, something terrible happened, and I am not ready to go out there again. I am not sure if I will ever be."

"Something terrible... the fire."

"No, the fire was a terrible thing, but it is not my terrible thing."

I lay my scarred palm across the wallpaper, proof of the fifteen minutes Nora and I spent carving at ourselves with the dull end of a paper clip, finished off with a pocketknife and a promise.

I make a new promise to myself, one that doesn't require a scar.

"You don't need to leave the wall," I tell her. "I'm coming in after you."

"Silvie!" A froth of bubbles spills from the heart's spout-like artery. *"You can't go in there by yourself. It's too dangerous."*

I cross the room and lift the jar. Bloody foam clings to its sides.

"I won't be alone," I tell the heart. "I'm taking you with me."

"That's a terrible idea."

"Better than staying out here and listening to you ramble on and on without actually saying anything."

"You'll be trading one cage for another," the heart cries, its voice sharp as an ice pick inside my head.

I wince and grip the jar tighter to keep from dropping it.

"The lock is important," Victor told me when I begged him not to shut me inside my room. "It keeps you safe."

"I feel like I'm in a cage," I murmured as he loomed over me, his shadow cast across the left side of my face, my chest, my torso, slicing me in half.

"Life is a series of cages," he said. "And this one is for your own good. I can't protect you out there, Silvie. I can't control what happens to you outside of this house."

No, he can't. My pulse quickens at the thought.

I put the heart back down on the bed and pluck the lamp from the table, throwing aside both the shade and the bulb. I'm left with a long, brass stand which curves at the end like a vase. I lift it up and down, testing its weight.

Victor is still with me, hovering like a phantom in the back of my mind, but he's white noise. I still hear him, but I don't flinch, I don't shrink back. Instead, I clench my fist and my knuckles burn white against the base of the lamp.

Pain spreads through my chest until it's hard to breath, and the anger from before, the hurt, floods through me.

A slice is too delicate for this feeling.

"You know how there are places where the wall goes soft, and it bends inward?" I call to the person in the wall.

"Yes, but Silvie. I am afraid that if you see me—"

"*When* I see you. Are there any soft spots in this room?"

She pauses and inhales sharply, as if she's taking a moment to consider.

"Let me check," she finally says before pacing around the perimeter, the wall buckling every few seconds. She pushes outward, marking the soft spots as she finds them. One by the bed, one next to the wardrobe, and finally next to the mirror.

"It is the softest here," she tells me. "By the mirror. The other spots I pointed out are weak as well."

"Okay, we'll try next to the mirror first then work our way around the room if it doesn't give way. Stand back."

I lift the base of the lamp again. It should be perfect. I drag the standing mirror away from the wall, careful to keep my fingers planted on the wooden frame and not brush them against the glass. I press into the soft spot, and it sinks beneath my fingers. I pull Nora's switchblade from my pocket and stab it repetitively into the wall.

The more I stab the wall—five, six, seven quick thrusts of the blade, the more I shake. A stab for each time Victor forced a pill down my throat. A stab for each time Nora pulled me along behind her, by the wrist, by the arm, by the corner of my shirt. As if I were a child.

A stab for each wave of pent-up rage.

And still, it feels wrong.

Still, I can't let myself really *feel* it.

In the back of my head, I still worry about what Victor would think—I can't snuff out his voice completely. But it's quieter now than ever before.

I pull away chunks of paper and plaster. My entire body reacts to the effort of it, and the riptide surges as I skin the house alive.

Soon, there's a hole the size of a fist, then a rib cage. My fingers, now covered in dust and grit, find the neck of the lamp. I hold it in one hand and press my other hand to my scar.

My anchor.

My one true thing.

"I am not sure if I am ready for this," the person in the wall admits. "We have never met face to face before. I do not... I look different from you."

"You don't need to be afraid. I don't care what you look like," I say, my voice level even though cold-water rushes through my veins. "As long as you promise to tell me the truth. I can't deal with any more lies."

"I will be honest with you if it means that we can be together, if it means I will no longer be alone."

"Then you don't have anything to worry about. Stay back. I'm almost done," I warn, and swing the lamp.

I smash the lamp into the wall again and again, pushing the plaster in until the hole grows to the size of a small child, and finally to something large enough to squeeze into.

I stare into the darkness.

"I'll be able to move around back there, right?" I ask. "I won't get stuck or anything?"

"Silvie don't. I promise that as soon as you drink my blood and strengthen our bond, all of this will make sense," the heart pleads as I pick it up from where it sits on the bed and cross back to the hole.

"Yes," the person in the wall tells me. "The passageway is narrow, but easy to navigate. You do not need to be afraid; I am not going to let anything hurt you."

A shiver runs down my spine. Didn't Nora say the same thing?

Your blood is in my veins, and my blood is in yours. I'm not going to let anything hurt you.

But I am hurt.

I stare into the aching darkness beyond the hole in the wall. I think of all the days I spent locked in my room or seated on the back porch staring at the sky—infinite blue—so close but just out of reach. I spent days thinking about what it would be like if I were strong enough to get up and leave. No more needles, no more pills. But Victor's love, all thorns and iron bars, kept me rooted in place better than any cage ever could.

"I'm coming in," I say with a small smile, despite the cold of the undertow, and the sharp cries of the heart, and the knowledge that everything I believed to be true is falling apart around me.

Despite Layla Mathis and the dead girl by the lake.

There's a passageway the width of a coffin behind the wall —resting between the wooden beams and a concrete slab that makes up the final layer of the Victorian's skeleton. I inch my way along inside it, breathing in dust and cobwebs. The only light comes from the hole in Nora's room, and the farther I creep, the more it dims.

Wooden planks creak beneath my feet, and with each step prickly fear shoots into my forehead. The planks are damp with rot, and it wouldn't take much for them to snap, to send me plunging into the depths of the house.

"No before, no before, no afterward," I call into the darkness ahead. "I'm here, I'm in the wall with you."

Finally. After what feels like an endless stretch of listening, searching, longing to know.

A hand reaches out from deep within the passageway. It's gray, with long, frail fingers. Curls of skin flake off it, not unlike a snake's shedding.

"Silvie," the person in the wall says quietly. "If you come with me to the labs, there is no going back. What I have to share could very well destroy you."

"I know."

I take her hand.

9

The passageway resembles a narrow vein, saturated with darkness the color of the ocean floor. Slivers of light filter in through pin pricks in the plaster, glinting wickedly, like needles or fishermen's hooks.

"You did not tell me that you had a heart with you," my new friend says casually as she guides me through the wall.

"You don't sound surprised." I keep my left hand wrapped around the jar, my free hand clasped between her thin, gray fingers. I strain to catch a glimpse of her, but she's nothing more than a silhouette.

"Hearts are a normal part of the Victorian," she explains. "I am not surprised that you have it. The one you call Nora took one with her after the fire. I knew she would bring it with her if she ever came back."

"Because the heart belongs to the thing she buried in the yard," I say breathlessly, *hearts* repeating over and over again inside my head. *Hearts,* meaning there's more than one.

"No, it does not. What Nora buried is not a thing, and it is not in the yard anymore. Mother gave it to me to protect, and I am taking you to it now so that you may understand."

There's a piece of myself buried out there.

I shiver, so focused on the fact that there are more hearts out there that I almost don't catch what she said. Mother. Mother meaning Layla. Layla meaning what exactly?

My new friend quickens her pace, and I hurry behind her. She pauses and runs her fingers over the back of my hand, gently pressing against each knuckle. "I always wondered what your hands would look like, what you would look like. I used to listen to you every day through the walls, so I knew your voice by heart, but not your hands, not your face."

She draws in a shaky breath. "I do not say this to disturb you, or to sound as if I am obsessed, but I have been waiting for this for a long time now, so I must be careful with how I relay information to you. Mother used to tell me that seeing is believing, so I must show you these things when we get to the labs. If I tell you anything before then it will sound like make believe."

"This is already like make believe," I mutter but let her pull me blindly through the bones of the house, and for a moment, disappointment burns the back of my throat. I'm still allowing myself to be led. But as we walk together, I realize that this is different. Her grip isn't the same as Nora or Victor's. Her touch is delicate, nothing like the way my brother would handle me. We're both holding onto each other.

Nora is always so much rougher when she grabs hold of me, pressing her scarred palm into mine anytime she needs something from me, anytime she feels like I'm slipping away from her. Nothing like my new friend. There's nothing possessive in the way she holds my hand.

I adjust my grip on her and the heart sputters. It's been giving me the silent treatment since we entered the wall, and while I'm not entirely unhappy with the prolonged silence, it does make me question whether it was ever speaking to begin with.

The scene from the mirror replays over and over inside my mind.

The blood on the table.

Layla.

She's the one who did this. She's the one who—

Killed me?

Raised me from the dead?

Some terrible combination of both?

The rage I felt in Nora's room continues to burn, a candle flickering in a sea cave—all rocks and waves and viciousness. Everything I didn't allow myself to feel before now, everything I kept buried continues to fight its way to the surface. It writhes beneath my skin.

I grip the jar as if it's a weapon, as if the heart inside is enough to keep me strong.

"Does the name Layla Mathis mean anything to you?" I ask, even though I already know it does. Even though I already know that she's—

"Mother. She did not mean for this to happen. She loved me so much, too much."

Beads of sweat break out across my forehead. You can love someone and still hurt them. I slip my hand from hers and press it to my surgical scar, my heartbeat rumbling beneath my fingers. "So, Layla is your mother?"

"Not by birth, but she is the reason why I am here."

The words are carefully chosen, carefully arranged, and the way they're strung together chills my insides.

"She's why I'm here too, isn't she? We're... related?" There's something about it that's so obvious, so terrible that my body seems to fold under the weight of it.

"In a way," she tells me. "We are like sisters, only closer."

We're sisters. Closer than sisters.

Nora's words. Our mantra. It's supposed to mean that she knows me, but she doesn't. She understands how I react to things—she understands what makes me tick to a certain extent—but she doesn't know me. I keep my expression level, even though inside I'm pulsing with electricity. I can't stop thinking about Nora. Our afternoons on the back porch, her legs stretched over mine until I didn't know where she ended and I began. Our twin scars, proof of our connection, evidence that it's the two of us against everything. Proof that I'll never be closer to anyone than her.

"Do you have a scar on your palm?" I ask, slowly, my pulse thrumming in my ears.

"No."

I don't know if I'm relieved or disappointed.

The passageway widens and I hurry next to her, craning my neck to try to catch a glimpse of her face. But her features morph, claylike in the dim light. I can just barely make out the faintest outline of hair, of clothing, of *someone* standing next to me.

"Please stop trying to look at me. You will see me once we reach the labs but give me these final moments in the dark. We were kept apart for a reason."

"Because it would upset me? I'm more upset by the fact that I don't know who you are, or what you look like. I don't even know what to call you." I wait, neck craned, anticipating her every word.

"Nix," she says. "That is what I am called."

My brow furrows. "Nix? Is that short for something?"

"No, it is the name that Mother gave me when she led me to the wall."

I do my best to picture Layla, face obscured, hair tossing in the wind like the dark flame of a candle.

She stands silhouetted against the sunset and stabs the little girl.

She stands over a bloody table and holds back tears.

She clutches Nix's hand and guides her toward the basement door, toward passageways that weave like veins.

The little girl's voice, so similar to mine.

The little girl's hands, gray like Nix's.

My eyes widen and I pull my fingers from my scar. "I watched her murder you. The mirror in my room showed me last night. She killed you and then dumped you in a lake."

My new friend, my almost sister, Nix. She turns and reaches for me, her arms nothing more than shadows, her body a faceless mass in the dark. "Mother did what she did because she loved me."

Her words roil my stomach.

Nix inches her way over to me and tentatively rests a hand on my shoulder. "The people she worked with wanted me dead. She had to make it seem as if she killed me, and perhaps she was making a true effort at first, but she could not follow through. I survived and after that, she protected me. Everything she has ever done is to protect me."

I shift the heart into my left arm and place my free hand on top of hers, squeezing it gently as she wades through the memory. I recognize the effort of it, the strain of her voice, it's the same as mine when I think about Victor—and the things he's done to me. It's exactly the same.

"Mother wrapped me in blankets and carried me back to the basement labs," she continues. "She nursed my wounds and raised me there. When this house was built, she created these passageways so she could keep an eye on things. The soft spots used to be places where she could look in, watch over everything. But once I was in the walls, the holes had to be sealed so that no one would find me."

"You love her even though she hurt you," I say, a lump in my throat. It's all I can do not to cry. For her. For me. For everything we've been through.

"Yes, I love her," Nix echoes, moving her hand from my

shoulder and weaving her fingers through mine before we continue through the passageway. "I know that my reasoning may seem flawed, but Mother was all I had. If I could not love the only person I had, then I would be alone. I would be angry. I would be nothing at all."

Victor's voice settles inside my ears, a static whine. His fingers tighten around my wrist as he draws my blood and arranges the vials like a funeral bouquet on our dining room table. Each memory is a fresh cut.

"Sometimes it's easier to love someone than be angry with them," I assure Nix.

Nix. To put an end to something.

There's more than one way to bury a body. Layla Mathis, Nix's mother, is the one who buried her. And I can't help but wonder who buried me.

Nix slows to a stop, but I take another step, my foot meeting open air.

I stumble, careening toward emptiness, but she grabs the collar of my dress and pulls me back.

A large gash opens within the passageway, between the wall, and the hall on the other side—as if the Victorian's been sawed in half. Cold wind blows into the passage, and I stay near the edge of oblivion, drawn by the soft light, the particles of dust and ash wafting in through the opening. But Nix shrinks back into the dark.

"It is the collapse. It runs through the entire building from the roof and second floor down to the first," she says, veering to the left, deeper into the wall. "The passageway branches off and continues this way to the labs. There is too much fire damage to keep going the way we have been moving."

The fire. Nora's half-truth.

I look down into the collapse.

Charred floorboards break off into oblivion.

A smell like burnt popcorn and mold wafts up to meet me.

A taste like graveyard dirt sits lodged in the back of my throat. I close my eyes, snowflakes falling across my face, cold wind in my hair. Nix's voice comes in through a filter, and I drift back through the kaleidoscope of red and blue inside my mind.

Flames lick the base of my neck.

A chorus of screams come from beneath the floorboards. Layers down, the others are roasted alive. I hum to myself as they cook, as the fire consumes and smoke floods the hallway. Is it evil if it's necessary? Is it necessary even though it's evil?

I'm not sure.

I hum and I wait.

My eyes snap open.

I remember the fire. I remember the spark of the match against the striker, and the way the flames grew and consumed.

I did this. Bile singes the back of my throat.

If I kill them, maybe it will all stop.

If I do this, maybe it will save us all.

The only release is death. Sacrifice. If I do this...

No, not me. It couldn't have been me. All this pain, all this destruction. The ruins left after the flames chewed this building down. I would never...

It's too much to take, I can't accept it.

I push my way out into the hallway, skirting around the edge of the collapse, the heart still cradled in my arms. My shoes squish into the damp carpet—red or royal purple, it's hard to tell in the dim light.

"Silvie," Nix calls as she chases me to the edge of the opening. She stops right before the gash in the wall, careful not to show her face. She reaches one thin, gray arm out into the hall, her fingers brushing against my sleeve.

"I need air." I need to remember what I've done.

The hole in the roof seems more menacing in the throes of the blizzard. Endless streams of white swirl in through the missing chunks of roof and fall to the first level. The occasional flake drifts over to where I stand and melts across my arms and cheeks, but I don't see any more images, I don't remember anything else.

Still, I did this.

I struck the match. I started the fire.

For a moment, all I want to do is drown in the storm. All I want to do is drop the heart through the broken floorboards and tumble down after it. Fall into a pile of ash and snow. I hold the jar out over the precipice and watch it beat wildly behind the glass before pulling the heart back and hugging it to my chest.

Drowning isn't an option.

"Silvie," the heart says, finally breaking its silence.

My body jolts and I scramble to keep hold of the jar. "You've been quiet for so long, I thought you forgot how to talk... I thought maybe you never spoke in the first place."

"I was wading through your memories, learning about who you are, who you've become since leaving this place... the things you have gone through. What I've learned disturbs me. That's why I didn't speak. I was processing everything... and still, I don't know what to say."

My scalp prickles. "Who gave you the right to look inside my mind?"

"You did, the moment you touched me."

I turn from the collapse and hold the jar level with my face. The heart rolls back from the glass and pulls away from the coagulated blood, the chunks of organic material squishing as it moves.

Behind it, Nix waits just beyond the hole in the wall, her arm—gray and wrinkled, the only part of her exposed. She continues to reach for me, her thin fingers bent at the knuckle. The red of the heart's flesh glistens viciously against the dark.

"Silvie, I'm disturbed."

"Well, we have that in common. You disturb me too."

"No, I'm not disturbed by you... I'm disturbed—I'm disgusted by what Victor has done to you. And I am so sorry."

Heat shoots up into my forehead and the hallway tilts. My fingers slip against the sides of the jar. It's the last thing I expected it to say.

His name.

The only thing sure to fuel both my rage and the salty panic of the undertow.

The only thing capable of ripping my control away.

A froth of bubbles spouts from the heart, and it continues as if reciting a eulogy. *"Our bond has grown stronger. It was a delayed link, so I didn't see it earlier—like how it took you awhile to see things the first time you touched the mirror."*

"How do you know about that?"

"The link. It's the same way that I understand what happened to you after you left this place. I understand that Victor took you with him. I know what he did. And I need you to believe me when I say that it was never part of the plan. I should have understood the extent of it when you mentioned your medication, but I didn't. That's my fault. Victor is a terrible man and what he did to you is inexcusable."

Heat pools beneath my skin, a sticky feeling—somewhere between shock and numbness. "And what do you think he did to me?"

"He hurt you, and I never wanted you to get hurt."

The hall tilts again, flashes of red and purple and ash gray. Flashes of heat. Ripples in the undertow. "What do you mean you didn't want me to get hurt? You're in a jar, you're a heart—you don't *want* anything. And you don't know my brother."

"I'm not a heart, and Victor isn't your brother."

The jar slips from my hands and hits the carpet with a muted thud.

"Silvie," the heart cries. *"He isn't your brother, and what he did to you—"*

This is all wrong.

The jar lays on its side, and as I pick it back up again, the heart hits the bottom with a wet plop. I hold it at arm's length, my hands shaking. "Why would you say that Victor isn't my brother?"

"Because he isn't. And it hurts me to see you in so much pain because of him."

After all of the progress I've made. After all of the pain and the rage, he's still so loud inside my head.

He still has complete control over me.

I step back, and back, and back.

Until there's nothing, until the floor disappears beneath me.

10

I fall into the dark, my hair whipping into my face. I only cry out once, a small gasp as I manage to grasp onto one of the decaying boards. I'm suspended over the edge of oblivion.

My other arm clutches the heart tightly against my chest. My heartbeat syncs with it until I'm not sure where I end and it begins.

"I'm so sorry," it says, its voice wavering. *"I didn't mean to put you in danger. I didn't know that mentioning Victor would cause you to fall."*

"Really? You spent all that time snooping through my memories and couldn't figure out the effect he has on me?"

"Silvie –"

"Save it," I say through gritted teeth as the jar slips, and I struggle to keep hold of it. "Unless you want me to drop you."

"If you were going to drop me, you would have already." It expels a blood bubble with a sickening pop. *"I think you like me."*

"And I don't think either of us are really in a position to talk right now." If I let the jar shatter—if I leave it to bleed out across the bottom floor of the Victorian—then holding onto it for this long would have been for nothing. I'll have nothing to confront Nora with, and as much as I hate to admit it, I've gotten used to its company.

I steal a glance down at the darkness. Below me is a hallway on the first floor—carpeted in jeweled shades of green. Only a sliver of the left wall is visible, and I swing myself slightly, trying to angle my body over the carpet.

More of the first floor slips into view. A line of portraits the size of my torso. There are at least a dozen disappearing into the darkened hall. Striped wallpaper the color of oxidized copper. Velvet accents. Dark and dangerous.

"Nix," I call, and the board cracks beneath my fingers. It's one bad move away from breaking completely. Splinters dig into my hands, and I grimace. "Help!"

"Silvie? I cannot see you, are you all right?"

"No, I'm really not." My eyes focus on the three portraits closest to me. More Nora originals. They watch as I hang on for dear life. The figures melt into the dimness. Is that me? Is that Layla? And someone, features clouded—who looks a lot like Victor?

The sight of him—of the blurred, claylike mass of his face—knocks the wind out of me and the board finally breaks.

My body pitches forward into the blackness and I shut my eyes, bracing myself for the impact. I wait to splatter against the deepest layer of the Victorian, my skull ready to cave in. I listen for the deafening crack, and the crunch of the jar as it shatters beneath me. Instead, I hit the carpeting, hard. Something—adrenaline? Panic?—keeps the pain at bay, and there's a buzz beneath my skin, like my nerves are set alight. I lay flat on my back. The jar is cradled, mercifully unbroken, in my hands.

"Silvie," the heart gurgles, bloody tears leaking from its aorta. *"Try not to move, you were damaged in the fall."*

"Don't talk about me like I'm an object." I roll away from the edge of the collapse and curl up at the foot of the portraits, my nose against one of the velvet stripes in the wallpaper. It smells of mold, and I twist so I'm lying on my back again. Each breath triggers an ache in my ribs.

"It wasn't my intention to make you feel like an object," the heart says, the jar propped up on my stomach. *"I only don't want to see you get hurt any further."*

"Nix," I yell, ignoring it. Snow continues to drift lazily through the hole in the roof, but I lie just out of reach. The snowflakes melt into the carpet, darkening the green.

"Silvie." Nix's voice is faint. "Where are you? What happened?"

"I fell through to the first floor." I stand, tentatively, sharp pain traveling through my legs and up my spine. I look up, cradling the jar in one arm, reaching the other above my head, but the second floor is at least eight feet above me.

Lowering my arm, I turn to the portraits. Each one is a little more than half my height and hung so that my eyes are level with the figures' chests.

Sure enough, the first one is of a girl who looks like me—like Nora. Her curly blond hair is pulled back into a bun, and her smile doesn't reach her eyes. She leans against a wall, her hands digging into the folds of her skirt.

The second one is of Layla, sitting on an overstuffed chair, her face turned toward the window, dark curls cascading down over her shoulder.

And the third.

Victor.

Victor with his mouth set in a thin, straight line. Victor with his hair slicked back, and his hands clasp tightly in his lap.

His eyes burn into mine.

My heart pounds in my throat.

He shouldn't be here.

"It sickens me to see the effect he has on you," the heart murmurs as I place the jar down on the floor.

"Silvie?" Nix calls again. "I have left the wall and will be there soon. Hold on."

My brother's face, on a wall with a mad woman and a girl who looks like me—who for all I know, *is* me.

Except he isn't my brother.

Another wave of pain travels up my spine and I double over, falling to my knees. I press my palms into the carpet.

The heart and Nix both cry out for me at the same time.

I lift my head to find Nix looking down at me, her face silhouetted against the gray sky.

"Are you hurt?" she asks, her voice shaking.

"A little." I rest my head against the carpeting before glancing tentatively over where the collapse continues down a third layer. The basement waits below, and all I can see is the vaguest outline of tile floors—dark stone. I look up again, squinting my eyes to try to catch a glimpse of Nix. All I can make out are the tendrils of her thin hair, hanging from her skull like spider's silk.

"Hold on," she says. "I will find a way to get you back up again—or else find a way to join you down there."

I inch my way back to the portraits and brace myself against the wall as I stand. My body aches, but the sharpness of the pain is already fading. The velvet stripes on the wallpaper are soft beneath my fingers, and the heart presses against the side of the jar as if leaning in to tell me a secret.

"It would be best if you sat down again and gave your body time to heal."

Though a dark purple bruise spreads from my left thigh down my leg, I don't think I have any broken bones, and I frown at the heart. "What difference is a few minutes going to make?"

I look up at Victor's portrait.

"You knew him," I say, lifting the jar and cradling it to my chest.

"Yes."

"He was here before the fire, and he knows the truth about who I am."

"*Yes.*"

He's here next to Layla and myself—or Nora, or some other girl with our face. I suck air in between my teeth.

"Silvie, I am trying to find something to pull you up with," Nix calls down to me.

"No, I'll meet you in the labs," I call up to her.

"You do not know how to navigate through the passageways."

"I can jump down to the basement, it isn't too far."

The heart cries out in protest, but its voice fades into the waning storm and I don't bother listening.

"Are you sure?" The concern in Nix's voice is almost too much to take. The basement is several feet beneath me, and I know it'll be a stretch to make it down another layer with the jar intact. Still, I press my thumb tentatively into the bruise on my thigh, and though I wince, it doesn't hurt as much as I expect.

I lock eyes with Victor's portrait. "Yes, I'm sure."

Floorboards creak as Nix paces the length of the hallway above. She travels back and forth a few times before coming back to the edge of the collapse. "I think I know where you will land. Once you are down there, wait for me. I will come to you."

"Okay."

"Are you certain that you are all right?" she asks. "If what I told you about Mother is what upset you, if it is what caused you to fall, then—"

"It's not that, Nix. It's my brother..." I run my fingers along the edge of the portrait.

"But you don't have a brother."

"Apparently not." He stares down at me, like he always has, only this time, I stare back. "I'll see you soon."

I wait until I hear her footsteps above me retreating to the passageway, before I pull Nora's knife from my pocket. The portrait captures Victor's likeness remarkably well. His serious, green eyes. His clenched jaw. The thought of how long he must have sat for it, how long Nora must have worked to commit his face to canvas fills me with another wave of anger. Because it wasn't only Victor, it was her too—they both lied to me.

"He doesn't look anything like me," I tell the heart. "I don't know why I never saw that we weren't related. It seems so obvious now. But I remember him being there for me since the first time I died, even if the memories are incomplete."

"I told you before," the heart says gently. *"You didn't die when you were a child—you died when you were seventeen."*

"How can I remember things that never happened?"

"Because it's what he wanted you to remember, it's what he filled your mind with when he stole you from this place."

My stomach twists. If he filled my head with lies, what did he erase in order to put them there?

I picture Victor's journal entry, the swooping cursive: his long, thin writing—like spider's legs crawling across the page. The words he used to describe my lifeless body, the pain he felt when he realized I was dead. The cutting, and slicing, and stitching that it took to make me breathe again. But if he isn't my brother, and I never died, if we *both* have been here before...

Whatever the truth is, he knows it. And he's kept it from me. Locked it away like my pills. Controlled it like my pre-portioned meals, like my schedule, like my whole damn life.

Victor's love is a razorblade dragged slowly across my open palm.

The kaleidoscope inside my mind shifts and all the broken glass inside it, all the shades of red and blue seem like a sick joke now. It's a half-finished science fair project. Let's give Silvie something to remember, but let's not try too hard—let's leave a mess of shattered moments inside her brain instead.

Victor coming home from work. Victor braiding my hair

and taking me to the park to play. Victor marking my growth with a thick black marker on our kitchen wall next to the stove. What kind of person could fabricate so much of my life?

Mark it in permanent ink so that there's no questioning the passage of time.

Who would tell a lie that damaging?

The same person who read me books before I went to sleep, who made sure I always took my pill. The same man who was so terrified of losing me that he tethered me close, and cut my wings, and inspired a hate in me as fierce as my affection. My love.

For him.

For us.

For our connection—our *family*.

I could kill him.

I stab the knife directly into his forehead and slash the paint. Peel the canvas from the stretcher boards. Pull the staples from the back and toss it to the floor, the strips of canvas falling like confetti. The entire time, I scream and howl, my chest heaving.

Nora's name is scrawled on the back of the boards in bleeding, black ink.

I throw it all down the hole in the floor and the stretcher bars clatter against the tile before I step up to the edge.

"About Victor," the heart begins, but I hush it, terrified of the things his name does to me, terrified that what the heart will tell me may cause me to break. For real this time, for good. I expect to crumble beneath the weight of not knowing, to recoil in fear, but the only thing that rushes through with the cold water of the riptide is regret. Regret that Victor's still my weakness. Regret for all the time I spent wishing for a different body, a different life. Regret for all the time I spent alive, but not living.

But not anymore. Never again.

I lift the heart up and take a deep breath.

I jump.

The hallway I drop into is dark, the only light coming from the opening above and a pinprick of brightness at the end. I trip over the remains of Victor's portrait and scrape my knees against the ruined tile floor, jagged bits of ceramic digging beneath my skin—but I manage to keep the jar safe and the heart intact.

I kick at the stretcher bars before rising to my feet.

The ceiling is surprisingly low, no more than six feet tall, which explains why I wasn't hurt as badly as my first fall.

Snow drifts down from layers above, melting in the dark.

"You can't be so reckless, Silvie. That could have been bad."

I stand for countless minutes in the narrow hallway, stale and damp and still smelling of mold. It's long enough to wonder if I've made a mistake, and question if I should try to find my way back up again.

Artificial light glows at the end of the hall and I watch it burn. Gentle, soft. So bright in all this decay.

Victor's eyes stare up at me from a scrap of ruined canvas. I grind my heel into them.

More time passes, convincing me that Nix isn't coming or that I didn't land where she thought I would.

"You don't have to wait for Nix, you know," the heart mumbles.

It's right. I don't need to wait for anyone, or listen to anyone, or do anything that I don't want to. For once in my life, it's okay to act on instinct. For once in my life, I can follow my gut instead of the man who claimed to be my brother.

Nora claimed to be my sister, closer than my sister. The thought simmers beneath my skin and I walk toward the light. My feet sink into the damp soil beneath the ruined tiles until I turn the corner and enter a room.

It's wide and round, with dark tile floors and high ceilings—more than double the height of where I entered from. There are two hallways on either side of the center, the one I emerged from, a glorified tunnel, and another across from it. Everything is lit by flickering florescent bulbs.

But these aren't labs—it's a surgical theater.

The only thing that reminds me that there's an entire house above it is the wooden board ceiling and a simple staircase to the left, which I can only assume leads to the first floor of the Victorian. Otherwise, this might as well be a different building entirely.

A single metal table sits in the center of the room, a white sheet draped over whatever lays on top of it. A surgical light sits positioned over it, flickering along with the fluorescents.

A viewer's balcony juts out overhead, spanning the perimeter of the room. A row of thin windows overlooking the center of the theater. The windows have been blacked out, but weak light still filters in through the dust and stale air, leaking in from some unseen source.

The walls are made of stone and lined with shelves.

And on the shelves...

Jars. Some empty, but others full of hearts, livers, lungs—no pickling liquid, no formaldehyde. Just like the jarred heart I cradle in my arms. They're brightly colored, too. Saturated with pigment—looking more like sculptures or blown glass. They're luminous.

"What are these?" I murmur, my stomach churning.

"Not what they look like."

"Nix?" I ask, turning to look for her, but finding the surgical theater empty.

My eyes settle on a large gash in the wall.

"I will be out in a moment, Silvie," her voice drifts from the opening. She shuffles around, her footsteps muffled. "You landed beneath the kitchen, not one of the halls like I initially thought. It took me longer to get here than I anticipated. Sorry for making you wait."

I glance up at the wooden board ceiling, the kitchen's underbelly.

"About Victor," the heart tries again, but I shake my head.

"I don't want to think about him right now, yet alone discuss him." I balance the jar against my hip and continue to inspect the room.

A tray sits next to the table lined with scalpels, clamps, bone saws. Everything a doctor would need for surgery—to reconstruct or destroy, to rip tumors from cavities, to give new life.

And the room.

Sharp tools. Empty jars. Too much history.

Nix reaches out and hooks her fingers around the edge of the frame, as I turn back to face the doorway.

"I am nervous," she says. "I worry that you will panic at the sight of my face."

"I meant what I said before, I don't care what you look like," I assure her. "I know what it's like to be afraid, but sometimes the only way past it is to face it head on."

She tightens her fingers around the threshold and lets out a deep breath before stepping into the room.

My eyes widen.

She's taller and even thinner than I expect, with limbs that stretch a little too far. Her neck is long, her blond hair patchy. Strands of hair extend down over her shoulders, all split ends. Chunks of malformed skull show beneath the matted nest.

Her skin peels like old parchment, slightly grayed. Spiderwebs of veins, blue and purple weave up through her cheeks.

She wears a simple shirt and slacks that cling to her thin frame. The curling skin around her neck forms a fleshy collar.

The most human thing about her are her eyes, wide and gray.

My eyes.

"You look like me," I say with more awe than horror. It's like looking at a clay version of myself, something sculpted by unpracticed hands.

She smiles, her teeth small and sharp. "All I have ever wanted is to look like you."

"*The first attempt didn't go as hoped,*" the heart rasps.

"First attempt?" I whisper into the lid, bracing myself against the swell of the riptide. I shouldn't be surprised though. I've begun to fear this moment because I've begun to think that maybe...

The gray child by the water.

The blood on the table.

It wasn't really Silvie.

The jars in the surgical theater. Heart, liver, lungs.

"Show me what I am," I say to Nix, my voice echoing through the room. "You said that once we were down here, you'd show me."

"The answer is laying on the table beneath the sheet. It is what Nora buried: what Mother gave me to protect." She reaches out and takes the jar from my hands, places it on the floor next to her, before nodding her head toward the center of the theater. "Go on, after you see it, we can talk candidly about this place."

"I think that I..." I think that I have an idea of what I'll find.

The water in my head surges, and even though I let it wash over me—numbing my core—I continue forward. Because there's fury beneath the fear. And the fury compels me to know.

I approach the table.

"I will help you through this," Nix tells me, and stretches out her arms as if to push me forward. "After all, we are sisters —closer than sisters."

Like me and Nora. Exactly like me and Nora.

Closer than sisters.

Even though Victor's miles away, I can still hear his voice in my ear insisting that no one will ever be closer to me than him.

He knows my heart; he's held it in his hands. He cradled me while I died and nursed me back to life. If he were here, he'd say that I'm too weak, too fragile for the truth. And maybe I was, maybe I used to be.

I press a hand against my scar, my anchor, my one true thing, and remind myself that I can handle whatever comes next.

I'm fragile, yes. But I'm not weak.

My hand moves from my scar to the white sheet, and I pull it back with a flick of my wrist. And beneath the sheet...

A person, a sprawled-out figure. Their features emerge in a haze of dust and moths with silvery wings.

The blond hair that falls in ringlets around her face. The pale gray eyes. The tiny frame.

It's me.

It's me laid out on the table.

I'm dead.

11

I thought I might be replicated, mutated... something. But seeing myself laid out on the table hurts worse than I thought it would. A soft pain spreads through the center of my chest, and I drop to my knees beside Nix. Her face comes to me in pieces, flashes of underdeveloped Polaroids. Her left cheekbone. Her lower lip. Wrists, and palms, and elbows.

The colors blur.

The faint toll of my heartbeat rings out. Somewhere.

But I can't reach it.

I hover in the back of my mind. With the riptide, the rush of salt water.

"Silvie, this is not what it looks like." Nix moves the girl off the table and props her up on the ground before sinking down next to me. She wraps her arms tentatively around my middle. The jarred heart sits on the floor nearby.

Her grip on me tightens, like I'm full of helium and might float away if she lets go.

The girl sits across from us, head leaning to the side. A life-size porcelain doll. She's dressed in the same deep burgundy colored dress that I found in the wardrobe. Her body shows no signs of decay. It's fresh. She looks as if she could be sleeping except that her eyes are open.

Nix leaves me sitting on the floor and brings the heart over next to the dead girl, motioning for me to follow. I inch forward.

"I am going to show you something," Nix says, crouching down beside the corpse. "It will help you understand. About her, and about the heart."

She gently unbuttons the girl's dress and reaches for the scalpel on the side table next to her.

My eyes focus on the girl's chest. She has the same scar as I do. From the dip of her collarbones to her navel. It's pale purple, thinner than mine, but it's still my scar. I inch my way closer to her. Reach out and brush my fingers across her cheek. It's warm. Alive. But she doesn't react to my touch.

Nix nudges me out of the way and slides the scalpel along the girl's chest.

She slices the scar open like she's opening a package. I watch with a sick kind of detached fascination. To my surprise, it doesn't bleed. The skin does, a little bit, but the deep gash only sweats a tiny amount of blood.

Nix kisses the girl on her forehead before she parts her ribs. The cracking sound sends a shudder through me. It's like what Victor did to me, the first time I died.

"Her heart drive is nonfunctional. It is broken somehow, that is why she is comatose."

Her heart drive...

"Here," Nix says. "Take a look."

I glance over her shoulder to get a better look at the girl's insides. Hot, sticky blood pulses between my ears, it swells until I'm sure that I'm going to drown. In my own blood. Inside myself.

The girl's heart is hooked up to wires. Blue, yellow, gold

wires. Inside her chest, there's a mix of meat and machinery. Random cogs and gears mixed in with the vital organs.

Her chest cavity is dry as a bone. There's no bleeding and the organs are too saturated. They're brilliant red, and deep, devastating shades of purple and blue. They're striking against the pale color of the wires. The wires mixed in with the meat... the machinery mixed in with the human parts...

"She was built to look like me." A hollow pain rings out inside my chest.

"She is an older model, so it is more accurate to say that you look like her. And I am a much older model than she is, the first in the Silvie series."

Nix leans down next to the girl and presses the side of her face against hers.

"Everyone is back together at last," she says, brushing a strand of hair out of the girl's eyes. She's a more aptly crafted version of Nix. "Silvie Seventeen, meet Silvie Fifteen."

"There's more than one Silvie..." The name tastes strange, like copper and burnt charcoal.

"I am sorry, I know this is a lot to process," Nix says as she pushes the girl's ribs back together, tucking the mess of meat and machinery back inside.

"Our surface tissue is the same as a normal person," she explains, running her fingers along my arm as if to illustrate. "Everything is natural down to the dermis. That is where things get messy. It is easier to slice us open, and our bones are strange. I am not sure what they are made of at this point, but they are different somehow."

Nix lifts the jar so it's level with our faces.

"This is a backup drive," she explains. "If anything happens to our bodies, we are still there, we are just saved separately for a while."

"Same thing with the ones inside us," she continues, lowering the heart and placing her hand over her chest. "Our hearts are not hearts: they are storage devices. They house all our data; they keep us safe when we are not in a body. We call them heart drives because they are like hard drives. The one you call Nora came up with it. Mother thought it was clever."

"The dead girl has my scar." *My* scar. My anchor. My one true thing, and it isn't even mine. None of it is mine. Hurt bubbles like a blood blister beneath my skin. A bruise. I run my fingers along the thick, purple bump and wonder if my chest would split open as easily as the girl with my face. The flick of a sharp, wicked blade and that's all it would take. Intestines and lungs and heart.

Not heart.

Heart drive.

"I have the scar also," Nix says gently. She pulls down the collar of her shirt and pushes aside the loose flesh around her neck to reveal her own purple scar. Hers is more jagged than mine, bumpier and larger and darker. But it's in the same spot. "So does the one you call Nora. I knew her as Sixteen, which is why I was confused when you called her by a different name."

Nora. I've never seen her wear anything other than turtlenecks, t-shirts with high collars, nothing that dips beneath the collarbone.

A different type of Gemini.

Mirror images.

I ache for the pull of the riptide—the salty sting of the waves—the wash of panic and the adrenaline that comes with it. Instead, heat singes my neck, my nerves, my entrails. Instead, the only salt comes from the tears that stream down my cheeks. The only sting comes from a pain so dark, so deep, that it's all I can do not to get lost in it.

Nix takes the heart from me and places the jar on the floor. The scalpel lays next to us: red, and blue, and dripping. Even though the dead girl doesn't bleed, the knife is still dirty with fluids. Coolant, and solvent, and other liquids that Nix tries to define but can't quite explain.

And where's Nora? We spent a year together and she never even hinted at anything like this. Even when we first got here, she lied. About her family. About the fire.

My body isn't mine. It was never mine. Not since Victor's been pumping me full of pills. Not since Nora's been dragging me along after her. In a way, there's comfort in the fact that even if they hadn't victimized me, I still wouldn't be myself.

I'm so much more than myself. The thought electrifies me, and the rush of connection that I feel with them, with Nix and my dead sister and her nonfunctional drive, is unlike anything I've felt before.

Nix sews up the dead girl—Fifteen's chest and her dress—using a needle and thread from the metal tray next to the table. A thin line of black thread runs the length of her scar, disappearing into the wine-colored fabric. Nix stays next to her, smoothing her hair back, adjusting her collar. It's as if she's trying to comfort our comatose sister as much as she's trying to comfort me.

The jarred heart rests in the center of the room between us.

Why didn't it say something? I think, cross my arms, and pick at a scab on my elbow, a reminder of my fall from the second floor. *It knows too much not to know about this.*

"I tried to tell you, but you dropped me," the heart says, and a chill runs down my spine. *"For the record, this isn't the way I would have told you. First, I would have explained what happened with Victor, then I would have eased you into this so as not to traumatize you. Though, you are handling it better than I expected."*

We're getting closer. It can hear my thoughts.

"What else can you tell me about us?" I ask, turning to Nix.

"We are organic and mechanical, a mix of both," she says. "A hybrid. Mother explained it to me once, but it was much too complicated for me to follow. Human, bionic. Both. They used the same source DNA for each of us, which is why we look the same. We *are* the same. We are Silvie. At first there was only me, then there were ten, then almost twenty. The group got whittled down after a while, of course. We are susceptible to illness... to death. We are test tube children, which makes things different from if we gestated inside of a womb. The animatronic parts do not grow the same way as the rest of us. A lot of us die before we get a chance to live, before we have the chance to be backed up onto heart drives. Most of us came out wrong and got torn apart shortly after for testing. You are the closest Mother ever came to success."

She gestures to where the hearts sit lined up along the shelf. "Those are five of our sisters. I have spent a lot of time combing through the labs, collecting them and bringing them here. But there are no bodies anywhere, no place to download their data."

"And here's another one of our sisters," I say, lifting the heart.

"I am not like the ones on the shelf," it rasps, dribbles of blood leaking out across the bottom of the jar.

What are you then? It doesn't answer.

Nix shakes her head. "If you take a look at our sisters, they are smaller, more purple than red. I am not sure if that one is from the same series. It is different somehow."

"If I touch the ones that belonged to our sisters, will I be able to hear them?" I ask Nix. "I could find out more about us."

"You don't want to do that. Not yet, you're not ready."

"Shut up. For the last time, you don't get to tell me what to do!" I snap and Nix shrinks back as if I slapped her. "Not you," I clarify. "The heart."

"It speaks to you?" Nix asks, her eyes wide. "You initiated a download?"

"I should have told you earlier, but I thought there was something wrong with me. I didn't know it was normal for me to hear it speak... I wasn't sure if it was even speaking at all." I look down at the pulsing red, the meaty bulk of the organ. "It doesn't tell me anything though, all it does is talk in circles."

"There is nothing wrong with you, Silvie." Nix rests a hand against the side of the jar and stares at it pensively. "I am not surprised that it called to you. It is like how the mirrors called to you. There are so many things that have been silenced, ignored, and abandoned when this place collapsed. They need someone to listen."

"So, the mirrors are...?"

"Data hubs. They cannot hold as much as the hearts but... back when this place was functional, Mother gave you each a mirror so that if something hurt to remember, you could leave it there, unburden yourself."

My brow furrows. "Those were someone's memories?"

She nods.

"Then someone watched Mother stab you... do you know who?"

She shakes her head. "There were not any other Silvies at that point. It was not one of us."

I look at the shelf, the hearts, livers, and lungs resting against the sides of their jars. They're lovely, like pieces of jewelry. And that's exactly what makes them different from the jarred heart. They seem more fragile—organs sculpted from stained glass. Organs that would crumble if I held them too closely. Meanwhile, the heart, despite its bright colors, feels more like it's molded from rubber.

"We can create a life together, Silvie," Nix offers. "We are already family, but I believe that in time, we can build a close friendship, a true bond. There are so many things down here that I want to show you, that I *will* show you. And we have all the time in the world, there is no rush."

Family.

A split-level ranch home, cracked pavement driveway. The

places where the grass creeps up through the gray, reaching and reaching for the sunlight.

The lock on my bedroom door, gray. The same as the walls in our hallway, the same as my dresses, my eyes.

Victor standing over me, scribbling in his journal as I eat my lunch. Victor watching as I take my medicine, checking to make sure I don't hide it beneath my tongue.

"I don't know if I can," I tell Nix.

"It is possible to survive down here," she adds. "There are entire rooms of canned preserves, freezers full of meat and vegetables. Just wait until you see the other end of the labs, it is like a little underground house. There are closets with gallons upon gallons of water. I have been fine for over two years, there is not a doubt in my mind that we will be fine for at least two more."

Victor smoothing my hair back. Victor smiling at me as I read a page from my biology textbook. Looking back, I realize it's the smile of a predator.

"It's not that..."

The floorboards above us creak and dust filters down into the surgical theater, falling gently like snow, like ashes on the wind.

Nix cranes her head and we both watch the person above move from one end of the kitchen to the other, pacing the length of the room—knocking dust loose as they wander.

A door slams.

A cabinet creaks.

The floors continue to sigh beneath the shifting figure's weight.

"That's Nora, isn't it?" I ask, my eyes narrowing.

Nix nods. "It appears she was outside, came in from through the back door and is now in the kitchen. Watch the way the boards move and the dust falls; you can trace her steps."

I follow Nix's gaze, and sure enough the depressions in the floor show her movements.

Nora continues to pace the length of the kitchen; the dust continues to fall.

The pain in my chest—the tightness, the burning rage—propels me forward. I scoop up the jar and rise, making my way toward the staircase in the corner of the room.

"Wait," Nix calls. "Where are you going?"

I hurry up the stairs, listening to Nora's footsteps above and Nix's footsteps as she rushes across the belly of the theater after me.

"Wait," she repeats. "Do not leave me. I am not finished explaining. I have not told you about the night of the fire. I have not shown you the rest of the labs. There are miles and miles of tunnels."

Miles of tunnels. My skin prickles, more from anticipation than fear, but I shake my head.

"You said it yourself, we have all the time in the world." I turn to her from the top of the stairs. "We've been together for less than twenty-four hours and you've already helped me so much. But Nora... she knew me for a year..."

I twist the locks on the door, my pulse pounding in my ears. "I'll be back, I promise. I just—I need to do this."

"Will confronting her make you feel better?" she asks. "Would it be so bad to start over, to leave her behind?"

I pause for a moment, listening to the sound of Nora's footsteps beyond the door. I'm already so far from her. She's already a ghost.

I could follow Nix back into the tunnels. I could spend a lifetime exploring the labs with her, learning about myself, my sisters. I could bury the memories of who Victor made me believe I was, pretend that it was all a bad dream.

In a way, it *was* a bad dream. That's why I can't walk away.

The only way to ensure that I don't wake up is to ignore my time with Victor and Nora, let it fester.

"I'm never going to feel better about any of this," I say as I exit into the kitchen.

It's unnaturally bright upstairs, a large picture window on the far side of the kitchen opens to the blizzard that rages outside, the sky a bright white against the storm.

The snow piled up against the windowpanes shines like crystalized sugar.

Nora stands in the corner by the back door, stomping it from her boots. I watch her pull off her scarf and hat, and it's like watching a stranger in a movie; I don't know who she is anymore.

I know what she is. She's my blood sister, my mirror image. Same brain, same body. But I'm farther away from her now than ever before.

Nora peels off her jacket and throws them all—scarf, hat, jacket—in a pile by the door. Her hair is wet, and her face is bleeding sunset red.

Heart in a jar red.

We're supposed to be closer than sisters, I think hollowly, the scar on my palm feeling as meaningless as the scar on my chest.

I wish there was a way to scrub it clean off my hand.

"Nora," I say, stepping into the center of the kitchen, aware that layers beneath me, Nix traces my movements.

She looks up and we lock eyes. Deep circles surround hers, all blue and purple, stained from lack of sleep.

"Hey Silvie," she says with a tentative smile. "You feeling okay? You look like hell."

"I feel like hell," I say.

"Look, about the snow, I really had no idea that there was going to be a storm. If I had, I wouldn't—" Her gaze falls on the ribbon in my hair. The blouse. The heart cradled against my chest. "Silvie, what are you... Where did you..."

Her expression morphs from confusion to fear.

"Why do you have that?" she asks, taking cautious steps toward me. She looks back to where the basement door hangs open. "Were you downstairs?"

I nod. "In the surgical theater."

The blood drains from her face and she sways, looking like she's about to pass out.

A strange thrill goes through me. It's my turn to weave the conversation, to keep her cornered, afraid, unbalanced. For the last year, she's been everything to me, my only friend, my constant companion. For the last year, I practically worshipped the ground she walked on, so convinced that everything she told me was true, real, proof of our connection. And we are connected. But it's nothing like I thought it was. "I met our sisters. The one in the wall, and the one that you buried."

"Excuse me?" she asks, her eyes wide.

I take another step toward her, wading through the riptide. It pulls at my ankles, it beckons me beneath the waves, but I remain steady, anchored.

I place the heart on the tile floor and reach into the pocket of my dress. My fingers trace the handle of her switchblade. This could get messy, and I almost wish that it would. I've never felt like this before, so certain of myself, so ready to draw blood.

"I know what we are, Nora."

12

Nora was my first friend, my only contact outside of Victor. She was my window to the world, my blueprint for how to be better. I used to spend hours lying awake at night, wishing that I could take on even a fraction of the confidence she had.

I'd roll onto my side, watching the time pass and the room darken.

Shadows cast by streetlights painting streaks of lonely gold across my bookshelf. Car headlights slicing through my windows, lighting up the rows of surgical textbooks, and cookbooks, and my secret sci-fi paperbacks. How to make the perfect grilled cheese. How to host the perfect dinner party. Crock pot recipes next to books about aliens and other worlds.

I always thought I might be better on another planet. Maybe I wasn't built for Earth. Until Nora. Until I realized that I wasn't trying hard enough, that if I really wanted to be stronger, braver, more confident—if I really wanted to be better—I had to find a way to change. I had to find a way to make myself more like her.

And now, even though we're the same—she's a stranger.

She stares at me, her eyes wide, her mouth open slightly.

She looks at me as if I'm the one who betrayed our blood oath, our sisterhood. My lip curls in disgust.

"I spoke to the person in the wall," I say as I take slow, calculated steps toward her. "Turns out you were wrong: she does exist. Her name is Nix. She's our sister too, except Mother hid her from us and she's been alone since before the fire."

"You know about Mother?" Nora's hands shake. With each step I take forward, she steps back until I corner her against the kitchen counter. I stop inches from her face, focused on the frantic pulsing of the vein in her neck, and the desperate way she grips the edge of the countertop, her knuckles burning white.

She's afraid of me.

Good.

"Let me ask you something: how did you come up with the name Nora and when did you start going by it? Because Nix says that you were only ever referred to as Sixteen while you were here... sixteenth in the series and all that. But you signed your name Nora on the backs of all your paintings. You really captured Victor's likeness by the way; I almost felt bad destroying the portrait."

"You don't understand. I never—"

"No." I clamp my hand down over her mouth, and her eyes widen in surprise. "You don't get to say *anything* until I'm finished."

A thrill rushes through me as she stands frozen beneath my touch. I think of the last time Victor brought me back from the dead. The way he pressed his hand down against my mouth, the power he must have felt, the complete and total control.

The fact that I can understand the feeling—the fact that I like it—terrifies me.

I pull away, and Nora, regaining her composure, pushes me back. Hard. Her palms strike me directly in the chest and I stumble, the air knocked from my lungs.

"What the hell, Silvie," she hisses. "This isn't like you."

"What do you know about me?" I say as I straighten up and catch my breath. "I for one didn't know *anything* about myself. Nix showed me everything. She's done more for me in the last few hours than you have in over a year."

Tears swell behind Nora's bloodshot eyes, and she curls her hands into fists.

Through the picture window, the storm has tapered off into a gentle flurry, and the grounds look almost peaceful beneath the blanket of snow. The holes we dug yesterday look like collapsed graves, pock marks on the white landscape. Nora's footsteps stretch back toward the forest, fresh snow already clouding the imprints.

I turn to meet her eyes. "Tell me what you were doing out there."

"I was digging." She glances down at her clenched fists and uncurls them slowly, like it's painful. Her palms face upward, and she extends them toward me. Her eyes are so red, so puffy, so full of misery. "I didn't know that someone already dug up what I was looking for."

"Our sister."

"Sure, our sister. If you take me to her now, we can still salvage this. There's a reason why I brought you here. I have a plan and if you would just listen to me then I can—"

"You really think I'm going to listen to you, after everything you've done?" I snap.

"Silvie..."

Our blood flows through each other's veins, our scars—on our chests and palms—declare us the same. My stolen childhood was spent here with her, and we're supposed to share not only skin, or hair, or eyes, but our minds. Even understanding these facts, I can't put myself in her position and make the same choices. I can't imagine a scenario where I'd leave my sister, my exact copy, my clone to suffer.

Light red foam bubbles out of the heart and though it remains silent, it leans against the side of the jar as if listening in on the conversation.

Nora's eyes dart to where it sits on the floor, and as she watches its flesh rise and fall, a pained expression spreads across her face. She reaches an arm out, leaning in to grab the jar, but I dart in front of it, catching her by the wrist.

"Don't," I warn.

"It shouldn't be beating," Nora says slowly. "I'm just trying to get a closer look."

I tighten my grip. "No."

She straightens up, and we stand locked in place for a moment, the heart's pulse barely audible through the glass. Then, Nora elbows me in the side, wrenching her wrist from my grasp. Sharp pain shoots through my ribs as Nora backs away, staring at me as if I'm gutting an animal.

"It's beating because of you, isn't it?" she hisses. "What did you do?"

"What did *I* do? What about everything you've done? You're the one who left me with Victor. You saw what he was doing to me, and you left me with him anyway."

"No, I didn't," Nora insists. "I got you away from him."

"And it only took you a year." I laugh bitterly. "Great job, Nora. You are *such* a good friend."

"You don't understand: I couldn't lose you again!" she cries. "What I told you yesterday about losing everyone I loved in the fire that destroyed this place? That was the truth. You are the only person who I've ever felt *anything* for, and I lost you."

She reaches for me again, her scarred palm stretched out like a sacrificial offering. My stomach churns as I look at it, it sickens me. *She* sickens me.

I step back, but that doesn't stop her from continuing to reach. It doesn't stop the numb feeling in my chest, the cold that's pumped out with each beat of my heart. The disgust.

"I was alone for so long," she continues. "All I could think about was finding you. I spent months searching, until I was convinced that I was the only one left. The only one left out of over a dozen versions of myself. Do you know how much it hurts to go from one of many to the *only* one? I *had* to find you; I couldn't keep going alone. And I when I finally did, when I finally saw you again, it was nothing like what I what I thought it would be. In a way it was worse than the fire."

She shakes her head. "I finally found you, the only person who could understand all the shit I've been through, and you *didn't* understand. You didn't remember any of it. You'd been wiped clean, and I had to mourn your death while I got to know you again. Do you get how hard that was for me?"

"I'm not dead, Nora. I'm right here!"

"But you're not the same." She holds her scarred palm up higher. "We're still closer than sisters, we still share blood, but you're different now. I know it's not your fault, but you...you aren't my Silvie anymore. I blame Victor. He's the one who wiped you. He clearly didn't know what he was doing and fried your circuits."

Her Silvie.

Like I'm an object. Like she owns me.

Nora inches closer and tries to lace her fingers through mine, but I slap her across the back of the hand, and she recoils.

"What the hell?" She pulls her hand against her chest, massaging it. "That really hurt."

"Good. It's what you get for working with Victor."

"I only worked with him so I could get close to you. I hate that man more than anything; he's basically a psychopath, and I still put up with him so I could be with you. Because I love you more than anything."

I curl my fingers into my palm so hard that my nails draw blood. She really has the audacity to claim that she loves me?

After everything? After all the hours she spent elbow to elbow with Victor, cataloguing my blood, and running tests on my samples, and lying to my face?

"So, Victor's the one who... wiped me. Broke me, made me into whatever the fuck this is... and the only reason why you're telling me any of this is because I found out and confronted you about it." I force her back against the cabinets, only this time she doesn't grip the countertop, she shrinks against it. I've never seen her look so small.

"Silvie, please. How can I make things right?" she asks, her voice trembling.

I press in so close to her that I can count the freckles across the bridge of her nose, and the pock marks along the edge of her jaw. Every beauty mark, every imperfection identical to my own. Even though she's nothing like me, nothing at all. "I'm not doing this so you can make things right. I'm doing this for me."

"But what about us?" she asks, pushing gently at my shoulders, making space between us. "Do you know why I'm always going on and on about our twin scars?"

"I don't need another story, Nora."

"This one is different. This story is everything." She tilts her palm so that the pale scar catches the light, glinting like ice. "You're the only one who ever understood me, Sil. Before you came along, I was so isolated. None of the others—none of our sisters—as you call them, liked me because they were all sick and broken, and I was the only one who came out okay."

I'm about to ask what she means by sick and broken, but then I remember Nix. And how she told me that the others in our series were prone to illness and death. None of the Silvies were quite right...

Nora continues. "I admit, it went to my head a bit. I was terrible in a lot of ways, and maybe I deserved to be cut off from the group, but it still hurt. I was so alone, but then you came along, and you weren't like the others."

My brow furrows. "Because I wasn't dying?"

"No, because of so much more than that."

"You're important," the heart gurgles from within the jar, still huddled up against the side of the glass.

"We found out about it by accident," Nora says, glancing out the window. The sun peaks through the clouds, hanging heavy in the sky—frosted shades of pink and orange dribbling through the tree line. "I don't know what they intended it for—or if it was intentional at all—but we decided to do the whole 'blood-sisters' thing."

"Fifteen minutes spent carving at ourselves with the dull end of a paper clip, finished off with a pocketknife and a promise."

"Exactly! Only when we shared blood, you went quiet. You convulsed. Your eyes rolled back, and I seriously thought that you were going to die, but instead something transferred over. When we shared blood, it was like a download. You *saw* me, Sil. All of me. My thoughts, my fears, my memories. You pulled pieces of me, pieces I could never share with anyone, into yourself."

The mirror. The heart. The images I've seen. Memories of Layla, of Nix, of the Victorian. It's all data. Code. What I'm made of—what I'm made for.

The heart blows a blood bubble and the loud smack of it popping against the side of the jar sounds like a smirk. *"I told you that everything reacts to your touch. I told you that your medication was preparing you for me—it was to evolve your ability to pull information from the other clones, and from the heart drives."*

Now I'm the one who reaches for Nora, my scarred palm held out like an olive branch.

"And you pulled the same sort of stuff from me? My thoughts, my fears, my memories?" I ask her. "You saw me too: that's why we were so close?"

She shakes her head. "You're the only one who can do it."

I drop my hand.

"It's like extreme empathy," Nora explains, the sun setting behind her. The colors melt together, a quiet violence. "You got me, Sil. You were able to understand everything because you were able to feel it. And you didn't judge me for any of it either, you were so patient with me—I think it was because you were able to see it from my perspective. Like I said, you *saw* me."

The first year after the fire, the year I spent alone with Victor being pumped full of false memories and medication—I was completely isolated. All I could do was watch him line pill bottles up along my side table, one after another, after another. All I could do was listen to him when he said how much work it was to keep me alive.

You're a lot to handle, Silvie.

You take up so much of my time.

Who else would do this for you?

"Do you understand?" Nora asks.

I do. "You liked me because I could soak up all your shitty feelings."

She shakes her head, the motion cartoonish and exaggerated. "I *like* you because you're the only one who's seen inside my head. You're the only one who can see things from my point of view."

I look down at my scarred palm and wonder about the scab that came before it. How did we hide it from Mother and the others? I picture us wrapping our hands in gauze and torn scraps of fabric. I picture us hiding the cuts beneath wool gloves and having hurried conversations on our way to the kitchen, whispered promises.

"How many times did we share blood?" I ask.

She tilts her head and stares out the window, watching the light fade behind the hemlocks. "Too many to count. You knew everything. And you lost it all in the wipe, and you don't know how long it would take to get back to that point. But you didn't even know what you were when I found you, so it didn't matter. Forget all the secrets I shared, all the thoughts, and memories, you didn't even know what we were."

She stays focused on the window, the last dregs of light straining through her hair. "When I first approached Victor about getting back in contact with you, he discouraged it. He thought it would cause more harm than good, and he wouldn't let me see you at first. And he was such an asshole. I couldn't stand the thought of you being trapped inside that house with him, being subjected to all that... stuff."

Stuff. The way she says it is so flippant. It damn near kills me.

The needles. The pills. The rough grip of his hands. The bruises he would leave on my wrists, and upper arms. The names he would call me, the passive aggressive remarks. How I never felt safe, not in my house, not in my body. Because of him.

"You knew what he was doing," I say through gritted teeth, burying my fingers in my palm, as if it's enough to contain the anger, the hurt. "You knew that he was experimenting on me, and you helped him. His project? It's me, isn't it? It's something to do with me... and you helped him."

"I didn't have a choice, and it wasn't easy for me. It was torture."

"Oh yeah, it was torture for you, right? It was torture for *you*." My cheeks burn. "You weren't the one getting their blood drawn every two weeks. You weren't the one he force-fed medication and kept under lock and key like some kind of animal!"

She finally turns from the window and gives me her full attention. Her eyes are still swollen, her cheeks flushed, two perfect lines of tears dripping down over her chin. She looks like a painting, a caricature of remorse.

And when she speaks, her voice is clipped. "It was awful for me to see you go through that, and I'm sorry I couldn't do more to get you away from him sooner. But I did get you out of that situation. I brought you here, and I think I deserve a little credit for that."

I wish I could break something, the rage that ripples beneath my skin is too much to contain. It's like nothing I say is getting through to her. "You were helping him!"

"For the thousandth time, not because I wanted to. You know how I feel about Victor."

"You think he's abusive," I say, my eyes narrowed.

She nods vigorously. "Right, he's an abusive dick!"

A spray of brine, of bitterness.

Dark water.

Cold.

"Your blood is in my veins, and my blood is in yours. I won't let anything hurt you," I say slowly, tracing the outline of my surgical scar. "Isn't that what you told me?"

She holds her hand to her chest, presses her palm to where her own surgical scar lays hidden. "Exactly. I won't let anything hurt you. Not now, not ever."

The current swells, waves cresting and breaking inside my mind.

Pain.

Cold.

"Except you did."

She drops her hand and frowns.

I picture them. Seated across from each other at our kitchen table while I was tucked away inside my room. This was before the padlock, but I would have been in my room as early as eight or nine and expected to stay for the remainder of the night.

As branches scraped my windowpanes, the noise burrowing beneath my eardrums.

As moths threw themselves against our porch lights, killing themselves for a taste of the glow.

All the while, Nora sat with Victor and begged him to let her speak with me. To befriend me. To reignite our sisterhood.

I hook my fingers against my scar. My anchor. Evidence that I'm not myself but one of many. Evidence that everything I've endured and forgotten has been shared by many minds—everything except for Victor. It burns me from the inside.

Nora pulls at the fabric of her turtleneck, her hidden scar, her hidden history. "This is so unfair. You're acting like all I've ever done is hurt you. I'm the one who stuck by your side through all your anxious bullshit. No one else would have put up with half the crap that I did, but I didn't give up on you. And I *did* get you away from Victor, so don't you dare try to make me the villain here."

I lean in close to Nora until we're nose to nose, searching her face for some trace of the girl I knew before. I try to find my beautiful, wild reflection. But now her eyes glint, her cheeks burn red and the pain in her voice doesn't reach her eyes. She's distorted, and I wonder if she's always been this way and if I was simply too blinded by her light to notice.

I can't keep arguing with her, it's only going to make me feel worse than I already do. She's never going to take responsibility for what she's done, and there are still things about this place that I don't understand. Nix can only know so much since she's been stuck in the wall since before the Victorian burned. Assuming Nora doesn't lie through her teeth, she's my chance to get answers. Something productive can still come from this conversation.

I take a deep breath, pushing the sick cocktail of betrayal and sadness down.

"You asked what you could do to make things right," I say slowly, even I know there's no way she'll ever make it up to me. "Explain why you buried our sister in the yard... did she die?" *Did you kill her?*

Nora shakes her head. "We can't die, not naturally anyway. I buried Fifteen because she tried to burn this place down. Mother and her team were going to decommission her, but she got the upper hand and torched them. Torched whatever she could. Fifteen was always a little bit weird, but about two years back she went full psycho. *I* think she had a thing going on with one of the scientists and Mother found out about it, which is her own damn fault. There were plenty of guys like us to choose from—plenty of other projects they were working on. She didn't have to go and sleep with one of the scientists."

The other jars in the surgical theater. Livers, and lungs, and massive coils of intestines.

"Other projects?" I ask.

"The Silvie Series—us, I mean—we were kind of like a side project, something the board of directors let Mother do to keep her happy. That thing in the jar—"

"It's like a backup drive, I know."

"Do you know who it belongs to?"

I shake my head. "Do you?"

"No. It doesn't look like the other hearts. It might not even belong to something from this location, it might be from the Beta facility."

The Beta facility?

Another house in the woods. More winding hallways, ornately carved mirrors, basement labs. More wallpaper, and passageways. More people—more *things* like us.

"There are other places like this?" I ask, my heart pounding. There are other experiments—*human* experiments—out there somewhere. If we can even be considered human at all...

Nora nods. "At least two others as far as I know. One of them was completely wrecked in a different fire, which makes you think they would have made the places less flammable. The other one is where they've taken up shop now. It's where Victor wants to take you."

Heat shoots up into my forehead, and my pulse is so loud

beneath my skin, it drowns me. Everything that Victor has done up until now, every pill, every slice of his scalpel... my breath comes in shallow bursts. "What do you mean he wants to take me there?"

"I brought you here with me so that he wouldn't. I saved you, truly. That's why I was freaking out last night when you came to my room about the painting. Victor figured out what I did. He called me and—"

Another burst of heat up into my forehead. "He called you? Your phone was working this whole time?"

"He's coming to collect you."

Collect me. Like I'm a taxidermy butterfly. Like I'm a corpse pinned against a cushion.

"What do you mean?" Numbness spreads from the center of my chest through the rest of my body.

Everything that I've worked so hard to overcome. Everything that I never thought I'd have to face...

"Victor's on his way here," Nora confirms. "And he won't stop until you leave with him."

13

Victor never left my side. He didn't go to work or out with friends; as far as I know, he doesn't have any friends. All he has are his journals, his research, and me. The three of us like siblings, a flock of birds that he has to watch over—our wings frail and hearts fragile.

We're everything to him.

A few weeks ago, I walked into the kitchen to find him leaning against the counter sipping a martini, his head tilted dreamily toward the window, the light casting half his face in shadow.

"It's ten in the morning," I said.

He turned to me and smirked.

"Come over here." He gestured with the drink. A splash of vodka spilled over the rim of the glass and splattered across the floor.

"You never drink before five." I inched up next to him and he draped his free arm around my shoulders. "What's going on?"

"I'm celebrating." He squeezed my shoulder, his fingers

digging into my flesh. "I had a very important phone call this morning, and it went much better than I thought it would."

There was a creeping feeling in my gut. I didn't like the way he kept glancing down at me, and I didn't like how glassy his eyes were. It was clear this wasn't his first martini; he was already drunk.

"What was the call about?" I asked, even though I wasn't sure if I wanted to know.

He gestured with the drink again, more vodka spilling out over the side. "Let's just say that we're finally nearing the end of all this."

Hope blossomed in the center of my chest. The end of all this could mean anything, and I was almost too afraid to ask, but I looked up at him, my eyes wide. "You know how to make me better?"

He took another sip of his drink and stared down at me, his gaze cold and clinical. "I already have."

"I'm not going anywhere with him," I say to Nora.

"You won't have a choice, Silvie. He'll sedate you—he'll do whatever it takes. Without you, there's no way for him to get back in with Mother's people and continue her research."

"Why are you telling me this?"

"Because I care about you—I really do. I wouldn't have brought you with me if I didn't, I would have just let him take you. But—but I'm sure that since you know the truth now, he'll let you be more like a partner than an experiment. We'll wait for him together, and when he shows up, we'll all leave together. It'll be fine."

"So, if I shut up and go along with it, that'll change things somehow?" My throat constricts. "You just said that it doesn't matter what I do. And with your track record, I can't believe you either way."

Tears stream down Nora's cheeks. She holds up her scarred palm and the pale mark is blurred as her hand shakes violently. "I messed up, I'm sorry. But we were so close, and I missed you so much, that I didn't know what to do when you didn't remember —and I know Victor, I know we can still work this out with him. We just need to stay calm and wait for him to get here."

I dig my hand into my pocket, fingers wrapping around the handle of the knife. I steady my breathing before I pull it out, my eyes burning into hers.

"Let me see then," I say.

"What hell, Sil?" Her gaze settles on the blade. "You took my knife?"

"Yeah, the knife isn't really what you should be focusing on right now. As I was saying, I can't trust a word that comes out of your mouth. So, show me. We'll pick up where we left off. Open the wound again: share blood. You can help me understand why you handled this the way that you did, and I'll know how to really feel about Victor coming here."

She drops her hand to her side. "I can't."

I narrow my eyes. "Because you're lying?"

"Because I shouldn't have to!" She shakes her head. "You know me—hell, you *are* me. It hurts that you don't think that you can rely on me when literally nothing has changed."

Except everything has changed. Even me... especially me.

"Okay," I say, and open my arms. "Come here. This is a lot for me to process, and I could really use my sister right now."

She's hesitant at first, and her back is rigid as I embrace her. Her body presses up against mine, both our heartbeats wild, slightly out of sync. I wrap my arms around her, the knife still gripped tightly in my fist, and wait until she starts to relax. I wait until her cheek is flush with mine, and she leans in against my shoulder, her body going slack. I wait until she's whispering to me about how glad she is that I've come to my senses and how she promises that everything will be okay.

Then, blood pulsing in my ears, I tighten my grip and spin her around. I back her into a wall next to the window and she cries out as her spine hits the plaster. She struggles, but I push her back hard, jamming my forearm into to her throat. "Give me your hand."

She squirms against me, and my arms and legs ache from the effort of keeping her in place—but I hold firm.

"You tricked me," she chokes.

My eyes burn into hers. "You tricked me first."

"Come on, this is crazy. If you would just calm down then we can figure this out."

"You should have told me that Victor was coming for me last night." I hold her tighter, feeling her heartbeat beneath mine. Still out of sync. We are not the same. "You used to tell me that I was obsessed with Victor, that I was so blindly devoted to him, but I'm not the one who's obsessed, Nora. You are."

A line of spittle drips down over her chin, and I release some of the pressure on her throat while keeping her pinned in place.

"He's not here, Nora. He has no control over either of us. You should have told me the truth and we should have run away together. Only you didn't. Because you're afraid of him."

She scoffs. "Oh, and you're not?"

I stare into her eyes—my eyes, layers of swirling gray.

"I'm terrified," I say. "But I'm not letting it stop me anymore."

I grip her wrist in my fist and slide the knife across—

Her palm.

My palm.

And press.

~

Bright colors. Endless burning.

A horsefly rests on a blade of grass, cleaning its back legs. A partly cloudy sky, crisp air. The Victorian—roof still intact, watches me as I look over the property.

I'm Nora.

I sit in the shade of a tree in the backyard and pick dirt from underneath my nails.

I watch the others play. Fourteen dragging her lame leg behind her like a wounded fawn. Thirteen flashing her three remaining teeth every time she laughs. It's disgusting.

I turn to where my Silvie sits next to me, the latest in Mother's long line of replicas. Silvie Seventeen. One of only three of us that aren't deformed, dying, or already dead. One of only three of us that are almost perfect.

We sit with our legs draped over one another, tangled up like we're an extension of each other rather than copies and the fly buzzes lazily around us.

Seventeen watches it.

"What do you suppose it's thinking about?" she asks.

I trace the scab that runs down the center of my palm. Our telephone line. Our tether. "Flies don't think."

Seventeen is different from the others. She asks more questions and isn't frightened when Mother occasionally snaps at us or when Victor shows off his dissection tools. It's impossible to get a rise out of her. It's like she knows that she was built to stay, that she's been safe since her inception.

She's reserved and chooses her words carefully as if she's picking flowers.

She loves flowers, admires how delicate they are. Roses are her favorite, then daffodils. She tells me more and more about herself each day, and a part of me thinks it's because she feels guilty that she can't share her thoughts the way I can share mine.

But I couldn't care less about what's inside her head—as long as she can see me. As long as she can understand. If it weren't for that, I think I'd hate her. She's Mother's favorite, the closest to being like the original Silvie. It takes a lot not to be jealous.

"Why don't you want to join in on the game?" she asks, gesturing to where the others run in circles around each other. Or try to, anyway. The majority of them hop, limp, crawl.

I roll my eyes. "Look at them, they won't be around for much longer. There's no use in getting attached; it'll only make things more difficult when Mother inevitably has to decommission them."

My Silvie picks a blade of grass and splits it, cautiously, down the middle. "She'll give them new bodies though. They won't really be gone, Sixteen—not forever anyway. No before, no forever, no afterward. We don't end or begin, we just are."

I shake my head. "She's not going to give them new bodies this time, she's not going to save the heart drives, they're going in the trash. It's not just their bodies that came out wrong, it's their minds too. It doesn't make sense to keep shuffling them from shell to shell. Fifteen was in the labs the other day and says that she saw them working on the next in the series. Mother's changing the process."

My Silvie tosses the two halves of grass aside and frowns. "In what way?"

I shrug. "I'll ask Fifteen later tonight."

"She's going to get herself into trouble if she keeps going down there."

"She's safe... for now. Her body is healthy, and her mind is sound... for the most part." I nod toward the others. "Not like them. For them it's only a matter of time."

"It's sad," she says. "I hate to think that they'll die."

I can't help but laugh. If I were with anyone else, they'd think I was callous, and I guess that's true. I feel about as much affection for them as a scientist would to a lab rat. Even so, it's not in good taste to mock them since we're built from the same code.

But I'm comfortable being myself around Seventeen, and as the laughter continues to trickle out of my mouth, she doesn't so much as raise an eyebrow.

"I think it's sweet how you get so upset about the others," I tell her. "It's not sad that they're going to be decommissioned; it's a necessary step. Mother almost has it right, you and I are proof of that. Pretty soon she'll create the perfect version, and we won't have to watch them die anymore."

My Silvie considers this for a moment, then tilts her head to the side. "You really think that she will get it right with the one she's working on now?"

I shrug. "If not this time, then the time after that. It'll happen soon."

To my surprise, a shudder runs through her, and she pulls her legs from mine, inching aside.

I reach for her, and she turns to me, her eyes shining on the verge of tears.

"Are you okay, Seventeen?" I ask.

She shakes her head. "When she gets it right, she won't need us anymore. And then what will happen to us?"

Bright colors. Endless burning.

Ash and smoke. In my clothes, in my hair, in my lungs. I can't breathe without tasting the fire. And I can't wait around for Victor to come back for me. I should have known he was lying, that he never intended to take me away from all of this.

I stand at the edge of the forest, watching the Victorian burn. It glows orange, and red, and yellow, lighting up the night.

The heart in the jar sits in the damp grass next to where I stand. Didn't he say that it was important? He wouldn't leave without it, not after everything he went through to retrieve it from the labs in the first place.

But the longer I wait, the more I question it. The mud dries against my palms and the backs of my hands; the blood dries beneath my fingernails. The flames climb to new heights, heat licking at the edges of the property.

Still, he doesn't come.

And I can't wait any longer.

I pick up the jar and turn from the inferno that eats away at the right side of the Victorian. I run into the thick pine forest, my lungs heaving from the effort.

The only thing I can think about is my Silvie, Seventeen. He said he was going back for her, that we would all leave together, but wasn't Seventeen already gone when the fire started? Wasn't she already outside?

She should have been.

So, he lied about that.

I wonder if he lied about Fifteen too. Maybe she wasn't as close to Mother as he claimed, maybe she didn't deserve what we did to her.

I think about how I buried her and hope that I didn't make a mistake.

~

Bright colors. Endless burning.

Victor sits across the table from me looking every bit as smug as I remember. The sun hangs low in the sky and his shadow falls in a long, inky veil across the lace tablecloth.

"I like what you've done with your hair. It suits you," he says casually, a light smile playing across his lips. His eyes travel the length of my face down to the collar of my turtleneck and it's all I can do not to squirm. "You look good."

I ball my fingers into my palm. "I want to see Seventeen."

"She doesn't remember you," he says, leaning back in his chair. "She doesn't remember any of it. I still need to work on her and seeing you would be too much of a shock; it would set my progress back."

"Why would you wipe her to begin with?" I ask. "She was perfect."

"You saw what happened with Fifteen. The less Seventeen knows about what she is, the less likely she is to snap and the easier it'll be for me to control the variables in the experiment. As far as she's concerned, her name is Silvie and I'm her doting older brother. It's actually kind of cute how she looks up to me."

"Her brother?" I ask, unable to mask my disgust.

"Do I look old enough to be her father?"

As if that's what I have a problem with. "Regardless of what she thinks... or what she remembers, I deserve to see her. I'm not leaving until I do."

Victor sighs and reaches a hand into his pocket. He pulls out his cell phone and slides it across the table to me. "Check the camera roll."

I scroll through the pictures and videos on his phone and even though it's Seventeen—even though it's my Silvie—she's nothing like the Seventeen I knew. She looks scared, and sad, and so much smaller than before. My insides burn. Victor broke her: he made her exactly like the others. Everything that made her special, everything that made her mine, has been extinguished and it takes all I have not to cry. But I can't show weakness in front of him, I can't let him know that I'm broken now too.

I push my chair back and rush toward the kitchen door, the fire in my gut working its way up into my head, making it hard to breathe.

"Where do you think you're going?" Victor asks, the amusement in his voice making the hairs on the back of my neck stand on end.

I twist around to face him, steeling my expression. "I'm finding Seventeen and getting her the hell out of here."

He grins, the smile slow and sick as it melts across his face. "No, you're not. She isn't here right now. And I have to say, I'm disappointed. You clearly had enough tenacity to survive on your own after the fire, but this?" He shakes his head. "You could ask me for anything, and you ask for her."

"What else could you possibly offer me?"

He doesn't respond and instead, waves his hand as if he's shooing a fly. "As much as I've enjoyed our little reunion, I think it's time you run along. I have work to do."

Except I anticipated this, and I smile at him as I play the ace up my sleeve. "I still have the heart drive, you know. The one you gave me that was so important. I've been holding onto it since the fire."

There's a sharp intake of breath and my heart thunders against my ribs.

"That's your missing piece, isn't it?" I continue. "Well, since you don't want anything to do with me, I guess I'll just have to take the heart to someone else. I tracked down your old lab assistant, maybe they'll be interested."

Victor shoots up out of his chair and barrels toward me, grabbing me roughly by the collar of my shirt, his face pressing down close to mine.

"Where is it?" His breath is sour, but I refuse to let him see how much it sickens me. I hold steady.

"Let's make a deal. You let me see Seventeen, I let you see the heart."

"I don't make deals with lab rats."

I pry his fingers from my shirt and push him, though it does as much good as pushing a brick wall. "Fine, no heart for you then."

He laughs, the sound sharp and acidic. "You think I don't know what you're doing? You don't actually have it; you're fucking with me."

"No, I have it," I say, slamming my phone down into his palm. "Check the camera roll."

He scrolls through the pictures, his jaw set in a hard line. "Where is it?"

I fold my arms over my chest. "Where's Seventeen?"

He deposits my phone on the table behind him before reaching into his pocket. He withdraws a scalpel and thumbs at the blade. "I could make you tell me, you know."

I pull out my switchblade, popping it from its handle. He glances down at the scar on his forearm. A thin silver line, a souvenir from the last time he tried to make me do something I didn't want to do. It's as if he's forgotten how much history we share or how far I'm willing to go to survive. But his expression shifts as he stares down the sharp edge of my knife, and he pockets his scalpel.

"Fine," he says. "Let's talk."

"After you let me see Seventeen."

He smirks. "I'll do you one better. I know why you want her so badly, and it doesn't actually have anything to do with her, does it? For example, if there were others in your series that could... see you, you'd be just as happy with one of them, wouldn't you? And let's say you help me with this, preparing her, building the others, you could customize one for yourself, make her your perfect little playmate."

"I don't want one of them," I say, my heart pounding. "I want all of them... I want all of them to see me."

Bright colors. Endless burning.

It's my first time back at the Victorian since the fire, and nothing's changed—but everything is different. I sit alone at the edge of my bed, staring down at my phone.

Three words.

'CALL. ME. BACK.'

Two words.

'PICK. UP.'

One word.

'BITCH.'

Text messages broken up by a barrage of angry voicemails and missed calls.

Victor calls again, and again, and again.

I let him go to voicemail again, and again, and again.

He's been trying to reach me since Silvie and I left for the Victorian earlier this afternoon. I let my phone's battery die so I wouldn't have to deal with it but once I plugged it in to charge, the missed messages came rolling in. Along with the new ones.

It was all I could do to keep the phone away from Silvie earlier. She kept begging me to try his number, to hand her the phone so she could dial the son of a bitch and check in. Now, I consider smashing the phone against the wall, grabbing Silvie and running. Except leaving now would mean giving up on everything I've worked for since the fire.

Leaving would mean nothing since she doesn't remember.

It's too difficult being alone—being unknown.

A few minutes pass, a few more missed calls, and I'm finally strong enough to answer the phone.

Victor doesn't even give me a chance to say hello. "You took her back there? What the hell were you thinking?"

My brow creases. "How do you know where we are?"

"I'm not an idiot. I've been tracking your phone since the moment you started working for me. Now why would you bring her back there?"

I pick at a loose thread on the comforter.

"Hello? Nora? Your little stunt is going to cost me two years of research. It's going to cost us everything!"

Moonlight spills through two tall, skinny windows casting shadows across the floor. The light falls across the standing mirror and I cringe at the way it's illuminated, like a blank eye through the dark. I threw a white sheet over it before I sat down, but I can't stop thinking about the glass beneath it, and how, if I rest my palm across its surface, I'll have to relive everything all over again.

"You better have a damn good excuse because I don't think you understand the full weight of what you've done."

I take a deep breath and recite the speech I've been practicing for months now. "Thank you for reuniting me with Silvie. Thank you for teaching me about our biology and how to manipulate it, and how to prep others in my series so that they can download multiple data streams, but I can take it from here. I'll be taking Silvie to the Beta facility, I'll be taking her before the board, and I'll be heading up the new experiments. I don't need you anymore."

He laughs. "You think you can screw me over? Really? You're nothing but old code at this point, Nora. You're dispensable."

"And you made me indispensable the moment you shared your research with me. I know what you were trying to do, Vic. Slipping pills into my food, trying to make me like her—experiment on me so that you could use us both as bargaining chips. You're smart, but I'm smarter. I figured out early on that you were never going to let me be a part of this, so I'm taking things into my own hands."

There's a sharp sound, like glass shattering, and I smile to myself, but then he hisses into the receiver, "You're not as smart as you think you are, little girl. How are you supposed to do any of this when you don't know where the Beta facility is?"

"Fifteen knows where it is." Which is why I need to find her, dig her up, and use Silvie to access the data.

"And I know where you are."

My breath catches in my throat.

"Judging by what you just said, you haven't dug Fifteen up yet, so you better hope you get what you need and get out of there before I catch up with you."

A shiver runs down my spine and I wish I could be strong, but I can't help it, I'm crying. I cry and cry, the tears tracing salty rivers down my face. I hate him. I clench my fist and think of all the ways I'd like to kill him. A knife to the gut, to the heart, to the throat.

But I'd also like more replicas that can do what Silvie does—more sisters who can see me, really see me.

"Maybe we could renegotiate the terms of our arrangement," I suggest.

He scoffs. "You're not really trying to negotiate with me after the shit you pulled, are you?"

"This whole thing has me so emotional, I don't know what I'm doing... but I know that I want this new series, and I'm sure we can figure something out." Even if it means Silvie ends up flayed open on a dissection table, even if it means I can never live outside of the Beta facility. Even if I'm an experiment for the rest of my life—I won't be alone. I refuse to be alone.

"Let me think about it. I'll be there tomorrow; you better hope I'm in a forgiving mood." He hangs up.

14

I surface from the data pull, gasping for air. Waves break across the surface of my skin, all salt water, spray, and surf. I jerk my hand away from Nora's and stumble back, gripping the knife so tightly that my knuckles burn white. The cut on my palm glares red.

"I told you not to do that, Silvie," Nora says, rubbing her neck. "This would have been so much easier if you'd listened to me."

My heart beats in my throat, and even though the pictures have faded, they continue to stir beneath my skin. A flicker of the fire, a flash of our dead sisters.

Everything that Nora saw, felt, thought.

I'm overflowing. Stuffed with teeth, and flesh, and insides which tighten and constrict. Far too much to contain. I need sharpened prongs and a steady hand to drain me of the heat and heaviness that's slowly taking over. The pin pricks, the warmth that pools in the back of my head and spreads. Spreads until I'm burning from the inside. Drowning in a white-hot ocean.

"You're sick," I yell at her, willing myself to stay standing despite the riptide, despite what I saw inside her head. "After all that, you're still going to sell me out to Victor? And even worse, you were going to use me as some kind of bargaining chip to get you in with the people who hurt us to begin with?"

She holds her hand against her chest, the red seeping into the fabric of her turtleneck. "I've been struggling with this for a long time. It's hard for me, but I'm trying to do the right thing."

"For yourself."

"I'm all I have!" she howls. "I'm the only one left who isn't deformed, or dead, or broken."

I clench my fist, my fingers digging into my split palm. "Which one of those categories do I fit into?"

"You're different, Silvie. That's the point." She takes slow, calculated steps toward me. "You saw me, you saw *us*. You can't pretend that you don't understand." She looks down at her blood-seeped turtleneck and flexes her fingers. She takes a deep breath. "I can't believe you cut me."

I hold the knife out in front of me and keep it pointed at her chest. "I can't believe you'd let Victor cut me open just so he can continue what Mother started. I can't believe you'd do all this for an experiment!"

She laughs, the wail of a siren. Behind her, the final dregs of sunset bleed crimson. "I don't give a shit about the experiment. I don't give a shit about what that woman was trying to accomplish; I want my sisters back. I want to be seen again." She stands between me and the basement labs, pivoting so that her body eclipses the doorway.

I bend to pick up the heart but its voice cuts into my head.

"You won't be able to hold me and defend yourself."

I can't leave you up here with her.

"I'll be fine, protect yourself. She won't hurt me, she needs to deliver me to Victor. I'm not the one in danger, you are."

And how exactly do you factor into all this?

It falls silent and I straighten up to face my clone. My wound stings, the cut bright and deep, the flesh around it aching. My bruise from earlier aches along with it. Falling through the collapse feels like it happened an eternity ago, but the marks remain. Some things never fade completely.

Nora's palm drips onto the tile floor and she runs a finger across the gash, her eyes watering as she presses into it. "It didn't have to be this way. All you had to do was calm down so we could wait for Victor to get here. Now things are going to get messy."

"You're right, they are." I rush at her, elbowing her hard in the ribs. There's a sink, then resistance as my arm makes contact, and she lets out a gasp.

I push past her to the basement door, but she catches my arm and jerks me around. There's a pop, an explosion of static in the back of my head and I grit my teeth as I swing the knife. It only cuts the air, but it's enough to get Nora to back off.

We twist to face each other, chests heaving, our twin wounds bright and angry against the pristine, white kitchen.

The heart beats wildly from behind the glass. Melodic. Maddening. It's the only thing that keeps me from collapsing in on myself. It's the only thing diluting the saline that pumps through my veins, the only thing fighting off the feverish toss of the waves.

Tears spring to Nora's eyes and she reaches for me, again—her bloody palm extended outward. "Come on, Sil. This is ridiculous."

Nora nudges the basement door closed and approaches where I stand, her palm dripping as she moves.

"What are you going to do when Victor gets here, huh?" she asks, casting quick glances toward the window, her face streaked with tears. "If you try to resist, he'll hurt you."

I squeeze my fingers into the cut on my palm, but I don't wince. "He's already hurt me."

"It'll be worse this time, believe me. Now that you know what you are, he's not going to hold back anymore." She wipes the tears from her eyes, leaving streaks of blood across her cheeks. "He'll pull apart your body and put your skin samples on slides. Maybe he'll keep you alive while he does it, it all depends on what the board wants. He could strap you to a table and keep you in some back closet somewhere until you run out of blood."

"And you'll let him do that to me." I glare at her.

She sighs. "Because I have to. And who knows, if you behave, maybe it'll be quick, maybe we can convince the board to let you live."

There's that word again... behave. It never really occurred to me before now, but maybe the reason why Victor has always been so obsessed with making sure I behave is because he knows what I'm capable of if I don't. And it's clear that Nora does too, or else she wouldn't seem so frazzled. I have the upper hand over her, despite everything going on inside my head. Because this skill of mine, this curse, not only means that I can understand her pain, it means I know her weaknesses.

I think of all the heart drives in the basement, catalogues for me to sort through. I don't need Nora anymore, and I think she knows that. I think she knows that I was always meant to evolve without her.

And I'm done behaving.

I swing the knife, but Nora grabs it by the blade. A fresh spurt of red erupts from her split palm and my body pitches forward as she wrenches it out of my hand. It clatters to the floor.

She lunges at me, her fingers knotting through my hair. I let out a cry as she yanks back, ripping strands out at the root. My scalp stings and tears prick the corners of my eyes.

She grabs another clump of my hair, but I thrust my elbow out, and she releases me as it hits her in the jaw. Her lip splits.

"What the hell, Sil." She bares her teeth and they're stained red, blood gushing down over her chin. I jerk to the side, but she pulls me back and we hit the tile floor together, our legs tangled like that afternoon in the grass so long ago. She pins my shoulders. "It'll be easier for you if you don't fight it."

I twist my face so that my cheek lies flat against the cool tile. Blood drips from my nose and I watch it snake out across the floor, I watch the heart strain against the jar. It rolls toward me, pressed up against the glass.

"Get up, Silvie."

I kick Nora in the stomach and roll aside, picking up the knife as I rise. I scoop the jar up with my free hand and scramble my way back to the door.

"I told you to leave me behind," it gurgles.

I couldn't do that.

"Damn," Nora says, blotting her sleeve against her split lip as she rises. It does little to stop the spurts of blood that now cover her lower jaw completely. "I didn't know you could fight like that; I'm impressed."

She takes a step forward, but I angle the blade.

"Don't," I warn. "I will cut out your heart drive, suck it dry, and pull all that you are into myself until there is no you anymore."

Her eyes widen and the look on her face, the fear, the panic, is intoxicating.

"What's the matter, Nora? Didn't you say that you wanted to be close to me?" I run my tongue along the flat side of the blade and her memories zap across the surface of my mind—*the sun beating down on a gravel path, Victor running a finger along her jawline, a strawberry coated in sugar*— "Let's get close."

Nora popping the heads off dandelions, Nora sliding the switch-

blade across her palm, and looking at me as if I'm the only one who can save her.

"It's sad. I used to be jealous of you," I say, lapping more of her thoughts and feelings from the knife. "But now I can see who you really are, and it's so pathetic. You're so pathetic. I can't believe I ever wanted to be like you."

Nora crying, Nora screaming, Nora completely alone.

As her memories recede, like the pull of a tide, I keep my eyes trained on the window. Outside, the sky bruises to deep purple before draining to black, giving way to a cloudless, starless night.

My guts churn and saltwater hums through my veins—a quiet, silken madness.

"You are the only person I have ever loved," Nora insists. "And I didn't want it to come to this. I've never wanted to fight you, Sil. I love you. We can still figure something out, we can still—"

"There is no *we*." Not unless I drink from her heart drive, but truth be told, I don't think I'd want to absorb her. I don't want that kind of poison inside me.

Outside, the velvety darkness deepens, and the fluorescent bulbs along the ceiling hum like insects.

Something in her seems to snap and she bares her teeth at me, her fist clenched, weeping red. "Why do I always have to be the bad guy? You just saw me, Sil, you should understand, so why am I still the villain here? You really are different than before; you don't understand the way that you used to."

I back up against the basement door and balance the jar against my hip while I fiddle with the door handle. It creaks open and Nora rushes at me, her eyes wild and glassy.

She flails her arms and spit flies from the corners of her mouth. "We need to bring them something! They're not going to let us back in unless we offer them *something*. Dammit, you'd benefit too if you just come with me and show them what he did to you, then we can both be happy, live with each other and be happy. If you'd just cooperate, they might not dissect you!"

I slam the door in her face, twist the locks, and press my back flat against it.

"Silvie!" She pounds against the metal. "You think you can continue like this? You think you have a place outside of the dissection table? You won't last on your own. You're too damn clingy."

She stops pounding against the door and grumbles. "You really messed up my lip."

"You messed me up too." I crouch down next to the door and run my fingers along the lid of the jar. "And you don't even care, Nora. That's the worst of it."

"I care too much." Footsteps sound from behind the door and I picture her pacing back and forth, Nix tracing her movements from the depths of the surgical theater. "I don't know what I'm doing anymore. I thought I knew, but I feel like I'm being torn apart."

"You can't guilt me into going back out there."

She scoffs. "You're gonna have to come out eventually. If you don't, Victor will find his way in." She curses under her breath. "You really fucked me up here, Silvie. I'm starting to bruise."

I'm already bruised. The heart in the jar beats gently and I cradle it against my chest, hold it against my own heartbeat. It syncs with mine in a way that Nora's never did. She kicks the door, and the sound reverberates through the tiny entryway at the top of the stairs.

"I hope you're ready when he gets here," she says. "Because you're not going to be able to beat the shit out of *him*, that's for sure."

Her footsteps disappear across the kitchen until I can't hear them anymore.

I sink down against the door and tilt my head back, hoping that my nose will stop bleeding. As the adrenaline from the fight fades, every inch of me shakes, but I smile despite the pain. I'm taking back my life. I'm taking back everything. And if I can pull data from her, if I can pull from the jars in the basement, what else can I do?

The people who did this, who made me, are still out there somewhere. They're planning on making more of me, of doing this to more of me. I won't let them. The Silvies won't suffer anymore. I press my bloody palm to my skirt; my nose continues to drip though the bleeding has slowed considerably, and red splatters against the floor.

I pick up the heart and hold it level with my face. "We should get back to Nix and my sleeping sister."

"I for one, don't approve of how Nix dotes on the dead one like she's a child." Flakes of blood cover it like a glaze. New scabs, old wounds—jellylike smears along the bottom of the jar. *"It isn't healthy to love someone that much, especially when they're unable to reciprocate."*

"Believe me, I get it. I loved Nora."

"I'm so sorry, Silvie. I can see how much she meant to you."

"You know what I don't understand, why you have access to my memories, but I don't have access to yours."

"That's not how the link works. It was designed so that I can be close to you, so that I can know you. It's a one-way line of communication... aside from our thought-talk."

The undertow sloshes beneath the surface of my skin, but I don't let it take me. It moves slowly, carving a path through the caverns of my chest, and I dig my fingers deep into my scarred chest, anchoring myself. "Have you ever known hurt like this?"

"Yes, a thousand times over," it says, popping another large blood bubble against the side of the jar. *"Which is exactly why I wanted to apologize for my part in what Victor did to you. He should have never been allowed to experiment on you. But I've been consid-*

ering our situation, Silvie, and I think I know how to make it up to you—how to make us both happy."

I frown. "I think I know what you're getting at, and I'm not drinking your blood, or letting you any further inside my head than you already are, especially if I don't have access to any of your information. What's to stop you from taking over my body completely?"

"I'm not capable of that, and even if I were, I would never do that to you. Besides, if we assimilated, I could help you confront Victor."

"You're supposed to be able to read my mind; how do you not get it?" I shake the jar, and the heart grumbles as it smacks against the lid. "I *can't* confront him; I can barely hear his name without spiraling back to where I started."

The heart falls back to the bottom of the jar. *"But Silvie, I can confront him for you. If you strengthen our bond, then we can both get what we're owed. I know exactly what to say to Victor to break him worse than he broke us."*

I give the jar a final shake before rising to my feet, and the heart grunts. "Because you know him *so* well, you just can't explain how—right?"

I stand over the jar, my chest heaving as it rolls along the bottom, and as I watch it writhe, I'm overcome with a wave of regret. Bending to pick it up, I hug it to my chest. The soft thump of it through the glass is almost soothing, and I remind myself that violence is a lack of control. If I allow myself to become cruel, I'm no better than Victor, or Nora. "I'm sorry, you didn't deserve that."

"No, I'm sorry for being cryptic." It rolls onto its side, rising and falling rapidly as if catching its breath.

I take my first step down onto the staircase.

"But how do expect us to get our revenge if—"

I grip the jar and move to shake it again, but the heart sputters and I pause. This isn't me. I'm not a monster. No matter how angry I am, I'm not a monster. "There is no *us*. There's me. My life and my choices."

"I understand that. And I'm trying to help you make decisions on how to best live that life. Of course, the choice is yours. What do you want to do with this new life of yours, Silvie?"

I hold the jar at eye level, and peer in through the streaks of blood coating the glass. "I'm going to destroy the people who did this to me. I'm going to burn them all to the ground, and make sure there's never another addition to the Silvie series ever again. All I need to do is revive Fifteen so we can find the Beta facility."

It twists away from me dismissively. *"That's not a possibility."*

"Yes, it is. When Nora and I linked, I found out that Fifteen knows where the Beta is, that's why Nora wanted to dig her up in the first place."

"I mean, that it's not possible to revive Fifteen."

"Even with the mirrors?" I ask, my stomach sinking when I realize there's no telling if I'd even be able to find the rooms Nora and I were staying in again. "I mean, I got an electric shock every time I touched the glass and if I put her hand up against it, it could act as a defibrillator of sorts, couldn't it? It could shock her back to life?"

"That's not scientifically accurate."

I balance the jar against my hip and carefully navigate down the stairs. "You didn't say that it's impossible."

"Using the mirror would require you to go back upstairs and break the glass. If Victor gets here before you make it back to the basement, it wouldn't matter if you got enough shards to revive a baker's dozen worth of the Silvie series. Besides, it would be a pointless endeavor. There isn't enough electric current running through the glass to revive anything. And beyond that, there's no need to revive the dead one at all—you can just pull the data from her drive."

I step down from the last stair and start across the surgical theater, a headache pounding in my left temple. A side effect of my fight with Nora, or strain from the heart listening in on my thoughts. "Despite what I said to Nora upstairs, I'd rather not pull anyone else into my head unless there's no other option."

"Well, you won't be able to revive her."

"What do you know about waking the dead?"

Its beating slows and it sits up a little higher inside the jar, puffing out smugly. *"More than you."*

15

"Silvie, I'm good at resurrecting things. Perhaps even better than Victor. If you drink my blood, I can show you what you need to know in order to revive your sister."

"I'm not doing that," I insist, as I carry the heart across the stomach of the surgical theater.

Nix stands next to where Fifteen lays on the table and waves enthusiastically as I approach.

"As it is, the power dynamic in our link is skewed," I whisper into the lid of the jar. "That's only going to get worse if I strengthen the bond. I've never had control over my body my entire life. I'm finally getting it back, and you think I'm going to hand it over to you like it's nothing?"

Thick, mucus-like strands of blood hang from the lid of the jar, residue from when I shook it. *"You wouldn't be giving up control. You'd be gaining necessary information."*

I pause, holding the jar level with my face. "The fact that you would even use this as leverage makes me want to chuck you in a dumpster, you get that, right?"

A strand of blood plops down onto the heart and it trembles slightly as the strand of red trails down its side. *"It's not leverage, it's a price. Everything has a price."*

"Yeah, well, that price is too high."

I make it to the table, and Nix throws her arms around me, pulling me in so tightly that the jar is wedged between us. "I was afraid that you would not come back."

I smile into her shoulder. "I wouldn't leave you alone again."

She squeezes me tighter, the jar digging into my sternum, and I wince.

Nix seems to sense my discomfort and pulls back. "Sorry, I did not mean to hurt you. I was only excited."

She notices the blood splattered across the front of my dress and frowns. "Are you okay? What happened up there?"

"I'll be fine, and I'll explain in a bit." I look past her at our sleeping sister. "But for now, we need to focus on her. And we can't keep calling her Fifteen, or sister... she deserves a name, same as us. Any ideas?"

Nix brightens at the question, rattling off a list of her favorite words—and it's so wholesome that my chest aches. After everything that happened with Nora, and the threat of Victor's arrival, my body is still buzzing, a headache pounding behind my eyes. Nix dulls some of the pain. I'm not sure if she'll ever understand how much she's done for me in the short time we've been together.

"What about Lily?" she says excitedly. "Lilies are my favorite flower. Mother gave me a bunch of them for my birthday once and they were the most beautiful things I had ever seen."

Lily.

It's a name fit for a life-size porcelain doll, and one I briefly consider taking for myself. Silvie tastes like ash, like bad memories. It rots inside my mouth, but I can't let it go yet. It would be easy to adopt a new name, pretend that I'm not connected to the original, but her blood still flows through my body and no matter how hard I try, I can't separate us.

I can't cut myself off from Nora either, not completely. I close her switchblade and slip it back into my dress like I'm pocketing a piece of her skeleton. Water rushes through my veins but I swim against it, fighting my way upstream. My headache softens, then fades.

Nix and I stand on either side of where Lily lays on the surgical table, directly beneath the viewer's balcony. I keep a calculated distance between us, and the jar sits perched on the table in the crook of Lily's arm.

"We're bringing her back to life," I tell Nix, looking down at the open wound in the center of my palm, "so that I can find the people who made us and make them pay for what they did. She's the only one who knows where they are."

Nix runs her fingers around the lid of the jar. She watches the heart as if it might burst through the glass at any moment. Once I mention my plan, she raises her eyes to meet mine, her forehead creasing. "You are going to leave me again? You promised that you would not..."

"I won't—I'm going to take you with me."

"I cannot go outside."

"It won't be for very long. Only enough time for us to take our revenge."

"But I do not want revenge." Nix looks at me with wide, pleading eyes. "All of that is in the past. And why would you want to seek out the people who did this to us? You are healthy. You are strong. You are the only one who can absorb data from the others in our series—"

"Through our blood."

"Through our blood," she echoes. "That is powerful. We will be okay from now on, as long as we are together."

Nix is right. I know the power that I hold now, but that doesn't change what's been done to me. It doesn't change that somewhere out there, people are planning to do much worse, if they haven't already. I would have never wanted this if I had a choice, and assuming the other Silvies are built of the same base code, they wouldn't either. That's not even acknowledging the pain that simmers through me, the white-hot rage. I deserve my revenge for all this.

"Do you know why I'm the only one who can do it, though?"

"A design flaw," Nix says. "Mother told me about it shortly before the fire. It was a mistake that became the new standard for the Silvie Series. The people upstairs, the people Mother was working with began to expect it from all clones going forward. They wanted it so our sisters could assume multiple personas, be many people at the same time. There were more... practical applications for it."

I stare up at the viewer's balcony and frown. I've only just begun to take control of my body. I can't imagine balancing multiple consciousnesses, dividing up precious real estate inside my mind. "I can't do that."

Nix lifts her fingers from the lid of the jar and tilts her head. "Your co-consciousness with the heart says otherwise."

"We can speak to one another; we're not sharing a mind."

"Perhaps not, but you have the ability to download and house multiple data streams. If we head into the tunnels now, we can look for any heart drives that I have missed. We can see if there is a way to read their code without you absorbing the data." She fiddles with the ruined ends of her hair. "I have been hoping that we may be reunited with our sisters, and you are our best chance of that, Silvie."

"Is that why you brought me down here?" I step back from the table, my mind reeling. All this time, I thought she was so innocent. All this time, I thought she had been victimized—same as me—and maybe she was, but that doesn't change the fact that she's no different than Nora after all; she's been working to advance her own agenda.

I can't believe I let myself think that someone would be nice to me without an ulterior motive. Have I learned nothing?

Why are Nix and Nora so obsessed with being tethered to the others, anyway? We're all built from the same code—we're already copies. I would think the pull would be in the other direction, a lust for individuality, a way to distinguish yourself from the herd, not be absorbed deeper into it.

My eyes widen as I realize that the original Silvie, at her core, really is clingy. The code we were given can't survive without connection, without feeling understood. Except I'm not that way. Maybe I really am different from my sisters. I know the thought should make me feel alone, but instead, my pulse quickens, because it means that I'm not limited the way they are.

"I brought you down here so that we may be together," Nix says, her bottom lip trembling.

"You want to use me to bring our sisters back."

"You want to bring them back too though. You just said that we were going to resurrect Lily."

"That's not the point," I spit. "You only brought me down here to use me. You're no different from Nora."

Nix shakes her head vigorously, her eyes wide. "I do not want to use you. I wanted to meet you. I wanted to know you. This is only a thought I had..."

I shake my head, still not completely convinced. "We don't have time to argue. Nora said that Victor's on his way, that he won't leave until he finds me. He'll take me to the other facility, and if he gets to me before I figure out a way to get there myself, then I won't be in any position to get my revenge or to save our sisters. I'll be dissected or worse..." I can't stop thinking about his scalpel. It's kissed my flesh more times than I can count, but never as punishment, never while I'm still conscious. I've never felt what it feels like to be taken apart. I've never felt the pain of my insides being butchered, only the tight grip of Victor's hands or the sting of a needle. But there's this terrible dread knotted through the core of me, this horrible part of me that knows that's what he has planned if I don't cooperate. And I don't intend to cooperate. Never again.

"Much worse," the heart agrees. *"Which is why we should strengthen our bond and confront him together."*

"Nix," I say, ignoring the heart. "I want to believe you when you say that you want to be a family..."

"Then believe me," she pleads. "It is the only thing I have ever wanted, to be a Silvie, one of the series. Silvie number one. Your sister!"

"That's the thing, being one of many is exactly what Nora wants too, and I can't trust her. We're copies of each other, but we're all so different..." I'm so different now, "... that it's impossible to know what's going on inside your head. I don't know you at all."

She picks at the split ends in her hair, further adding to its frayed appearance. "It hurts to hear you say that. I have only ever wanted to be your family."

"It's the only thing any of us have ever wanted," the heart echoes.

I slam the switchblade down on the table, the noise reverberating through the surgical theater. "This isn't about you. Or the heart." I glare at it pointedly.

"This is about cleaning up the mess that they made when they created us; this is about making sure that there aren't any more of us that are left to suffer," I tell Nix. "And if you want to help me, then great. If not, stay out of my way."

Nix reaches out and rests her hand on my wrist. "I want to stand beside you as you build your future."

"Then show me." I raise my bloody palm. "Show me who you are and that I can trust you."

My body tenses as I brace myself for how she's bound to resist. How I'll need to wrestle with her, force her to share her data. I plan it out, calculating the steps it will take to grab back the knife, rush Nix, and forcibly slice the blade across her palm. But to my surprise, she nods—a faint smile tugging at her lips.

"Okay," she tells me. "I will do whatever you need me to."

I pass her the switchblade and she lifts it, turning her hand on its side. She drags the blade along the inside of her palm, and though her skin puckers rather than slicing open, her blood is the same and it drips out in a fat, crimson line. I reach across the table and take the knife, reopening my own wound.

"I cannot control what you see," she says, weaving her fingers through mine.

"I wouldn't be able to trust you otherwise."

We press our palms together.

~

Bright colors. Endless burning.

I am Nix, and I am small—nothing more than a child. My thoughts come in disjointed spurts, as if each word is fed to me through a machine. It is a constant reminder that I am not what Mother wanted me to be, I am broken.

Mother cradles me in her arms as blood congeals against the front of my dress. It is tacky, gummy. She will not stop crying, her hot tears splattering against my cheek. Against my forehead.

It hurts me to see her cry, almost as much as the gashes that pepper my stomach. The stab wounds.

"I'm so sorry," she says, holding me tight against her chest. "They told me to nix you..."

I am not familiar with the word, but Mother seems agitated by it, her body trembling as she squeezes me closer.

"What am I going to do?" she says quietly, more to herself than to me. "There are going to be major consequences for this."

"What are consequences?" I ask, looking up at her.

"Trouble."

"You will be in trouble?" My brow furrows. I do not want Mother to get in trouble, and I do not want her to hurt.

"Yes," she says softly. "Big trouble."

"Then you should nix me," I say. "If it will keep you out of trouble. I don't mind."

She chokes back a sob.

"Mother?" I ask, confused. "Why are you sad?"

"I can't kill you."

"Then do not. Nix me." But I can tell by her reaction that I have said the wrong thing, and I want to ask what nix means but I am too weak, my vision blurring. I like the way it sounds though, so it cannot be that bad. I do not know how such a pretty word could be so upsetting. I repeat it again and again inside my head, fighting off the urge to sleep.

Nix. Nix. Nix.

Me.

If I am Nix, then Mother will stay out of trouble. She will be happy.

She brings me down to the labs and hides me away in the nursery room while she goes to find a way to stop the bleeding.

Even as the blood on my dress dries, my wounds continue to weep, soaking the sheets beneath me, dripping down to the floor of the nursery. The pain fades, all feeling fades, and I drift, half asleep and waiting for her to return.

It seems as if hours pass in this room.

She created it a few weeks back for my new sisters, so they can acclimate after she brings them into the world, so she can make sure they are not broken like me before they are allowed upstairs.

Before the awfulness by the lake, before the stinging pain, Mother swore that I would have sisters soon and that I would not be alone ever again.

But that was before I became Nix for her.

That was before the knife.

And when she finally comes back into the room, her mouth is set in a thin line.

As she lays out the medical supplies, as she stitches my wounds shut and I slowly regain feeling in my body, I realize that everything has changed.

I know that I am not really Silvie, I will never be Silvie.

And I will always be alone.

"You can't ever go back upstairs again, do you understand me?" she says, her voice grave. "They will kill you."

"Like you tried to..."

"I'm so sorry, but you didn't come out right. I tried, but you're broken. As far as they're concerned, you're a monster."

The words should hurt more than the wounds do, but I accept her diagnosis, her death sentence.

"You'll be safe down here, I promise. I'm the only one who has the key to this room. There have been fires at the other facilities," she tells me, as the last of my scabs flake and peel. "But we've fireproofed the basement levels, even if the house above burns, you'll be okay down here. I promise, I've thought of everything. I'm not going to let anything hurt you again."

I do not have the heart to tell her that I am hurt.

I do not have the heart to tell her that even as she dressed my wounds, even as she nursed me back to health, she hurt me.

Bright colors. Endless burning.

I sit with Mother as she braids my thinning hair. I am twelve or thirteen at this point. It is easy to lose track of time down here. There is no way to tell for sure how old I am, or how long I have been locked away. Mother says that the others do not age like I do. She says that they are in the same bodies all their lives. At first this makes me sad, because I am not like the others, and I do not want to be older than they are. But Mother promises that I will reach a point where I stop changing, and my sisters and I will be the same physical age. Though part of me fears she only says it to keep me calm.

We are in my room, a small rectangle hidden deep within the labs, behind my special door, a door that only Mother can open. She assures me that I only need to spend a few more weeks shut inside. Soon she will give me free rein of the corridors within the Victorian.

"You're the most important thing in my life, you know that?" she coos.

"What about the original?" I ask, wanting desperately to believe her. "Or the others in the series that are more like the original than I am?"

"Shhh," she says, smoothing my hair, her palm stroking the exposed portion of my scalp—the area where my hair has thinned to the point of nonexistence. "Thinking about that will only upset you."

She pats me once on the top of the head and I scoot over, glancing into the small, circular mirror which hangs above my dresser. The skin beneath my eyes is bruised black and purple. It sags like the rest of my face, and I quickly turn away. I turn back to Mother, with her beautiful skin, her glossy hair.

"Am I still a monster? Do the people upstairs still want me dead?" I ask. "It has been years, surely you can introduce me to my sisters now."

"We've been over this. I'm sealing the holes in the walls so that you—"

"So that I can move freely through the house, to be with my sisters," I say quietly, sitting back down on the edge of the bed. I pick at a loose thread in the flowered comforter.

Mother rests her hand on my shoulder. "To be near them, yes, but still safe, still separate."

I pull the thread loose and look up at her, tears welling up behind my eyes. "I am sure that enough time has passed by now. I am sure that they have forgotten about me."

"Only to the point where you're a scary story."

The tears drip down my cheeks, and I wipe them away with the backs of my hands, turning slightly so she cannot see. "I do not want my life to be a scary story, Mother."

She hooks her hand beneath my chin and gently turns my face back toward her. "We don't get to decide what kind of story our life will be. Not everyone gets a happily ever after."

"I want to play with the others. I want to be with them. It will not be enough to walk through the walls next to them if I cannot meet them."

"You know that's impossible; it would frighten them too much. And you don't want to frighten your sisters, do you?"

I shake my head and lower my eyes. "Why do you not tell them about me though? We could talk through the wall, even if I am to stay separate. I am Silvie number one after all."

Even though I know that I am not. I am Nix. And even that is not enough to make Mother happy.

"I do not want to be alone," I try again, inching close to her. "I love you, Mother, but as you create more of my sisters, you visit me less and less."

"Which is why I'm making it so you can hear the others through the wall. It's why I've been sealing the holes and creating this for you, so you're not trapped down here anymore."

"Do you love the others more than me? Is that why you are neglecting me?"

She rests her hands on either side of my face and kisses me lightly on the forehead. "I'm not neglecting you. I love you, all of you, your sisters included."

"How are they?" I ask, because she has told me about their health issues, about Seven and her degenerative bone condition, Nine and her skin disease. I know that they are still slightly broken, and I worry for them. Because she has not brought any of them down to be with me, even though I have begged. When the people upstairs tell her to nix them, she kills them.

"I'm getting better at making them," she says with a small smile.

"They're better every time, and I'm sure it won't be long before I perfect the recipe."

"What is a recipe?" I ask, my brow furrowed.

"Remember when I first made you and you had free rein of the house upstairs?"

I nod, my chest aching at the memory of being able to wander the halls freely.

"Remember when we'd bake together in the kitchen?" she asks, and I nod again. "Well, recipes are instructions, so that what you're baking turns out right."

The recipe. Like I am a cake or cookie, and if Mother had only added the right amount of baking soda, then I would be perfect.

A pinch of salt.

Half a cup of sugar.

Blood, and guts, and homemade dough.

"Are they beautiful?" I ask. "Are my sisters beautiful?"

She nods.

"Can you make me beautiful too? Can you make it so they will not be afraid when they see my face?"

Her eyes stay trained straight ahead, and she strokes the side of my skull absently.

"Mother?" I tug on the corner of her shirt. "Can you fix me?"

She does not look at me. Instead, she pulls her hand away as if I am contagious. She stands and crosses the room, her back to me as she unlocks the door. She does not look back.

"Thinking about that will only upset you," she says.

Bright colors. Endless burning.

I listen to the others all day, every day. I trace their movements from below the floorboards and hurry through the walls after them, alongside them. Their laughter is my music, my poetry. I love them so much, almost as much as I love Mother.

I know them by their voices, the cadence, the melodies of their speech different depending on which one is speaking.

Fifteen with honey in her voice, Sixteen with ice, and Seventeen with a voice full of endless curiosity.

In all my years within the walls—hidden away in the labs—they are the only things that keep me from being lonely.

I wonder what they look like—if parts of their skin sag and peels like mine, or if they are rosy cheeked and normal as Mother says they are. I assume that they must be better than I am since they have lasted this long. But still, I worry.

Something is wrong. It is early evening, and usually the Silvie series would be settling in for the night, brushing their teeth and hair, running up and down the hallways as the men upstairs work to corral them into their rooms. Not an easy task when dealing with teen girls. Usually, there would be laughter and gossip, a cacophony of sound. Instead, there is quiet.

Quiet, punctured by far-off, high-pitched cries. I stand within the passageway on the second floor and press my ear to the wall, my heart drive pounding.

I smell the smoke before I see it. Acrid and pungent. I twist within the passageway, but the smell drifts up from below, thin tendrils of gray float into the dark and I hear Sixteen rush into the hall.

She calls for Victor.

"Where the hell are you?" Footsteps. An exasperated sigh. "I got the heart drive like you asked, but we can't stay in here much longer or we're gonna roast."

"I told you to wait for me outside," he responds.

"You told me to get the heart drive while you got Seventeen."

I choke on the smoke, hurrying along the inside of the corridor, until the smoke thickens to the point where I cannot breathe; I rush out into the hall. Empty. Thank goodness. I hurry to the window and the men upstairs, my sisters, they all run from the building.

I know what I must do, hide down in my nursery room where it is fireproof and safe. Bury myself within the house to save my life, because if I go outside, the men upstairs will kill me. Even now, they line up my sisters, corral them into the woods, and I have a feeling that I know what waits for them there.

The fire hisses. The fire grows. And I know that this is my last chance, watching them pour like ants from the belly of a fallen tree. It will be the last time.

I turn from the window and take one last deep breath before diving back into the passageway. Tears sting my eyes. From the smoke. From the heat. From the understanding that Mother did not come for me, that my sisters very well may not be coming back here again.

After tonight, I will truly be alone.

16

When I surface from the data pull, Nix is crying. Fat tears stream down her face and I wipe them away with the back of my hand before wrapping my arms around her.

"Sister," I say into her shoulder, smoothing back her hair the way she likes. Guilt chews me up for being so angry with her, for not believing her when all she's ever done is tell me the truth.

"I do not want you to look at me like I am damaged, and I do not want you to pity me." She pulls back, clutching her palm to the scar on her chest. "I am not some monster to be pitied."

"You're not a monster at all." I grab a roll of gauze from the medical tray to the side of the table and motion for Nix to give me her hand. She hesitates at first, but eventually pries her bloody palm from her chest and gives it to me.

I wrap the gauze around the wound while she calms down.

"I'm sorry you had to relive that, but it was necessary," I tell Nix, snipping the end of the gauze and placing the roll along with the surgical scissors back on the table. At least I know that I can trust her now. Even though she's every bit as obsessed with connection as Nora is, I didn't feel any malice in her longing.

"Was it really necessary, Silvie?" the heart asks, a tinge of disgust in its voice. *"Whatever you pulled from her must have been devastating if she's reacting like this."*

"Just more of Layla being an asshole, which is pretty par for the course at this point." I lift the jar, my hand leaving a sticky print across the glass. "You don't get to judge me. I had to make sure that I could trust Nix, and you don't get to dictate how I do that."

"I'm not trying to limit or control you."

"Could have fooled me."

"The heart drive is arguing with you?" Nix asks, her brow furrowing.

"It doesn't think I should have downloaded from you."

Nix reaches out and lifts the jar, her palm layering a print over mine. "You are wrong, heart drive. It was the right thing to do. We must make sure that we are comfortable with each other."

She holds the jar out to me, but I shake my head.

"Hold onto it for now. I need to download from Lily next." As I say it, a lump forms in my throat.

"You do not want to revive her after all? I am confused," Nix says, cradling the jar in her left arm. She uses her free hand to smooth back Lily's hair, before tracing the outline of her face.

"What's there to be confused about?" I ask. "I never said that I wasn't going to revive her. But Victor is on his way, and I need to know where the Beta facility is." What I don't want to admit is that I like the way it feels when I download data, that my body is still humming from my link with Nix, that I crave the way it makes me feel—powerful, knowing.

I run my fingers along Lily's wrists.

"It would be better to link with me than download from the dead girl," the heart rasps from the crook of Nix's arm.

I motion for Nix to give me the jar. "It's spouting more of its nonsense. Can you pass it over?"

She hands me the jar.

"I don't get it." I tilt the jar horizontally and the heart plops against the side of the glass. "You're the one who said I didn't need to revive Lily to find out where the Beta facility is and I could just download the information from her."

"I didn't think that you would actually do it." It rolls to the opposite end of the jar. *"It would be better for us to link and confront Victor."*

I frown. "Do you want to be close to me, or beat the shit out of Victor? Because if this is all part of some weird revenge fantasy, I'm definitely not linking with you."

"Says the girl who's acting on her own revenge fantasy."

"Exactly. *Mine*, not yours."

"It could be your fantasy too." It gurgles for a moment before a blood bubble deflates like a sigh. *"Why do I have to want one thing or the other? I can want to be close to you and to take revenge on Victor. Much like how you want to download from Lily and revive her."*

"That isn't anywhere close to the same thing." I go to shake the jar again, but Nix catches me by the wrist. Though she keeps her touch light, it reminds me too much of Nora, and I pull away.

"What is the heart drive asking you to do, sister?" Nix asks, lowering her face down close to the jar. I flip it vertical again and the heart hits the bottom with a wet thump.

"It wants me to forget about Lily and strengthen the link between us."

"You're pushing yourself too hard. You need to rest and recuperate from your last download before jumping right into the next."

Unless I link with you, right? Then I can dive right in. I roll my eyes.

Nix tilts her head to the side, her long, thin hair falling

across her gray shoulders. She closes her eyes for a moment and takes a deep breath, before opening them again. "Silvie, I know you are concerned about resurrecting her, but perhaps the heart is right. I am not sure that a download is the right thing to do..."

I look down at my palm, at the tacky blood—only slightly congealed.

"Are you worried that I won't be able to pull memories from her?" I ask Nix. "Because the heart says that it will take a toll on me if I try to do too many downloads back-to-back."

"Her file is corrupted," she says, running her fingers through Lily's hair one more time before pulling her hand away. "It is dangerous to try."

"Corrupted how?"

"I am not sure, but when Mother came back, when she brought Lily to me, she said that she was broken and that the inside of her head is dangerous."

"What's the worst that could happen?"

Nix walks around the table and rests her hand on my shoulder. "You lose your mind or get lost in hers."

"At least Victor wouldn't find me."

"He would find you comatose, and you would be easier to take away."

A shiver runs down my spine. "You wouldn't let that happen; you'd protect me."

I turn Lily's hand on its side and slide the knife along her palm before lowering the knife onto the table next to her. I lace my fingers through Lily's, my palm hovered above hers, my blood dripping into her wound.

And then I press down.

Bright colors. Endless burning.

The only time I feel alive is when I'm helping Mother kill us.

She says that it isn't healthy for me to think of us as a hivemind, that every Silvie is different. We speak differently, we think differently, we feel differently. That's the problem. We're base code branched off in a thousand directions until it becomes impossible to trace us back to the source. But sometimes I wonder if Mother just isn't looking close enough. Sometimes I feel like we really are the same, and when I kill one of us, I kill all of us.

It's almost midnight. The others are asleep while I'm down in the labs, wrist-deep in Twelve's chest cavity. My fingers trace the contours of her ribs, (our ribs) and her lungs (our lungs), before settling on her heart drive (our heart drive). Three quick cuts with the scalpel, then I twist and pull. There's a wet pop as the drive comes loose, and I lift it, still beating, from what used to be my sister.

Mother stands next to me, jotting notes down on her clipboard as I work. Most nights she quizzes me on our anatomy or critiques the way I wield my scalpel, but tonight she's silent.

My skin prickles.

She's usually so chatty. Something must be bothering her.

I hand her the drive, and wordlessly, she seals it in a plastic biohazard bag. A squirt of blood coats the plastic, obscuring the heart from view and it writhes, one, two, three times before going still. Mother disposes of it in an orange bin to the left of where we stand.

"Good job, Fifteen," she says, as I peel off my plastic gloves—slick with Twelve's blood (our blood). "That was a near perfect extraction."

Mother's praise used to mean something to me, but now it's just noise. I sigh, staring down at my once sister, an extension of myself. Her eyes (our eyes) stare blankly up at the ceiling.

"Why do you look upset?" Mother asks.

It's a fair question. I shouldn't be upset at all. I love taking us apart, I love learning about our biology and how Mother builds us... and a thrill goes through me when I help her kill us. I shouldn't be so wrecked over it. Not when Mother has taken me on as a makeshift apprentice, not when she says that I'm nearly perfect.

I place my bloodied gloves down next to the shell that used to be Twelve and I can't help but feel like I betrayed her, I betrayed all of us.

"The others would never do this to us," I tell Mother. "They'd never decommission one of our sisters."

"Which is why I asked you to help me, not the others." She wraps an arm around my shoulders and pulls me in against her side. "And I shouldn't have to remind you that the Silvie series isn't a hivemind. There is no 'us'; there's you and them—you're separate."

"I know." I snuggle in, savoring the closeness. Mother rarely touches the others; she's hardly ever in the same room as them unless they're flayed open on a table. She told me the reason for it once, something about her first attempt and how she got too close, but I was only half listening. I tend to tune out when I'm not actively doing something. It's part of the reason why I love dissections, and the other projects that Mother allows me to assist on, they keep my hands busy enough that my mind doesn't wander.

I get it though, emotions are tricky. It's harder to take us apart when you care.

"You shouldn't feel guilty." Mother runs her fingers through my hair, and I smile into her shirt. "In fact, you remind me a lot of the original Silvie."

"Really?"

"You're curious like she was. Smart too. When you first started coming down here, asking questions about how your series is made, I was advised not to encourage you. But I saw so much of her in you, and I was right. Look at everything you've accomplished. You know more about your series than any of your sisters, and your insights have been invaluable as I move on to the next phase of your evolution."

I bury my face deeper into her shirt, breathing in smell of her perfume—citrus with notes of vanilla.

"If I'm so much like the original, why make Sixteen and Seventeen?" I ask, my voice muffled. "Plus, it's clear that you like Seventeen

best... you give her more attention than the rest of us—even if she is unconscious most of the time. It's like you're always locked away with her somewhere. You work on her more than any of us."

"That's because Seventeen is different and studying her will help me as I continue the series." She squeezes me closer. "Don't tell your sisters, but you're my favorite. You're the most like the original Silvie."

Maybe there was a time I would have believed her but hearing her say it now just makes me sad.

I love Mother, but she's so focused on getting it right, that she doesn't understand that she won't. It's not possible. We're the same, me and my sisters—but what we are and what the original was...

"What's going through that head of yours?" Mother asks.

There's no way for me to explain, not so that she would understand.

I pull back slightly, my eyes flicking to the hollow shell of my sister, her chest cracked open, the spray of red down her sides. "I wish I could show you."

~

Bright colors. Endless burning.

A needle in my neck, stuck into the flesh at the base of my skull. It's pulled out and replaced by a longer, thinner needle. It hurts worse than bee stings, worse than whole swarms of angry summer insects. There are varying degrees of pinching and pain, but I grit my teeth and endure it.

I lay stomach-down on a cold metal table, the edges of my vision blurred. The room smells like bleach.

"That's enough for now," Mother says, her voice low and smoky. "Don't go crazy with it."

"Quit hovering and let me do my job," a deep voice responds. Victor. I hate it when she involves him on our projects. And that's what this is, our project. He shouldn't have anything to do with it, but Mother insists that he's a necessary evil, and he's the only one

skilled enough to help us get what we want. He chuckles softly, sending a flurry of discomfort up my spine. "This is the fun part."

"Only a sociopath like you would find this enjoyable. How are you feeling, Fifteen?" Mother asks me.

"Fine," I say, my voice muffled by the table.

"No discomfort?" she asks, resting her hand on my back.

Yes, yes. Oh, yes. Insects, sharp teeth—blistering pain. But I shake my head. I tell her that it isn't anything I can't handle. I can't give her any reason to go back on the project.

Mother removes her hand.

I want to lift my head and see her, but my body won't let me. I stay on the table—splayed out like a corpse, pain pulsing down my neck. Whatever Victor injected me with sloshes through my insides. A cold, slick liquid, somehow heavier, more present in my body than my own blood. Shoes click against the tile, high heels followed by loafers.

"What's all this about, doc?" Victor asks, and I strain to make out the words. They're almost out of earshot.

"Don't call me doc, it's disrespectful."

"What's all this about, Dr. Mathis?" he exaggerates the last bit, pulls at the vowels like he's ripping the legs off a spider.

"Silvie. It's always been about Silvie. I don't think I'm ever going to get her back. There's always something wrong, a little off. No matter what I do, it's never really her."

"I told you as much when you first insisted on starting this thing. But what does that have to do with the injections? What are you having me pump her full of?"

"I'm trying something new. Maybe then I'll know what's wrong; I'll understand why she's not quite right."

"Meaning what exactly, Layla?"

"Dr. Mathis!" Mother snaps.

"Dr. Mathis," Victor says, and I can practically hear him roll his eyes. "I'll tell you what I think you're doing, and I'll tell you why it's a bad idea. You can't—"

~

Bright colors. Endless burning.

A smell.

A sharp, gummy, gristly smell. Like dirt and blood—wet and terrible.

It's in the air, and in my mouth. A bubbling, burning, human smell.

Faces turn to soup and spill across the tile, and oak, and carpeting. They soak in, steep like tea. The fire slurps them up in waves of red, and orange and yellow. I run past them, through them. My vision clouds, and the faces come and go through smoke the color of the night sky.

Mother runs alongside me. She grips my hand in hers, afraid that if she lets go, I'll melt away into the floor and join the faces that stick like tar to the bottom of our shoes.

"I understand why you did it," she tells me, and I believe her. I have to believe her. After all, we're linked. She feels what I feel and knows what I know. We're in this together.

The flames dwindle the farther we run. The smoke thins, but the smell remains. I don't think I'll ever get the smell out of my nose.

We turn a corner and find Victor pacing back and forth in the entryway directly in front of the main door. His hair is disheveled, and his shirt sleeve torn. Darkness flashes across his eyes when he sees me. He says my name, but I don't answer. I know I shouldn't.

He curses.

Mother hurries to meet him.

"Layla! I thought you didn't make it out. Both my lab partners are done for. More than half our staff is missing. I managed to close the fire door so the left side should be okay, but the rest of the building..."

She shakes her head. There is no rest of the building, not anymore.

"I had Sixteen carry your back up drive out just in case," Victor

tells her. "I'm glad it wasn't necessary, but you were really cutting it close."

"I couldn't leave without her." Mother squeezes my hand. "What are you still doing here? It's not safe, the labs may be safe, but the fire is still spreading through the upper floors."

"Yeah, no shit." Victor motions for us to come up next to him and we step forward. "There are a few who made it out into the woods. You should go tell them that you're okay, find a place to regroup with whoever else managed to make it out."

"What about her?" she asks and gives my hand another squeeze. "If they see her, they'll hurt her."

"Can you blame them? She tried to kill us!"

"That's not what happened..." Mother says, but she can't begin to explain. She's too tired, too broken from all of this. I am too. I ache knowing that I've hurt her.

"Give her to me, I'll take care of her," he says, and his hand clamps down over my wrist before she can answer.

"No," I say, my insides churning. "Mother, please."

Not him. Anyone but him. I stare up at her, pleadingly. She has to understand how much I hate him—she hates him too after all, in her own way. I know that she doesn't trust him, not completely. But she still lets him drag me away from her.

She lets him pull me tight against his chest, and I stand squirming as he addresses her, as if I don't matter at all, as if I'm not even there.

"Get out there and find the others," he tells her. "Let them know that none of this can be salvaged and we'll have to speed up renovations on the Beta facility."

"I can't leave without—"

"Yes, you can," he cuts her off. "This place won't survive without you. We'll catch up to you once I'm sure there aren't any other stragglers."

She casts a worried glance in my direction but nods curtly.

"Keep her safe," she says, and disappears out the door. "Protect her at all costs."

But he doesn't. Instead, we race back through the flesh-colored hallways, and he drags me after him through heat and across blistering floorboards.

"I know what you are. I know what she turned you into," he spits. "Damn bitch really did it this time."

"She'll know," I warn him, my voice small and buried in the sounds of the fire. The pop, crackle, hiss. "She'll know if you hurt me."

"You're nothing more than a backup copy. She's already got her drive. She'll get over it."

I try to tell him that I'm not a backup, not completely. I'm her, and I'm me. I have her blood in my veins and she has my memories. We're linked. I try to tell him to let go of my wrist, but he keeps running until we're out in the backyard, until the right side of the house is bright as a birthday cake, and the heat clashes against the cold. We find another Silvie at the edge of the yard by the woods, a heart drive resting in a jar at her feet, a shovel balanced against a tree behind her. My stomach churns and I wonder where our final sister is. There should be three of us.

Victor pushes me toward the other Silvie—it's Sixteen, I realize that now—and picks up the jar.

"You know what to do," he says, nodding toward the shovel.

I don't like the way he says it.

I don't like the way she stares at me.

I pull my hand back from Lily's, but the images keep coming. Fire, and dirt, and screaming.

I'm back in the surgical theater with Nix, with the heart, with the viewer's balcony—dark windows watching as I thrash.

I'm back and I'm me again. But the images wrap tightly over the theater, the walls, and the heart in a cellophane-thin layer. I look up from underwater and they rush across my eyes, over my skin, and down between my bones.

"Silvie," the heart pleads. *"Come back to us."*

I fall away from Lily and Nix reaches out to catch me, her breath coming in shallow gasps. "Silvie, please. I warned you that her heart drive was corrupt."

"You knew the risks," the heart says solemnly. *"The inside of that girl's head is a war zone. This was the only possible result of pulling from it."*

Nix clutches me to her chest, her skin waxy and coated in sweat. She does her best to hold me steady, but I continue to shake. The room melts around me, the jars on the wall glinting like polished stones. Images overlap. Water rushes through my veins.

Dirt. A long sleep, a dying breath.

"They're not stopping," I say through gritted teeth.

Dirt. My arms covered in flies.

"The images won't stop coming." I thrash, and the water carves rivers through my core. "They're still flooding in."

A horsefly.

It looks at me.

It crawls over my cheek. And the other Silvie—Sixteen, Nora, my sister. My clone. She looks down at me, her hands calloused from digging.

"Silvie!" the heart cries and the images shatter, the surgical theater comes tumbling back into focus. I choke back bile, and collapse, my head falling in Nix's lap.

She brushes my hair back from my eyes, as my breath comes in shallow gasps. My stomach clenches, an ache that shoots up into my forehead. It consumes all of me. I lay immobile, my eyes darting from Lily to the heart, to the spotlight above the operating table. Just beyond my sightline, jars line the shelves—full of our sister's minds—and other organs from other projects.

So much work went into building this nightmare, and now, even though it's been left to rot, it endures. The jars remain. The labs continue to stretch back into the dark of the underground.

"Can you stand?" Nix asks.

I sit up tentatively and am met with the crash of a wave through my body.

"Not yet," I say and lean against her shoulder again for support, letting the surf retreat.

"Silvie," the heart says. *"What did you see?"*

"Layla," I say, and it shudders. "Layla Mathis. You're a copy of her mind. You're her back-up drive—that's why you're different."

I look up at Nix, who's eyes shine with concern.

"The heart," I tell them. "It's Layla."

Layla Mathis. Mother. My creator. All this time, Nora's been holding what's left of her hostage and didn't even know it.

"Please, Silvie."

That's why it didn't want me to communicate with Lily. That's why it didn't want me to come back down into the labs, why it wanted me to drink its blood so that it could flood my mind with whatever it wished. It didn't want me to know.

"You belong to the woman who made us..." I whisper. "You did this to me... to us... you linked with Lily and it drove her insane."

"That's not what happened."

"I saw it—I saw everything! She was like me. You made it so that she could communicate through blood. You forced her to share your mind, and she couldn't handle it so she..."

"She was never meant to hold another's memories. She wasn't like you, but she wanted to be, and I wanted to help her evolve. I couldn't do the same for Nora—she was too volatile. But Fifteen—"

"Lily."

"She was my best chance at replicating what we accomplished with you. She spent a lot of time with me down here: she knew the experiment. I didn't force her to do anything, it was something we decided together."

I examine Lily's expressionless face, her blank eyes.

"You broke her."

"I only wanted to be close to you," the heart, Layla's backup drive, whimpers. *"I only loved you too much."*

It's what Nix said, isn't it? *Mother only loved me too much.*

You don't love me, I think slowly, my mind reeling. *And you don't love Lily, or Nix, or Nora. You love Silvie, the original Silvie. You tortured all of us because whoever she is, you can't stand to let her go.*

I rise from Nix's lap, and she stands with me, her eyes welling up with tears. She links her arms through mine, so that although I struggle to find my footing, I don't fall.

"What is it telling you?" she asks, their voice wavering. "Is it really Mother?" She tightens her hold on me. "Does she remember who I am? Does she still love me?"

"I love you all."

"She doesn't know what love is."

Nix shakes her head. "Mother saved me. You saw it yourself when you downloaded my memories."

"I watched her try to kill you. I watched her isolate you from me and the others in the series. I watched her leave you behind when this place burned. Then she came back just to leave you all over again. That's not love."

"Please Silvie, now is not the time to fight. Be angry with me later, but for now we must plan for when Victor gets here."

That's right, Victor is on his way. And I failed to pull the information I needed from Lily; I still don't know where the Beta facility is.

I turn to the heart. "You can tell me where it is though, can't you? You're a copy of Layla, so you must know."

"I can't, and I don't. That information is hidden inside Fifteen. There are certain things that the original did not store on me."

I'm not sure if I believe it, but I don't have time to argue. I glance feverishly toward the basement door, then up at the viewer's balcony, the line of blacked out windows staring down like the beady eyes of an insect. The only way he could know that I'm down here is if Nora tells him, and even then, she probably assumes that I fled through the tunnels after our confrontation.

Still, I shiver when I think of Victor.

How far away is he? Is he already inside the Victorian? I picture him rushing from hallway to hallway, calling my name over and over.

Nix picks the jar up off the table with her free hand and lifts it in front of her face, tears streaming down her cheeks. "Why did you leave me, Mother? After the fire, you came back, you brought me Lily, you told me to wait for you—but you never returned. Is what Silvie saying correct, do you not love me?"

The heart droops mournfully. *"I don't have any memory of that happening. My last upload was right after Fifteen set the fire. I'm not sure what the original Layla did after that."*

Nix watches it beat for a few moments then turns to me. "Did Mother answer?"

"The last time it received a download was right after the fire was set. And it's not like it has all of Layla's memories from before then either."

She lowers the jar back onto the table. "It is not really Mother..."

"Nix, I know this is hard for you," I say, still leaning on her for support. "But Victor is still on his way, we need to figure out what to do when he gets here."

I keep seeing the malice in his eyes, the white-hot hatred from the memory. No, the hate was directed toward Lily. Murderous Lily who set the fire that almost killed him. And

Nora was the one with the shovel. I wasn't even there; I was long gone by that point.

I strain my brain trying to remember.

Wet grass against my bare legs. The house lit up, birthday cake bright. Me, in the front yard watching it burn and thinking if only it were really a birthday cake and not a house. Then if I blew on the right side and made a wish...

Is that my memory or Layla's? Or Lily's? Or Nora's?

I shake my head and fall against Nix, who holds me steady though my feet hang limp.

"Maybe you should sit down again."

"We don't have time; Victor will be here soon." I steady myself. "I'm good; I can walk. If you grab Lily, I'll carry the jar."

The heart flops over on its side. *"I'm so sorry for what he did to you, Silvie."*

And I'm sorry for what you did to Nix.

"Not me," it rasps. *"The original Layla."*

"No," I pull away from Nix and stumble over to the table, placing my hands on either side of the jar. "You're a copy of her mind. Even if you didn't do it directly, you're still the same consciousness. You're still responsible." Because *someone* has to be responsible. Someone has to answer for all the pain.

"Silvie, please stop arguing with her," Nix says quietly, wiping her tears with the back of her hands. "She is not Mother. Taking out your anger on her would be like you being angry with me for what Nora did."

"My anger? What about your anger?"

Nix steps up next to me and looks down at the jar, fighting back another stream of tears. "Mother cared for me, more than anything in the world. She hurt me, but she loved me even more, and I do not have the right to be angry with her."

"From what I've seen, that may be true. But people can care for the wrong reasons, people can care and still do damage." My eyes burn into hers. "You have *every* right to be angry."

Nix smiles and swats at her remaining tears. "I am so glad we are together, even if we do not agree."

She walks around to the other side of the operating table and lifts Lily, cradling her in her arms. Her head slumps against Nix's chest, her curls falling in front of her eyes. It looks as if she's sleeping.

"I'm surprised that you can carry her," I say, half expecting Nix to snap in half at any moment.

"I am stronger than I look."

A spurt of blood erupts from the heart, coating the bottom of the jar.

I pick it up and follow Nix across the tile floor.

"You're taking me with you?"

I still have questions about what it was like here before the fire. Might as well ask Layla.

"I don't want to be Layla," the heart says, sloshing in the fluid. *"I'm trying to change, but she's the code on which my mind was based so it's difficult. But I don't want to be that woman."*

I'm about to disagree with it, to reiterate the fact that it *is* Layla because of its code, because of the memories injected into its veins, but that wouldn't be true. Nix is right. I can't get mad at her for what Nora did, even though they share the same code. It's the same with the heart.

Besides, I share the same code as my sisters and I'm continuing to change.

I see with bright, bleeding clarity for the first time. The heart and Layla are different in the same way that Nora and Nix are different.

I let the tide wash over me, the cold sting of the water piercing my skin. I let it suck me in and spit me back out again, the dark water mine and mine alone.

Perhaps inside Nora's mind there's a deep hole with dirt floors and dirt walls. Perhaps there's earth so smothering that she crushes it into pigment, spreads it across a canvas to keep it from pressing down on her.

Perhaps in what's left of Lily's mind there's a fire so vicious, so hot that she sleeps to escape the raw bite of the flames.

We're the same. But we're also so much more.

Layla's voice, the voice from the memory drifts through my ears again. *"There's always something wrong—a little off."*

Because while we're Silvie, we're also more than the original could ever hope to be. We're born of her base code, we share her blood, but that's as far as it goes.

We grow.

We evolve.

We suffer separately.

I spent so long trying to unravel the past, and now that I know my history, that's all it is. A history. It's not an omen of what's to come. I'm not limited by it.

"Are you okay, Silvie?" Nix asks, pausing in front of the entrance to the tunnel.

"I'm okay," I say, and I mean it. "I'm just thinking about us."

Nix's smile stretches wider, into a more confident grin. "We are the same."

I shake my head. "We're both part of the Silvie series, but you're unique and so am I. There's only one of me."

The heart's voice trickles through the back of my head, and I reassure it that I'm fine. I don't hate it. I understand everything now.

Above us, the floorboards creak. Dust falls like ash from the ceiling. Heavy footsteps.

I thought we would have more time.

I focus on Nix, on Lily, on the tunnels stretching out before us. *No before, no forever, no afterward.* Flesh that never stretches, never wrinkles. No infancy, no childhood, no numbered days. No time before or after.

Above my head, the dust continues to fall.

Blood smears from my arms down the sides of Lily's dress. It darkens and disappears into the bruised red of the velvet. The riptide tugs at my ankles but I remind myself that the water belongs to me, I don't belong to it.

No before, no forever, no afterward. A faint headache blooms in the center of my forehead.

"He's here."

17

Nix and I watch his movements while my heart goes numb.

"Victor," she whispers, her voice shaking. "He was the one who cut them up."

Her eyes shimmer on the verge of tears again and I reach for her. "How do you know what he did to them?"

"I heard. I heard everything." She balls her hand into a fist, flakes of skin falling to the floor like ashes. "How he would cut them up, how he would sever their tendons and rip out their heart drives. Break them."

"We need to move," I say. But I'm frozen, watching as he crosses the kitchen, watching as the doorknob shakes and the hinges ache, and it hits him that the door is locked.

Nix steps forward into the mouth of the tunnels and waits for me, our sister cradled in her arms.

Even after everything, Victor still sends flashes of cold through me. This man who kept me locked away and medicated. This man who ruined me.

He pounds against the door.

Each crash of knuckle against wood sends a shudder through my core. Fear, anticipation.

"Baby sister," his voice drifts down the stairs, leaks between my ears. Slick and vicious. "Silvie darling, won't you unlock the door? Your big brother has come to take you home."

"How does he know you are down here?" Nix asks, her mouth slightly agape. "You could be anywhere; he should not have been able to narrow it down so quickly."

My eyes narrow. "Nora probably told him."

"Are you really surprised?" the heart mutters. *"She was never going to protect you; she said as much when we were upstairs."*

"I don't need her to protect me," I say even as Victor's voice sends waves of dread through me.

He pounds against the steel again. "Damn it, Silvie. Open. The. Door."

My fingers tighten around the jar, and I cross the remainder of floor to come up next to Nix.

She squeezes my shoulder. "I cannot imagine what this must be like for you. He is a monster."

Except he isn't. It's not in his DNA; it's not part of his base code. He's not fighting some urge that's been programmed into him from the start. He's just a man. And somehow that makes it worse.

"Calling him a monster gives him power that he doesn't deserve," I say quietly.

The door buckles, then gives way.

It smashes against the wall, light tumbles down the staircase, and at first—nothing. Brightness. Emptiness.

Then, a silhouette. A long, dark shadow.

"You're sure she's down there?" His voice. The same voice that's played on repeat through the static in my mind. The same voice that's crippled me too many times to count. I wince against it. "She didn't fucking answer me."

"You seriously thought she would? I told you how insane she was acting earlier." A second shadow—Nora. "She's definitely down here. She slammed the door in my face."

"And you didn't stop her."

"I tried to, but she locked me out."

He laughs, a sound that sends a shudder through me. "Beat you up pretty good too. I expected more from you."

Cold water floods my lungs and I clench my fist, swim against the current, but my control slips and the riptide pulls me apart.

"I don't know what to do," I whisper to Nix. "I thought I would, but I'm not sure if I can confront him. What do we do?"

"We run." Nix grabs my arm and pulls me into the depths of the basement.

The tunnel is more like a hallway, lit by the same florescent bulbs that line the surgical theater. They flicker like the flames of a candle, seconds from burning out. Nix's movements drift back to me in flashes.

She adjusts our sister, and Lily's arm drops down, her fingers reaching to the earth.

Nix glances back at me.

"This way, quickly," she mouths, because footsteps sound out not too far behind.

"The acoustics in this place were not built for hiding. And there are only two halls branching out from the theater."

But there are more options as we go, right? This isn't all there is?

"Let's hope that we make it that far."

I hurry to catch up with Nix and lean in close to her, my shoulder brushing against Lily's crumpled form.

The hallway shifts, the dark tiles from the theater change abruptly to bright white. Tiny squares. Gray walls, a line of identical steel doors down the left side of the hallway—nothing on the right.

"We should hide in one of these rooms," I suggest. "If we keep moving like this, they're going to catch up to us eventually. We should get out of their line of sight."

Nix shakes her head. "The doors are locked from the inside.

Further down the hall, there are open rooms, but it will be another few minutes."

"Do we have another few minutes?"

Behind us, voices soak into the hallway, abstractions of the people I once considered family. Victor's deep baritone. Nora's voice—my voice—high and birdlike, distorted as if through an echo chamber.

The further we go, the less certain my footsteps become, and the jar slips between my sweaty palms. My legs cramp, knees threatening to buckle and drag me down. A sharp headache drills into my temple, the right side of my skull enflamed from the transfer. A fine layer of perspiration gathers on my face and the backs of my arms.

"Are you all right, Silvie?" Nix asks. "You do not look well."

"I don't feel well." I slump against the wall, the cool concrete doing little to soothe the fire in my mind.

"It's the strain from attempting multiple transfers, you need to rest," the heart rasps. *"Or I could help relieve the burden. Bite into me and drink. I promise that you'll feel better."*

"If this is what happens when I link with Lily, linking with you would kill me."

The headache digs into the area above my eye, and I flinch.

"The heart still wants you to link with it?"

Lily's palm drips red onto the tile floor, and Nix adjusts her hand so that it rests in her lap.

"The heart thinks it'll help, but I..."

Victor's voice drifts closer and I shudder. Lily's blood pools on the floor.

"I can't keep going like this," I tell Nix. I open my mouth wide and suck in air, but no matter how deeply I breathe, it's not enough. Spots cloud my vision, and I sway, one bad breath away from passing out.

Nix tries the handles on the surrounding doors, without success.

"I could try to break one down," she suggests.

"Or Silvie, you could drink from me and feel better," the heart urges. *"I know that you don't agree with what I did—what the original Layla did to Nix. But I'm not like that, I'm different. I promise that I will help you face Victor. For both of us—for all of us."*

His voice grows louder. Nix continues to try doors, venturing to the far end of the hallway, Lily still cradled in her arms like an oversized porcelain doll.

I huddle my body around the heart.

I'll never forgive the original Layla for what she did to Nix... what she did to us.

"I don't expect you to." It curls up next to my chest and my heartbeat melds with it.

Nix hurries back to where I remain slumped against the wall.

"Can you walk?" she asks. "I found an open door."

I lean on her shoulder, and we move down the hall to where a door on the left hangs open.

We hurry inside, shutting it softly behind us—hoping that the sound doesn't carry. At first, I barely notice the room. I keep my ear pressed to the door, waiting for a sign that Victor and Nora have found us.

"Silvie," Nix whispers. "I think you should look at this."

I turn. The room is an exact copy of my room upstairs, with the same wardrobe, same bed, same standing mirror. A darkened window takes up the far side of the wall, half of it shattered to reveal a small room beyond it, with two overstuffed chairs, an old desk, and a computer monitor just beyond the shattered remnants.

Shards of glass lay spilled across the floor. It's an ocean of brightness, of color reflecting the ceiling, the torn wallpaper, and the ornately carved wooden frame of the mirror—so much like the one upstairs. Jagged shards cling to the edges of the window like loose teeth, a gentle tug away from falling.

"We would observe you here until you were ready to up to the main house," the heart says, its voice cutting past the fog inside my brain. *"Sometimes we would take the series back here as they regressed, but only if they were too sick for general population. There are other rooms like this throughout the labs."*

I turn from the one-way glass, I'm not looking at the mirror, or the wallpaper—identical to the walls upstairs. My eyes are trained on the righthand corner of the room, where Nix stands at the base of a massacre. Wallpaper bubbled and peeled from the plaster, fire damage leaving a blackened trail up to the first floor, second floor, third floor of the Victorian. And finally, a patch of sky, of missing roof, eating up half the room.

Parts of the floor are rotted, the blackened edges of the wallpaper damp from the storm earlier. The far corners are dry, but evidence of the years left to the elements permeate the room.

Nix lifts Lily beneath her armpits and holds her in place so that her feet brush against the floor.

"Help me," she says, face craned toward the hole in the roof. "She needs to see it too."

I nod. I understand.

I gently lift Lily's head so that she can look with us, in case she's still in there somewhere watching. The deep black sky stretches over us, speckled with stars. It's cold and wild and seems so far away from where we stand, layers beneath it. So far away from the skinned knee of a roof, the boards blackened, morphed, and destroyed—damage done by my dead sister.

The building has been eaten away to its core. Killed by a whisper of a girl, barely five feet tall.

How can anything be that fragile?

I picture the flames beneath Lily's skin and imagine that's why her flesh is so warm despite her extended sleep; her death that isn't death. I lower her chin and Nix carries her over to the bed, laying her down so that her head rests on the pillow.

My eyes stay fixed on the damage. I crave the crisp yawning

of the sky. Clear and dark. Empty like Lily, infinite like my sisters and myself.

The sky back home never looked like this.

Back home, I never felt like this.

My medication dulled my senses, my blind obedience dulled my heart.

I wonder if as Nora follows Victor through the tunnels, she wishes she had approached this whole thing differently.

A hollow pang of regret rings out inside my chest. I wish that she had.

"We will be okay here," Nix says, smoothing back Lily's hair. "We should push the wardrobe in front of the door in case they try to find us. But we should be able to wait them out."

"I don't think I can push anything right now," I say as the headache continues to throb in my right temple.

I turn from the ruined roof and walk up to the one-way glass. I examine my reflection, grimacing against the sharp pain left over from the download. Nix was right, I don't look well. The dull gray of my eyes, the greasy sweep of my hair, and the velvet ribbon that tugs it back from my forehead—all of it comes together to form a broken doll of a girl. A body that looks pale and on the verge of collapse. My gaze travels to the dirt on my neck and the red sprayed across my collar.

I blot at it with a crumpled corner of my skirt until it looks less like blood and more like a marker run through the washing machine one too many times. The cuts on my legs are not as easily concealed and I give up after a few moments of wiping away the streaks, and willing the blood to congeal, plug up, stop. Because even though I fell from the second floor what feels like hours ago, my body hasn't had time to heal yet. The bruise on my thigh remains. A fine spray of blood tints the front of my dress, and the undersides of my arms are covered in shallow cuts from my fight with Nora earlier. A living catalogue of damage.

I pick at my cuts, and the tart screaming of the wounds makes me dizzy, and my heart rate picks up—the rapid flutter of wings against my ribs.

I watch Nix through the mirror, tending to Lily, casting nervous glances in my direction.

I look down at the heart, all that we have left of Layla.

"We can't hide here forever, Silvie," it gurgles. *"I knew that man before the fire, and he doesn't stop until he gets what he wants."*

I knew him too; I'm well aware. I lean against the wall, dizziness washing over me in waves.

I hold a hand against my forehead, trying without success to stop the pain. It drills into me; it radiates through the back of my skull, down to the tips of my fingers. There are so many layers to it that once my headache dulls or my dizziness fades, I'm hit by another sharper pain. The second that pain starts to dull, another wave, stronger than the one before, comes in to overwhelm me.

"Silvie," Nix turns to where I stand, shivering against the wall. "Your lips are blue. You should sit down." She motions me over to the bed, but I shake my head.

"I can't stay here, Nix," I say.

"Victor will not find you here."

"That's not why." I try to explain but the words die behind my lips and my teeth chatter as my body's overcome by chills. If I don't face him now, he'll always be a ghost in the back of my head.

"You are not in any condition to leave this room. He will give up eventually. Then he will leave, and you will never need to see him again."

"No, I need to..." The words slip away.

"You are still recovering from the download. You must take it easy."

I bring the heart over to Nix and sit it at the end of the bed by Lily's feet. I inch my way onto the comforter next to the jar, glancing over at where Lily lays, head propped up against the pillow. One of her eyes droops, half-closed. A crescent moon of dull gray, hidden beneath long lashes. Her arm splays out and her fingers uncurl. She reaches for me and if I had the strength, I would reach back.

"Silvie, do not go out there alone," the heart warns. *"You're weak from the downloads, you need to rest."*

I close my eyes. The tingling in the back of my skull reaches a fever pitch, and the only thing I can think about with any clarity is the way that Victor's hands felt when they would tighten around my arms or the way his brow arched as he stuck the needle in to draw my blood. My eyes snap open, tears pricking the corners of my vision. I cry out, a long, exasperated howl as the tears pour forth, salty streaks down the contours of my face. I cry and I cry, until my chest heaves, until my eyes burn. The release is unlike anything. I'm a storm. I'm the riptide. This is who I am now, broken and ready to break. I will be his destruction… I'll destroy them all. It won't erase anything that's already happened, it won't take back the years that were stolen from me, but it's something. It's the only thing. My fury. My vengeance.

"I won't be alone," I whisper. "You're coming with me."

I unscrew the lid to the jar, Nix looking on in confusion.

"What are you doing, Silvie?" Nix asks.

The static in the back of my head surges. "I need to go out there and face him. And Layla has the right to confront him too."

The heart's beat quickens. *"Are you saying what I think you are?"*

It's time to strengthen our bond.

"Do not let Layla pressure you into doing something you are not comfortable with."

"I'm not comfortable with any of this." I look down at the coagulated blood that clots my wound, at the red streaks on my skirt, the color so bright in the dim light. I'm hit by another wave of dizziness and brace myself against the bed. But this is the only way for me to ruin him the way he ruined me. This is the only way not to fold in on myself. I pushed my body to its limits, and this is the only way to get some semblance of control back... by relinquishing it completely.

I cry out, digging my nails into my palms, screaming until my throat bleeds. I take deep, ragged breaths, forcing myself to calm down. Nix reaches for me, but I swat her away. I need to do this before I change my mind.

It's my choice. I'm in control of the decision. If I repeat it enough times, I'll start to believe it.

"I'm not just doing it for me, or for the heart, it's important for all of us. Layla is the only one here who knows how we're made. She can help us wake up Lily, we can build bodies for our sisters—maybe eventually we can get her a body of her own. And I can find the people who did this to us and ruin them."

Nix looks to the sky, to the charred walls and floors and dripping, exposed pipes. "How will you link with her?"

"I need to drink its blood." I pull the jar closer and the heart hums with anticipation.

Nix rests her hand on my arm, gently as if she's afraid I may collapse into pieces. "Will you be okay? ... Will Layla?"

"Yes," I assure her even though my stomach flutters and my pulse races. A fine sheen of sweat breaks out across my forehead.

"I'll be fine, Silvie. No matter what happens, I'll be with you."

"She'll be fine," I repeat, reaching into the jar and pull the heart from the crusts of blood at the bottom. "She isn't human."

"You are not human either," Nix comments.

"Not completely." I bite into the heart.

18

Bright colors. Endless burning.

Blood that doesn't taste like blood. It's too sweet, with a bitter note at the end: flowers charred by flames.

I close my eyes, but they are not my eyes—they're hers.

We meld together. I can't speak. I can't breathe. I burn.

And I wade through her memories.

My baby sister is six years old. I'm eleven. Even though we're five years apart, we're like twins—everyone says we're so similar that it's frightening. Not in the way we look, but in the way we think, the way we talk and relate to one another. It's like we shared a womb, like we share a mind.

There's no one in the world I love more than her.

We sit on our front porch watching our father mow the lawn. The air smells like freshly cut grass, and chlorine, and sun on pavement. We lick at ice pops and drape our legs over each other. The blades beneath the lawn tractor whirling in a way that sends shivers through me. There's so much violence in the sound.

I adjust my body so that Silvie's legs stick straight out across mine. Her knees are bruised, a hello-kitty bandage barely covering a scrape on her left ankle.

Her ice pop is cherry, mine blue raspberry.

Red and blue.

"I wish my hair was dark like yours, Layla," she says, juice dripping down her chin, her lips stained red. "It's like Snow White's."

"Well, I wish I had your hair," I say, mussing her golden curls. "It's so pretty."

She grins, her teeth red as her lips. "It's like Sleeping Beauty's, but Snow White is my favorite."

"I know she is."

"When we go to Disney World, we should dress up like Sleeping Beauty and Snow White. Only we should make them sisters, so we can be sister princesses."

I smile and nod. "Sister princesses."

She sighs dreamily, the red continuing to bleed down over her chin. "Maybe we'll meet princes there. There are princes at Disney World, right?"

"I'm not sure. My friends went last summer, and they only took pictures with princesses and Mickey Mouse."

Our father shoots us a look from the back of the lawn tractor, and I know that we should probably go inside and get started on chores. The sun beats down on us. A bead of sweat drips down my forehead.

"We will meet princes there, I'm sure of it!" Silvie cries. "And they'll be the best princes, and have the best castles, and a bunch of horses. And when they marry us, they'll be best friends so that we can always be together. It'll be happily ever after."

The lawn tractor circles back, blades whirling.

"Happily ever after," I agree as my ice pop bleeds blue over my fingers.

~

My baby sister is sixteen. I'm twenty-one. My class schedule is packed, and she doesn't understand why I refuse to come home for the weekends. I've been thinking a lot about home lately and what things were like growing up. I'm not sure if Silvie understands yet; she's too far in it to grasp the possibility of anything else.

"It's only an hour drive," she says, her voice tinny through the phone; my reception keeps cutting in and out. "And I miss you. I don't feel like myself when you're not here."

"You should come stay with me then," I suggest again, the last in a long series of offers. "You know that I have an apartment off campus, and more than enough space for both of us."

"And you know that I can't." In the background a dog barks, a door slams. Muffled voices—excited or afraid—blend with the dog's high-pitched yipping.

"Just a sec, I'm gonna move to my room," she says, and the line goes fuzzy as I wait for her to relocate.

I lean back in my desk chair and stare at the ceiling. Two long cracks in the plaster stare back down at me. My upstairs neighbors cross the room, and the cracks seem to widen beneath their shifting weight.

I look down at my nail polish, left hand painted red—the right one blue. It's started to chip.

A door shuts. A lock clicks.

"All good," she says, though she keeps her voice low, and I picture her cradling the phone to her ear, hand over her mouth and the receiver.

"I'm graduating soon," I assure her. "We'll be together after that."

"No, we won't, Layla. You're gonna be there for another three years in the grad program—more than three if you decide to get your PhD."

"And you'll be in college soon too, Sil. I'm sure you'll get into the same program, and then you'll be right here with me."

She sighs. "We'll see."

In the background the dog continues to bark, something like a snare drum sounds, and Silvie draws in a sharp breath.

"Hey, when I graduate—I'm going to make so much money we won't know what to do with it," I tell her, my grip tightening around the phone. "We'll buy a huge penthouse apartment, and you'll spend all day lounging on the sofa drinking white wine and watching trashy reality TV. And I'll be a big shot in the medical community and take you to all my fancy charity dinners. It'll be our happily ever after."

"Happily ever after," she repeats, though it doesn't sound like she quite believes it.

~

My baby sister is dead.

I'm twenty-two, and now I'm all alone.

I stand over her grave, staring down at the simple rectangular marker, reading the dates, her name, and the inscription over and over again.

"I hate to leave you all behind, but we'll meet again someday"; empty words carved into marble.

I don't cry.

I cried enough the night it happened. In the glow of the police lights. Red and blue. Red and blue. Flashes of tears, and screams, and nameless feelings.

Now everything is numb. Now I don't have enough of a voice left to tell her everything I never said. About home. About us. About all of it.

It starts to rain. A gray drizzle.

I kneel next to where she sleeps within the earth, layers down. Away from me.

I sink my fingers into the dirt and as the rain bloats to fat, cold droplets.

"I hate to leave you all behind, but we'll meet again someday."

"We will," I promise her, thinking of our happily ever after.

Snap. Pop. Fizzle. Colors on top of colors. Fingers lacing through the depths of me until we're both... alive and dead, unique and the same.

Layla, I think, and the thought is mine as much as it is hers.

My blood whispers. It calls to her blood and strains for her answer.

I'm with you now, she responds, and we swirl together.

Mother and daughter.

Natural and unnatural.

Our data is ours. We are together.

Water rushes in to meet the blood, until it dilutes to blush tinted waves. We float together. Me and Layla. Two minds, one body.

My blood whispers and hers responds.

It bursts through me, and she fills the empty spaces between my bones. It doesn't hurt. It doesn't drown me. We swirl and swirl until we're the same.

I try to focus on the feeling of it—the stitching together of our minds. Instead, I replay every memory of the original Silvie, my oldest sister, my reason for being. Again, and again.

We are not the same, but I have her face, her skeleton, and her older sister—who gave me life, and now lives within me.

I'm sorry that I'm not her, I tell Layla.

"I'm sorry for all of this," she answers, and we continue to meld. *"I only loved you too much."*

Layla rests in the back of my head and I blink my eyes open. Nix stands in front of me, her eyes wide.

Despite the shock of the link, I feel much better now. Stronger. Less likely to collapse.

I digest everything I saw, picking apart the images until they settle like algae on a pond.

"Take it slow at first," Layla says, her voice a gentle sway behind my ears. *"Your body may need some time to adjust to the change."*

"Is she okay?" Nix asks. "Are you?"

I nod and wipe blood from my mouth with the back of my hand. Red coats my arms up to the elbows, gloves of fluid. "We are."

The jar lays on its side, tipped over next to the bedframe—scabs of blood already drying against its sides. I nudge it with my foot, and it rolls beneath the bed. What's left of the heart, chunks of muscle and flecks of meat, stain the bedsheets. I tore it apart with my teeth and fingers, cracked it open like a pomegranate and sucked until the taste of bad metal soaked my throat.

Time will tell if I live to regret this.

Nix wraps her arms around me. She clutches me to her chest, hands pressed against my back. "I thought you were going to die. Your eyes rolled up into the back of your head and I could not keep you from convulsing. That is why..." She shifts so that only one arm is wrapped around me, and gestures to the crumpled-up comforter at the foot of the bed, Lily huddled on the other end looking like she's curled up in a cocoon. "You were flailing, I had to keep you away from each other, and make sure you had plenty of cushion, so you would not hurt your head."

"I'm feeling much better," I assure her, pulling out of the hug.

Layla kept her promise. The dizziness is gone, and I sit up straight while she hovers in the back of my head, a slight prickling in my lower skull the only indication that she's here with me. Only there isn't pain like there was before, just presence.

"How long was I out?" I ask.

"Not long. I heard them walk down the hallway a few moments ago."

I stand and make my way into the center of the room. "Then I'll have to catch up with them."

"Are you sure you will be okay?"

I nod. "Layla wasn't lying about taking some of the strain of the download away. I feel great."

"That is not what I meant," Nix says, her brow furrowed. "Will you be all right seeing Victor again?"

A knot forms in the center of my stomach, his name tangled up in the meat and machinery. Layla reaches out, soaks up some of the pain, dulling it to an ache, an uneasiness. And while I'll never be completely free from all the things that I feel, I don't shoulder the burden alone anymore—even if that does unlock fresh concerns.

I crane my neck to the collapsed ceiling, the clear dark sky, glasslike above me, above us. Crisp air filters down through the opening, and I breathe in deeply. It chills the back of my throat, and I ready myself for what comes next.

"Stay with Lily," I tell Nix. "We'll deal with Victor."

19

This link will be the end of me.

Layla prickles along the base of my skull. She's in my blood, and my spit, and my psyche. She feels like ants, like insects with thousands of legs. When we first linked, it didn't feel like this, and while it doesn't exactly hurt, it's not comfortable either.

I exit into the hallway alone. No Lily, no Nix. Only me and my creator. I shudder when I realize that I'm not actually alone, that I'll never be alone again.

"It'll get easier," Layla says, her voice weaving through my gray matter.

I don't believe her. And she knows it. She flips through my thoughts easily, picking apart my past, shredding into me. Meanwhile, no matter how hard I try, I only get flashes of color, and numbers, and names, when I try to access her mind.

Red and blue. Four, three, nine. Silvie, and Victor, and Theo.

"Wait, who's Theo?" I ask, but she doesn't respond. When I try to press in deeper, she puts up a wall and the flashes cut to black.

I pause, blinking rapidly. *How did you shut me out like that?*

"The original Layla linked with Fifteen, so even though this is

my first time, I have memories from her experience," she tells me. *"I know how to guard my thoughts; you'll learn how to in time as well."*

I shouldn't have to. You should have the decency not to snoop, I think.

"I'm sorry. I only want to know you."

We'll have plenty of time to get to know each other. Give me some space until we're finished with Victor.

She doesn't though. She continues to sift through my memories, and it feels like long, boney fingers pressing into the soft parts of my brain, kneading it like dough.

"You initiated a download before you entered the house?" Layla asks. *"Without a blood share?"*

It takes me a moment to understand what she means. With everything that's happened, I hadn't given much thought to the pull I felt in front of the Victorian—or how I absorbed memories without slicing open my palm first. I'm not sure who's memories they were or why they filtered through to me, and I shiver.

I guess, I tell Layla. *I had already been feeling a pull beneath my skin before I got here but it was more intense out in the yard, like the Victorian was crying out to me.*

"Hmmm..."

My skin prickles. *What?*

"Nothing." She sinks even deeper into the back of my head, combing through the weeks leading up to my arrival here with more fervor.

I knock my hand against the side of my head. *Quit it.*

This link...

There are only two upsides: I'm no longer eroding internally from my multiple downloads, and the voice that beckons to me from the salty sweep of the riptide has been blissfully quiet. It's still there, still promising that sea-sickened oblivion is better than whatever terrors wait for me outside my head, but Layla dulls the rush of water.

Even with two minds to share the burden, there's no erasing it completely. But it is better now. It's bearable.

I navigate the labyrinthine halls. The long gray hallway with the steel doors empties into a narrow passage that more closely resembles the hallways above. It's wrapped in wallpaper and boasts honey-colored floorboards. If it weren't for the lack of windows, I would swear we were upstairs.

"Why does it look like this?" I ask Layla.

"See for yourself."

Images trickle in.

The rooms in this hall belonged to the scientists who lived and worked here. There's an entire replica of the Victorian on this level—a house beneath a house. Thanks to Layla, I know the anatomy of this building—all the cogs and chords that line its skeleton, all the passages and empty rooms. It's easy to see how Nix survived down here alone for so long; it's built like a body. The surgical theater at the heart, labs branching out on either side, spilling into more comfortable living quarters.

Layla has full control over what she shows me though, so I take the images at face value. I scratch at the back of my neck. She's completely invaded this space that's supposed to be mine, and unless I find some way to get the power back, this is going to be bad. Even though so far, the worst she's done is snoop. Even though so far, she's been nice.

But Victor was nice too at first.

A hallway to the right is obscured by debris, charred boards and concrete that collapsed during the fire. So many of the people who lived down here died, eaten by the flames. Entire chunks of the right side are eaten away, through to the starless sky and I'm amazed that it doesn't all collapse in on itself.

"This house was built to survive," Layla says, her voice a hurried whisper in my head. *"You were built to survive too."*

We continue through the hallway, pausing only so I can run my fingers over the wallpaper and its flowered accents. Velvet, and foil, and silk. Not an inch of movement from within. No voices. At first, the blood on my arms smears off onto the flowers, painting them deep and dangerous colors. Eventually, it dries to a crust, and I turn from the walls, face forward, and continue to search for Victor and Nora.

The hallway opens up ahead and ends in a wide doorway. I continue forward, the dim lights flickering as I approach the doorway. I can just barely make out a tiled floor beyond the threshold.

I stop mid-step. *That's the kitchen, isn't it? The same as upstairs, only on the right side this time.*

"As above, so below."

The closer I get, the more the room slips into focus. It has the same floors and cabinets as the kitchen upstairs, only built on a smaller scale. The curved edge of a table pokes out around the doorway, and voices drift back to where I stand. Nora's voice —high, birdlike, exactly like my own.

And Victor's.

Except it doesn't sound anything like Victor. The cocky arrogance in the voice is wrong. It's a little too deep, the pronunciation of vowels too harsh. It's like how the bed upstairs mirrors my room back home, how the house above mirrors the house below. Similar, but not the same. Warped. Wrong.

Heat pools in the back of my head.

His voice drifts out into the hall. "... still your fault. If you had left Silvie home with me where she belongs, we wouldn't be in this position right now."

He says my name and it's a rush of saline.

Tension.

Tightness.

My lungs and ribs. All the meaty pieces inside myself expand until they're far too big for my body. Until I can't think, or breathe, or move. Until all I have is the water, the sandy floor of the ocean—seashells tangled in my hair while I writhe through a pain too big for my body.

Layla reaches out to me from deep inside my mind, pushing back against the waves, but it isn't enough.

The riptide pulls at the red on my collar, washes over my neck and pools in my clavicles.

"Let me take some of that for you," Layla whispers and she tries again, holding me through the rush of the waves, keeping us steady as the current swells.

"You feel what you feel," she tells me. *"But we will continue through it."*

I know she's right. And even though the water continues to lash out at me, no matter how hard it tugs—no matter how badly I want to breathe it in—I stay anchored in place.

"Victor..." I say quietly, my voice straining through the deep mud and thick algae. I press a hand to my scar and the scabs on my arms sting against the cotton of my blouse.

Brine. Gypsum and halite. My body crashing into the waves, sinking, down, down, down. The pressure causing my ears to pop. Dark water. Deep, endless black.

No. My fingers press deeper into my scar.

Salt in my lungs—chunks of it—clogging my insides. Weighing me down.

No, I'm strong, I tell myself. *I'm stronger than this.*

"And I'm here with you," Layla adds even though she should know it gives me little comfort. *"You don't have to feel it alone. You don't have to fight against the—"*

Water.

Pushing.

Me down.

I'm stronger now, hearing his voice shouldn't be enough for the riptide to grip me around the waist and pull until—

I shake my head.

Water rushes back and forth across the surface of my skin

but it doesn't drown me, I won't let it. There's no getting rid of it, but there's coping. There's a way to function despite it—move with the waves, not against them. Breathe in and out, count to ten, repeat again.

"Move with the waves, not against them," I whisper to myself. "The feeling will pass." There's high tide and low tide; I won't be underwater forever.

"I can surface and carry the burden completely," Layla reminds me. *"We're together now, but if you need me to take over for this, I'm more than willing to. I would love nothing more than to confront him."*

I shake my head. *It's my body, I'm the one in charge. And I need to be in control for this. I'll let you take over once I get a chance to speak to him.*

Layla is being so pushy about taking over that I'm terrified that once she does, she won't relinquish control again. I'll be a prisoner in my own body. I'll be worse off than before I got here.

"I would never do that to you," she insists, but her words don't mean anything, not when she refuses to let me see for myself.

I glance around the doorframe.

I already know that this man isn't my brother. All those years he spent pretending to be are washed away and I see him for what he truly is, what he's always been. He sits across from Nora at a round table in the center of the room, his face visible from the hall, Nora's back to where I stand. He flashes her a cold grin, the smile stopping just shy of his eyes.

This man is the kind of person who feels at home holding a scalpel, who gets a kick out of making a cut for the sole purpose of stitching it back up again.

This man doesn't know what love is.

"You're lucky I'm hearing you out at all, Nora."

"You're only hearing me out because you need whatever

data you've hidden inside me," she says quietly. "I'm not an idiot, I know it's not because you've suddenly grown a soul."

His grin widens, his teeth shockingly white. It's the smile of a predator. "I shouldn't be involving a lab rat at all, especially after the shit you pulled. I'm doing you a favor by even considering keeping you on as an assistant instead of a specimen."

"I'm more than just another of the series though."

He clucks his tongue. "You're a copy of a copy. Silvie is the special one, and you've already seen what I'm willing to do to her."

A flurry of chills run down my spine.

"Why are you hesitating?" Layla asks.

See for yourself. I flood her with images of my false brother, of the tallies in the wall behind my bed frame, of how I need to hear it for myself—not through one of Nora's memories, not through Lily. I need to hear what he really thinks of me. I need to work to sever him from me, bleach his voice from my memory, and finally become what I was built to be.

So that I can avenge us, so that I can destroy the others like him, and this can all finally end.

My eyes stay trained on Victor.

He's dressed in a cheap suit and wears white rubber gloves. A worn leather doctor's bag sits on the table in front of him, the cracks in its surface looking too much like animal bites.

My eyes stay on the bag, on the cracks, on the white gloves.

He reaches out and pats the bag affectionately.

"Brought along some goodies for when we track down Silvie," he says, smirking. "Gosh, I could tell you stories about her you wouldn't believe. I know the inside of that girl's ribcage better than I know myself."

"You haven't performed surgery on her in months," Nora grumbles. "You're being dramatic."

My skin prickles. So Nora knows about all the times I died... of course she does.

"Yeah well, that last time I spent three hours bringing her back. It was truly a labor of love. Her insides leave an impression—all that meat and machinery, I can never get enough of it. It's hard to forget what she looks like on the dissection table, flayed open like that. I've done some of my best work on her."

Layla reaches out to me, but I push her back.

I feel the weight of this alone.

"You always liked her best," Nora says, her voice full of disdain. "You and Mother. I guess I liked her too, but it was always such a bitch being second to her."

Victor shrugs. "In the end, it worked out in your favor though. Since you're second best, you're not going to be the one on the table."

"If you keep your word."

He laughs. "I may be a bastard, but I'm an honest bastard. If we can agree on the terms, I'll keep you on as my assistant. I swear."

My bottom lip quivers and all the wires, all the slick organic matter inside me, hemorrhages.

There's blood gummed up inside my veins. Blood splashed across the front of my dress. Blood scabbing down my arms. Blood, blood, blood. I chew the inside of my cheek, adding to the mess. Worse than a mess, a massacre.

I keep waiting for Victor to notice me, to glance over at the doorway and realize that however he planned on pulling me in, it isn't going to work. I keep waiting for the anger that never comes. The rush of fear. Instead, there's a click through my machinery, a steady ticking—too much like a bomb. A countdown to self-destruct.

"It sucks that she needs to die. I'm never going to completely agree with it," Nora tells Victor. "I don't get why we can't both be part of your team and she just like, I don't know, volunteers for blood tests and all that other crap you'll need to make the others like her."

"You never really understand how to build something until you've taken it apart. I've gotten this far with blood tests and medical trials, but I need to dig in to get to the next phase. Do you remember what I said last time we had a disagreement like this?" He leans across the table. "I told you that all this would be worth it in the end. And do you remember what you told me?"

She nods. "Of course. I said that I'd do whatever it takes to get more sisters. Even if it means losing Silvie. I know I had a... lapse earlier, and I know I shouldn't have brought her here, but I'm past that now. It doesn't matter how I feel about her. I'm excited for the next phase."

"Then do me a favor and try to show a little enthusiasm!" He says with a wave of his hand. "This is what we've been waiting for. This is what I've been working towards since before the fire—try not to look like you're going to a funeral."

"How do you even know she's still here?" Nora shifts in her seat, and it's like I'm watching a ghost of myself.

"How much longer are you going to drag this out?" Layla asks. She's getting impatient and the tingling in the base of my skull spreads, a feeling like TV static reaching the tips of my fingers.

I'm not ready yet. I push her back, focus on Victor.

"Even though the tunnels continue past the kitchen," he tells Nora. "There are only two hallways. And you forget, I spent the majority of my time down here when this place was still active. Everything beyond the kitchen is a dead end. So, we wait for her to loop back around and then, well you know." He pats his bag again.

"It won't be easy, she's different now. She has such an... attitude. It's like when she was stashing the pills only worse."

"She only started stashing the pills because you were trying to poison her against me. Regardless, I corrected her easily enough." He laughs, a booming sound that rises from the depths of his belly and I flinch. "It was actually kind of fun, smothering her. The way the body thrashes, oh, it was the most incredible thing. She didn't even question me when I told her it was because she was skipping her medicine."

He killed me.

It wasn't my fault. It wasn't because I skipped my pills.

He killed me.

Thick, wine-colored liquid leaks from my left nostril, and I wipe it away with the back of my hand.

Static motion.

A buzz, a beat, a boom.

A tick of the clock.

One minute closer to meltdown.

Something snaps inside me. And even though I won't ever be ready, the way he dreamily tilts his head back, the way he so lovingly remembers something that haunts me... it gives me the strength I need.

I burst into the kitchen, slamming my palm against the doorframe as I enter. I cry out and they turn to look at me, both heads swiveling at the same time.

Nora's eyes widen.

Victor smiles, slowly—showing off too many teeth. "There you are baby sister. We've been waiting for you."

He doesn't rise from his seat; he doesn't tense up or look surprised. He's perfectly relaxed and regards me with the cool detachment of a predator.

"We figured you had continued back through the labs," he continues, waving his hand nonchalantly. "I guess it doesn't matter. You found your way to us."

"Silvie," Nora pushes her chair back and rises slowly, her eyes locked with mine. Despite the way her voice shakes, her expression remains stoic. They're not puffy or bloodshot, or on the verge of tears. The corner of her turtleneck is ripped, and the entire front is stained with blood from earlier. Hers, mine. Her lip is swollen and crusted in red.

She eases away from the table, approaching me with outstretched arms until I fix my gaze on her. My stare stops her before my words. "You should know by now that we're past that."

She drops her arms. She sits back down, this time pulling her chair next to Victor, her eyes trained on me.

"Is that Nora's blood?" he asks, his eyes traveling from the stains on my collar to the ones on my skirt. He sounds almost proud.

"It's mine," I say, balling my hand into a fist. "Most of it, anyway."

He's not your family, I remind myself. *Don't feel hurt. Don't feel anything.*

"Nora and I did get into a fight earlier though," I tell him, struggling to keep my voice above a whisper, a whimper, the kind of sound a wounded animal would make. "I beat the shit out of her."

"You always were a handful," he chuckles. "It's crazy to think that you all come from the same source. The dead one is a murderous bitch—there's more Layla in her head than anyone else—and we both know what's wrong with you, Silvie."

"What's wrong with me, Victor?" I ball my fist tighter. *Don't feel hurt. Don't feel anything.*

"You're broken—you've always been broken." He cracks the knuckles on his left hand one at a time, pulling his fingers until they pop. He switches to his right hand, notices me staring and flashes me another smile. "Come on now, don't look at me like that."

"Like what?"

"Like you hate me," Victor says leaning back in his chair. "Nora's the same way, she gives me the same look. God, it was written all over her face when she opened the front door. 'Oh, it's *this* asshole'... but she's not any better than me, are you Nora?"

"No, she's not any better at all," Layla says, and I advance to where Victor sits, staying on the opposite side of the table, ignoring the cold sweat that's broken out across my forehead, the salt water that rises over my hips and pools along the divots in my skin.

He's not your family. Don't feel hurt. Don't feel anything.

The room tilts, and multi-colored spots cloud my vision. I shut my eyes and count to three. Images flash through the kaleidoscope in shades of red and blue. The click of a polaroid camera. Our mother's casket. Water drip, drip, dripping through the darkness.

False memories, all of them.

I open my eyes.

Victor stands, stretches, and walks across the room to the light switch. He flicks it on and off a few times and shakes his head, a small half smile playing on his lips. "I always thought it was damn stupid of them to keep paying the bills for this place after what happened, but I guess it worked out in your favor. Can you imagine how much worse all this would have been in the dark?"

I run my tongue along the rough backs of my teeth, letting the sour flavor drown out the taste of the name. The flavor of flies, of resurrection, of long, fitful sleeps.

Victor still won't step up to meet me and instead saunters over to his bag, undoing the clasp with a flick of his wrist. It opens to reveal an array of devious looking instruments. All steel and chrome, sharp and shining.

Nora stays seated with her back straight, her hands carefully clasped in front of her. Her face is empty. She's empty, nothing like the sunrise of a girl I used to call my best and only friend.

"It's only a small portion of my collection, but it should be enough to get the job done," Victor says with a smirk. "Worst case scenario we make our way back to the surgical theater and get what we need from there."

Water floods my lungs. I sputter against it. Saline twists through my wiring, bashing me into rocks, drowning me in the depths of the sea.

He reaches into his bag and pulls out a scalpel, its blade gleaming in the glow of the fluorescent bulbs. He points it at me, and phantom pain travels the length of my scar. It takes everything I have not to let the rush of the water take me.

"Let me talk to him," Layla pleads. *"Let me help you."*

Soon, we need to be strategic.

"I won't let you cut me open," I tell him, my voice still a hoarse whisper.

"Unfortunately, you don't really get a choice in this, Silvie. You're my creation, I *own* you."

His creation. This man who raised me, kept me, filled my head with false memories—with years of fabricated tenderness. Love. Protection.

No, there was no love.

I was a possession. A slide on his microscope. A caged animal serving a life sentence until its dissection.

"I'm not your creation, Victor. Mother's the one who made me, just like she made my sisters—the other girls in the Silvie series."

He scowls and flicks the scalpel, sending it into a vicious spiral. It scrapes against the table. "It's pathetic that you call that woman Mother."

Nora stays still as a porcelain doll, the rise and fall of her chest the only indication that she's still breathing.

"It was Mother, Silvie's right," she mutters, her lips barely moving, her eyes trained on the table. "You were the surgeon; she was the brains of the whole thing. You're good with a knife, that's all."

He smacks her upside the head with a quick flick of his wrist, and she flinches.

"You don't get to talk to me like that," he says through gritted teeth.

"Just do it, already," she begs, turning to look up at him. "Just cut her open so I don't have to keep worrying about what it will be like to see it."

"Shut up." He hits her again, this time across the face, and I flinch as if it's me. Phantom pain. Memories. Layla continues to tug at the tips of my fingers, begging for her chance to take over.

Not yet, I think as Victor locks eyes with me.

"Layla can't take all the credit," he says. "If it weren't for me, all of you would still be a twinkle in that bitch's eye."

"I'm not that happy with her either," I say, "but I understand her now. It's hard not to when we share a mind."

"Excuse me?" he asks.

"I told you earlier, most of this blood is mine. The rest belongs to my new roommate." I wipe blood from the corners of my mouth and Nora's eyes travel from the blood caked on my chin to the red streaks on my arms. Too much blood to be from our fight.

"What did you... oh no, Silvie." Her face drains of color.

"What the fuck is going on?" Victor demands.

"The heart..." Nora says, massaging her cheek where a bruise is already beginning to form. "She had the heart drive you gave me; she took the heart drive and she..."

"I ate it," I say, smiling, hoping that there are still bits of it stuck in my teeth, red and meaty. Hoping that my grin is pink. Hoping that it horrifies him.

"It's what you wanted isn't it?" I ask. "Pump my head full of other consciousnesses? It's what I was made for, isn't it?"

"No, Silvie," Layla tells me. *"That's not what he was trying to do at all. He was setting up a remote transfer. So that you could pull*

data without a blood share. I wasn't sure at first but now I'm certain. That's why you pulled data without a blood share when you first got here—something must have triggered the remote download. He was setting it up so that they could turn you into whatever they wanted, whenever they wanted with the flick of a switch."

My breath hitches. *Can he do that to me now?*

"I don't think so. He may claim otherwise, but from what I've seen, he hasn't perfected it. Not in the slightest. You may have been pulling data remotely, but it happened organically, he didn't control it."

Control. That's what this has been all about. But even with the power he had over me, even with the way he manipulated my abilities, he couldn't control me or them. I run my tongue along the blood crusted across my upper lip. No one can control me now.

Nora gags and a glob of phlegm hits the floorboards. She turns to Victor. "You can fix this though, right? You can still fix her! Or... or no, they'll see what you accomplished... this can still work, right?"

Victor shakes his head. "This isn't what I promised them."

"But we can still make it work, right?" she says, looking up at him. "There's a way to fix this."

He raises his hand again and she flinches. "Don't you dare say another word, this is your fault. You fucked this up, Nora."

"There has to be a way to fix it," she murmurs as his hand comes down again.

"There's nothing to fix," I say quietly. "Isn't this what you wanted, brother dearest? You changed me, you made me like this."

"I'm not your brother, Silvie."

"And I'm not Silvie," I tell him. "Not really, not anymore."

They look at me, my false family, they look at the red slathered up my arms and think of the heart, of Layla, but they don't see us. Meanwhile, I see everything.

Nora's mascara is smudged, her eyes puffy. Finally, she starts to cry.

I give her a half smile, but she doesn't know. There's no reason to cry for me. I am not Silvie. I am not my reflection, or the heart, or Layla, or anything that's come before.

Victor tilts Nora's chin so that she's looking up at him and examines her face as if he's searching for something. And although his face is turned three quarters away from me, in the split second before he grabs her hand, it's written all over his face. She's his new muse, his next victim. He's already thinking of the pills inside his bag, he's already measuring the days, months, years it will take to condition her—fix her the way he fixed me.

Only it won't work. She's not like me, so she won't take well to it. It will destroy her.

I stare at them, as if through a filter, an uncrossable veil, and for a moment I want to run to Nora, pull her away from him—but I know that she wouldn't believe me, and I know I might be wrong. And after everything, a selfish part of me wants her to finally understand. I run a finger along the gash in my palm. It's finally beginning to scab over.

Nora and I will forever be connected by the blood that gave us life, and a history that scarred us both in different ways. But for now, there's only me and my creator. There's only a future that I will build for myself.

Layla, I think. *It's time.*

20

She reaches out, and I let her. As her fingers wrap around my heart and dig into the meaty center of my being, I step away. I float.

My body falls to the floor, my forehead hitting the tile, as tingling spreads from the back of my skull through the highways of my veins, and she takes over.

I hover in the back of my head. Watching. Listening. It feels as if I'm underwater, while she picks my body up off the floor. She stands taller than I would, with her shoulders back and chin lifted and when she steps forward, there's power in her stride.

I don't mind looking on from a distance—feeling everything but saying nothing. Even though I know that for all its twisted beauty, there's something sick about our arrangement.

You'll be trading one cage for another. Isn't that what Layla told me when I first took Nix's hand and stepped into the wall? I think she's right. And I think that once all this is over, we'll need to work on finding a balance within our new dynamic.

"Silvie?" Victor asks.

"No," Layla says with my voice. "Silvie told you what she did, Victor. You should know who I am."

Nora's eyes widen. "Is that..."

Layla pulls the corners of my mouth up into a smile. "Why do you call yourself Nora, Sixteen? You never told me before."

Tears stream down Nora's cheeks. "Because I'm not Silvie, I'm not anywhere close to the original—you'd never let me forget that. I couldn't keep her name after everything that happened."

"I kept calling mine Silvie," Victor says picking the scalpel up off the table. "It seemed like too much of a hassle to rename her. Especially with the nature of the trials. I thought you'd be happy that I didn't discard her, that I'm keeping your little pet project alive."

Layla looks from where Nora sits at the table, to where Victor stands with the knife. Images filter and a sick sort of satisfaction washes over me as she confirms what I suspected.

"Ah," she says. "I finally understand why you've kept her around."

"What do you mean?" Nora asks, testing her fingers against the bruise on her cheek, now a mosaic of purple and blue.

"You can't properly run a trial—any experiment in fact—without a control group." She glances at Nora. "If there's a new medication on trial, for example, placebos are needed. One must remain the same so that the other's changes may be properly accounted for. Sixteen—Nora, I don't think that Victor has your best interests in mind."

He cracks his knuckles again and the sound grates on me. "I'm glad that Nora is willing to put the past behind us. I always did feel bad for her, always so alone, always so much more capable than her siblings."

He hooks his thumb beneath her chin and tilts her head again, his other hand still clasps the scalpel. "You'll soon have the sisters you deserve. A whole new crop of the Silvie series.

Once we get back to the Beta facility, I'm thinking we'll get the green light pretty quickly."

"But you said that I messed it up," Nora murmurs. "Silvie isn't what you promised them."

"They don't have to know about this. I have plenty of documentation from the trials, and based on those results, it would be safe to start with three more and work our way up from there. Of course, as director of the operation I can plan it out however I see fit."

"I'm the director," Layla says, our vision blurred by tears—angry, mourning. "And you ruined the Silvie series, destroyed my life's work, the most important thing in my—"

"Oh, please." He scoffs, releasing Nora's chin and advancing toward her—us, scalpel in hand. "You're nothing but a cheap imitation, a clone of her consciousness. And I refuse to be intimidated by a clone." He stops a few inches from us and slices the scalpel through the air, just a hair away from slitting our face in two. "You don't know shit about what's happened since the fire. Layla's last back up was what? Two weeks before it even happened?"

"I was backed up before she fled the building, and I know she survived the fire," Layla says, stepping back. "Dr. Mathis knew it was going to happen, or she wouldn't have created me. She wasn't going to allow herself to die."

He smiles again, and his teeth gleam from within the reflection of the scalpel. "Oh, Layla's still alive, sure. But she's about to be retired, so to speak. Once the board sees what I've managed to accomplish, they'll hand me the keys to the whole operation. You'll be impressed too once you see what I've managed to turn Silvie into."

What not who.

Layla clenches our fist.

"You should be proud of me." He tilts the scalpel, and it

catches light from the fluorescent bulbs. "I perfected your recipe; I made her better."

After the first time I died, I lay recovering from my surgery, delirious with fever. My stitches itched, my eyesight flickered like the flames of a candle, and while I lay writhing in my own sweat, Victor sat by my side and told me about our mother. I burned from the inside, the room rippling around me, and his voice was the only thing that cut through the haze.

Our mother was...

Kind, beautiful, generous.

Tears sprung into his eyes while he explained that all my memories of her were scooped out with the shredded fatty tissue, that to save my life the surgeons had to erase her. He told me that the fuzzy pictures I had left were all there was, that it wasn't my fault, but if I hadn't gotten so sick, I wouldn't have lost her. His voice trembled, and the tears fell hotly against my forehead.

How could I question the pain he felt?

How could I deny that my own stubborn body had unleashed this cruelty, and as a soul trapped in this shell it was my responsibility to tame it... to keep it from eating away at more of me.

"You don't want to lose me too, do you?" he asked. "You might think you remember horrible things about me, but they aren't true, it's the sickness. It's the sickness that followed you when you resurrected. It's going to try to take me away in any way that it can."

In the beginning there were memories of Victor that didn't make any sense. Him digging a scalpel along the back of my hand. He and I walking along the edge of a lake, his hand clamped around my shoulder like a vice. But they weren't real.

They were the result of my unnamed, incurable illness trying to steal him away.

My family, born through tragedy. My mother lost to the same mysterious illness that caused me to die again and again, and my brother was the only one I could trust to protect me, keep me well, to resurrect me.

It was all a carefully crafted lie. The memory of the lie itself isn't even real. Instead, it's a clever way to erase any data I had left. Not that he needed to. It was clear that I already trusted him, depended on him completely.

He killed me, then he killed me again. Just for the fun of it, not even to make sure that I was really dead.

Victor's eyes sparkle and I wish I could claw them from his skull and feel nothing. I wish I could look at him without my blood freezing—without feeling so small, and scared, and used.

"This isn't the way things were supposed to be, Victor," Layla says. "You weren't supposed to hurt her."

"Does the original Dr. Mathis know about what you've been doing?" she asks, fighting to keep me steady, calm. Static buzzes through our body—radio feedback, a high-pitched whirl through our machinery.

"Layla doesn't matter. She hasn't been the same since the fire. I think it's the link between her and the dead one. It's left her a little muddled."

Ask him if there's a way to cut the connection, I say.

"Is there a way to cut the connection?"

"Who cares? Makes things easier for me, for both of us. My work with Silvie has been acknowledged, and all we need to do is get her back to headquarters and I'll be crowned the new head of the organization. Layla lost the title the second the fire started."

"Of course," he continues, raising the scalpel again. "There's one thing left to take care of before Nora and I head on our way."

Water. Filling my belly, inflating it to the size of a balloon. Only the thinnest layer keeps me from bursting. Only the smallest murmur of sanity keeps me from diving deep into myself and drowning there.

Water. A tall, sweating glass twice a day. Pills in various shades housed in thin plastic bottles. Kept in our medicine cabinet, the mirror slicing me in half as I reached for them. Because my shaking hands told me I was ill. And the tar-colored blood, and wine-colored drippings let me know something was wrong.

The bitter taste.

The pills hitting my stomach like stones, like concrete blocks.

The pills dragging me down into that dark, deep nowhere in the back of my head.

Victor telling me that it's for my own good, that I need to behave and take them and not ask questions. *No questions, Silvie. No questions or you'll die again. You'll die, and you'll stay dead.*

I'm not myself. I'm so much more than the original could ever dream of being. So many voices. So many possibilities.

Layla shifts our body as Victor lunges with the scalpel. I reach up from the depths of our body and grab hold just as his shoulder slams into me.

Static.

Electricity.

Layla retreating back to the base of my skull as Victor knocks me down.

I hit the floor hard and lay on my back for a few moments, spots dancing in front of my eyes. I reach out and clamp my hand around his ankle. He spins around and kicks me once in the ribs, sharp pain traveling up my side. My fingers fall away from his leg, and he crouches next to me, the scalpel poised above my chest.

“Victor,” I say, my voice shaking.

“So you’re my Silvie again, huh?” he asks, but I shake my head.

“Not yours.”

“We’ll see.” He reaches out with his free hand and pins my hands above my head. His fingers squeeze into my flesh, and I wince. “I know you think you’ve done something smart by downloading the information on that drive, but you’ve really just made things more difficult for yourself. Originally, this would have been a quick operation, minimally invasive. Check to see if everything’s the way it should be, and we’d be on our way—that sort of thing. But now…”

I flail my legs, kick them out in every direction, but all they do is slide against the floor.

“Now, I’m going have to take my time, really dig through everything and see if there’s a way to sever your connection with Layla’s backup drive, or at least make it so that it isn’t glaringly obvious to the board. It could take hours. And you know what the real bitch of it is? I don’t think there’s any anesthetic down here.”

My heart thunders inside my chest, each beat sending a fresh twinge of pain through my body.

“And honestly, this is a real bitch for me too. It’s going to eat up a lot of time that I don’t have. I need to get you to the Beta facility and claim my rightful place as director. The experiment has been stalled since the fire, and we can’t have that, can we? We need to continue.”

He leans in close, his breath hot against my cheek. “It’s going to be so much fun to compare your insides with Nora’s.”

My eyes widen. He plans to dissect her too, and while it would serve her right, while every bone inside my body aches for vengeance, I know that it wouldn’t be right. It won’t help me make it out of this situation for her to suffer too.

I shouldn't have to break someone else in order to make myself whole.

"What about the deal you had with her?" I choke, fighting to make my voice loud enough that she can hear. "She's supposed to work alongside you at the Beta facility."

"That's the thing, sweetheart," he leans in so that his face is inches from mine, his sour breath sending a shudder through me. "If you're going to work with me, you need to be willing to actually do the work. And I don't think she has what it takes."

He pushes the tip of the blade into the top of my scar and a tiny bead of red blooms over my collar. I grimace against the pain.

I twist my face to the side so that my cheek presses into the cool tile floor.

Nora's finally left her seat and stands to the right of where I lay, her hand resting on the table.

"Nora." Tears cloud my vision and I close my eyes. "He never planned on letting you work with him; he's going to take you apart the same as me!"

She stares down at me, her head tilted to the side as Victor continues to glide the scalpel across my skin. Hurt sears through my chest. Layla absorbs some of it, but that doesn't dull the wet soak of blood through my blouse, or the way my arms ache beneath his grasp. It doesn't block out how close Victor's body is to mine—how his sour breath invades my nostrils, and I almost wish I could die again just to get away from him.

"Please, Nora. We're sisters. Closer than sisters."

A fresh set of tears trace lines of mascara down her face and she picks Victor's bag up off the table. A hollow ache rings out in my chest. She's choosing him, she's going to help him cut me open while I'm still alive.

She steps up next to where he has me pinned and sinks down to her knees beside us. She dips her head down next to mine and I glare at her, but then she whispers, "Your blood is in my veins, and my blood is in yours. I shouldn't have let him hurt you."

Then she rises, pulling a bone saw from the bag and digging it into Victor's shoulder.

He howls releasing his grip on my wrists as she yanks the saw back and pulls him off me by the hair. The scalpel hits the tile, the noise sharp as the blade. She slashes into him again and again. The bone saw doesn't cut deep, but it does enough damage to keep him from rising to his feet.

"Damn it!" Victor screams, hunched over on his knees. He grabs at his shoulder, his chest, all the places where Nora hit him, blood pouring through his fingers.

"Are you okay, Silvie?" Nora asks, and offers down her hand, but I swat it away and stand on my own, hand pressed against my scar. It's torn open, and red weeps through my fingers, but I'm alive. I'm still alive.

Victor looks up at me from his place on the floor, his eyes wide.

"You've come such a long way," he says, a mix of pride and awe ringing through his voice. The way he looks at me, the way his eyes crinkle around the edges, is almost like before. He almost looks like my brother again. "You really are the next step in their evolution."

I turn to Nora. She still grips the bone saw tightly in her fist.

She stomps over to Victor, fire in her eyes. "Stay away from her. If you so much as look at her the wrong way, I swear I'll end you."

He sits hunched over, bleeding, and his eyes focus on his scalpel, but I kick it across the floor.

"Don't try anything." I take a step forward, but Nora's arm shoots out and she pushes me back.

"He's dangerous," she warns.

"You think I haven't figured that out by now?"

Water. Velvety darkness swells beneath my skin. The cold invites me, numbs me, calls for me to sink into it. I let the numbness enter my veins, my marrow, the swirl of my fingerprints. I let it guard me from a pain too harsh, too sudden to breathe through.

My ribs still ache from where Victor kicked me. Even with Layla numbing the pain of his incision, it still burns, and it's almost too much to take.

Victor rises slowly, and a sick grin stretches across his face. His eyes glisten as he faces Nora. "You need to figure out where your loyalties lie, you stupid girl. You can't play both sides, it won't end well for you."

Nora drops the saw, grabs his bag, and swings it full force. It hits Victor squarely in the side of the jaw. He stumbles back into the wall, and spits out a glob of saliva, tinted pink. He wipes the back of his hand along his mouth.

"You're going to regret that," he growls.

"Like I'd give you a chance to make me." She crouches low, grabbing his scalpel before charging at him. She stabs it deep into his side, and even though he bats her away easily enough, ripping the blade out, there's a lot of blood. He's covered in cuts and clearly disoriented.

"You may be good with a knife, but so am I," Nora says, and he shoots her a look that I can't quite read. "Or have you forgotten?"

There's something in the way they stare each other down that chills me to my core. Blood continues to squirt from Victor's wound, and his face goes white as a sheet. Then his eyes roll up into his head and he falls face first into the tile. A loud crack, and he lays splayed out, silent.

Nora walks up next to me, breathing heavily. "I'm sorry, Sil. We should have done this from the beginning."

"Done what?"

"Kill him." She drops the bag and scalpel to the floor and

kicks them across the tile. They clatter into the bone saw.

"If you hate him enough to kill him, then why were you going along with it? Why were you letting him control you like that?"

She lets out a bitter laugh. "That's rich coming from you. You let him control you for years and now you're nothing more than a glorified meat puppet for the psychopath who made us."

"That's different," I say, even though I'm not sure if I believe it. "Layla is what I need right now, and if there comes a time when I don't need her anymore, I'll find a way to sever the connection."

"There is no way to sever us. We are the same."

A wave of cold washes over me. Another shiver. A high-pitched whine rings out inside my head as Layla attempts to help me find comfort in our connection.

"None of this is malicious, Silvie. You can't let her put thoughts in your head. You know by now that I would never do anything to intentionally harm you."

Intentionally...it's a word like a bullet wound.

"Nora," I say over the static buzz of Layla's voice. "I can almost understand why you want to be seen, and understood, but I can't understand why you would want this to continue."

Her scar peaks out from the rip in her turtleneck and she presses her scabbed palm to it. "You don't? You don't want more people *exactly* like you? People who can understand what you're thinking and feeling, without ever needing to explain? You don't want a connection that runs deeper than blood?"

"I have a connection that runs deeper than blood," I say, Layla humming beneath my skin. "And that's what I'm trying to say. It doesn't change things. It's not going to be enough for you... it's never going to be enough for you."

She looks down at where Victor lays and shakes her head. "He's going punish me when he wakes up, but I've wanted to do that for a long time."

"When he wakes up? But I thought..." I inch back across the tile floor, but she reaches out and grabs my wrist.

Her eyes lock with mine. "I thought so too, for a second. But he's still breathing, and after thinking about it for a little bit longer, I came up with a wonderful idea. It's been really hard for me, I keep going back and forth, but I think I've made up my mind now. Maybe you don't get how lonely it is because you've been separated from the collective for so long," she continues. "But our connection is unlike anything. And without it—without our sisters—it's unbearable."

"You *killed* our other sister! And you said it yourself, there were only three of us left. The rest are dead."

Nora scoffs. "Fifteen was fucked up in the head, and after what she did to this place there's no way Victor would have been allowed to help us evolve. We had to get rid of her, and he had to take you so he could keep trying to perfect us... and I had to keep the heart safe until the time was right. We were supposed to leave as a group, but I guess it worked out in the end, huh?" Her grip tightens and her eyes shine feverishly. "There are going to be more of us, Silvie. Victor's made sure of it. We'll never be alone again."

I jerk out of her grasp and back up.

"The way I saw it, I had three options. One, we kill him together and run away. Two, I go along with his plan and hope that he keeps his word about letting me live. Three, I do it myself. I brought you here to get away from him, Silvie. To do it on my own. I already had the jarred heart, I had you, all I needed was the information that Fifteen had about the Beta facility. Then I wouldn't need him anymore. Once he perfected you, that's when I knew I had to act. I had to find a way to get us back to the Beta without him. If I could show them how much better you are, if I could offer up the dead one for comparison. It's that first night when things got complicated."

She takes a deep breath before continuing. "I shouldn't have picked up the phone when he called, but I was afraid. And the more time I spent with you here, the more I realized that I couldn't handle you on my own. I needed him. So, I made a decision and crossed my fingers hoping that it was a decision that would allow me to survive. Except, as you just said, he plans on cutting me open too. So, what are my options now?"

I shake my head. "You still don't know what you want."

"I want you, I've always wanted you—or someone like you, anyway. Silvie, please. I tried to find another way. That's why I took you here in the first place. So you could remember, so you could get away from Victor. And in the back of my mind, I always hoped that with the enhancements Victor made to you, we'd be able to work there. They wouldn't experiment on us anymore. We'd be the ones doing the experimenting. Imagine that, Silvie! Working alongside the people who created us, help them make us more sisters, each one more spectacular than the last! Imagine an entire network of people who understand you—really, truly understand. You'll never be alone again!"

My eyes stay on Victor the entire time she's ranting, waving her hands and talking herself in circles trying to justify everything that she's done. But the water beneath my skin is calm, I am calm as I watch my false brother.

It starts with his fingers, a cautious twitch.

Then his left leg.

And as her voice climbs in volume, he rises off the floor and wipes the blood from his chin.

"Shouldn't you warn her?" Layla asks.

I'm not loyal to either of them, I'm loyal to myself.

Victor limps over to her, his shadow consuming hers, until both are twisted and dark across the tile floor. Still, she doesn't notice, and I catch his eye just before he brings his fists down against her head.

21

I pick at the scabs on my arms while he drags Nora along the tiles.

"What are planning to do?" Layla asks.

See for yourself.

She scrolls through the images as the riptide swirls beneath my skin. Chlorine. Sodium. A quiet hum of brackish water.

"You shouldn't have done that, Silvie," Victor says, pulling Nora off to the side of the room. He drops her against the doorframe, her head hitting the edge of it with a hollow thud. "You shouldn't have provoked her like that."

"She still doesn't know what she wants," I say, eyes cast down.

"Are you sure about this, Silvie?" Layla asks once she's finished soaking in the images.

Trust me.

"I don't think she ever will, not that it matters." Victor reaches into the back pocket of his pants and withdraws a syringe and a small vial of purple liquid. After filling up the needle, he taps the side, then digs it into Nora's neck.

I massage my fingers into my ribs and wait for the pain to

fade, but it stays like a stain. The wound on my chest keeps bleeding. "What are you going to do with her?"

He stabs the needle back into the vial and fills it up again before turning to me.

"I wouldn't be concerned about her if I were in your position, I'd be more worried about yourself."

"This is where you should let me take over again, Silvie. This will be too painful for you."

No, I need to do this.

He advances, forcing me into the corner of the room until my back's pressed up against the wall.

"Now," he says. "Are you going to be a good girl and take your medicine?" He lunges at me, the needle poised to pierce my skin, but I dodge out of the way, and he grabs me by the collar. The needle moves through the air, and my windpipe closes. I choke.

He pulls me close and holds me in place against his chest.

I squirm against him, kicking, doing my best to scratch at his arms, but I'm too small and he's too strong.

"You need to hold still, or the injection won't go in properly." He grabs my chin and roughly turns my face to the side, exposing the vein on my neck. "I know that you hate needles, but this would be a lot less painful if you'd cooperate."

"Silvie!" Layla calls from the back of my mind and I agree.

My body spasms, and Victor releases me as I fall to the floor. The back of my head hits the tile. My face is craned toward the ceiling. Only this time, Layla doesn't take over, only sends my body into a shock temporarily so that Victor will back off.

I peel myself up off the floor and pry the needle from his hand—ripping one of his plastic gloves. He sheds it like a snakeskin and his fingers, calloused and rough, wrap around mine.

I bite the fleshy webbing between his fingers, and he releases his grip as I stick the needle into his neck.

He falls back and claws at his jugular. I watch him writhe, until his body goes still—and even though his chest continues to rise and fall, I'm confident that he won't be getting up again. I drag Nora out of the kitchen and into the hall as Layla continues to chew away at the pain that runs the length of my scar.

"You're losing a lot of blood, Silvie," she warns.

The Silvie series heals quickly, I'll be fine. I'm more focused on what I need to do next, what I told Layla I would do no matter what. I'm too caught up in my thoughts about the fire, about the tally marks carved into my wall back home.

All the years spent in quiet desperation.

"Are you sure that you want to do this, Silvie?"

I nod, my guts in knots. Down in the depths of my body, Layla reaches out. A hand on my heart. An arm around my core. She fights back the riptide as it rolls over my ankles, wrestles with it so I don't have to. There's no getting rid of it, there's no expelling the anxiety that tries to drown me, but there's coping. There's sharing the burden. I don't need to fight it alone. She shows me how to handle what comes next. She shows me accelerant and matches and reminds me of what waits for us back down the hall.

Once this is over, will we ever be able to resurrect my sister? I ask.

"I know your anatomy, Silvie. I gave you life. If she can be fixed, I will find a way to fix her. I promise." Images wash over me in a wave. Layla walking hand in hand with Lily. The three of us lined up in front of the house. Layla standing in front of a mirror, tears in her eyes.

You really do care about us.

"I do. And no matter what happens after this, I'll help you any way I can. We'll be okay."

You're not Layla, not really, I remind her.

"And you're not Silvie."

I nod and take a step forward. For the first time, my life is mine. For the first time, my decisions are my own. And if I should fail, it will be my fault and no one else's. The fear of the unknown, the riptide boils, down layers deep. But it's my journey, and I'll take it no matter what happens.

"You'll be okay."

"I'll try," I whisper, throwing open the kitchen cabinets, searching for what Layla keeps whispering to me about...a book of matches and the accelerant.

"Silvie, wait." I flinch at the sound of the voice and turn to find Victor standing in the center of the kitchen, his hand held to his neck.

The sick curl of his lips. His gloved hand. Nausea rushes over me and I freeze in place.

He advances toward me and my heart screams inside my chest.

"How?" I ask, the blood draining from my face.

"You didn't inject the needle, you just stabbed me in the fucking neck."

"But you were unconscious..."

"I was just pretending, you stupid girl."

My skin burns. My hand balls into a fist and tears tug at the corners of my eyes. It's worse than Nora trying to sell me to scientists. It's like she's killed me. It's like she's left me to bleed out on the side of the road.

"Don't give me that look, Silvie," Victor says and reaches out his hand. "I know I said some awful things before, but I'll make it up to you. We don't have to make this difficult, we can make this as painless as possible."

I shake my head. "I'm not letting you hurt me anymore."

"Hurt you? I have done *everything* for you." He advances,

and I back up so that I stand on the threshold between the kitchen and the hall.

"You *tortured* me," I scream, and Layla's presence is the only thing that keeps me from losing my footing and bashing open my skull.

"I *fixed* you," he spits.

"I was never broken." With that, I splash him with the accelerant, coating him in the fluid, and he screeches as it hits his wounds. His greasy hair falls wildly across his forehead, and he flails, reaching for me. He's in so much pain, it's beautiful to see.

I understand what the heart meant, back before we linked together. I understand why it was so desperate. I'm desperate now too. Now that we share a connection deeper than anything that's come before us. Deeper than any of us ever shared with the original.

I am the beginning and the end.

Nix waits for me on the other side of the labs, hidden away in our secret room. She waits with Lily, and inside Lily is the location of the Beta facility and the people who hurt us. I smile, a slow festering grin. I'll burn it down. I'll burn them all.

I pull a match from the matchbook, strike it, toss it. It catches Victor by the shoulder first, a delicate, glowing light. Then it crackles, chews, tears into him and he screams. Victor screams my name over the howl of red, and yellow, and orange. I'll put him out once I'm sure he's gone so that the fire won't spread, but there's so much pleasure in watching him burn.

Black smoke curls up from the heat and pop, crackle, hiss. So much noise, so much screaming. I watch him shrivel in on himself, I watch him cocoon and crumble.

This is the end. Of being afraid, of feeling helpless, of him getting to decide how I'm going to live my life.

This is the beginning. Of my revenge, my reckoning.

I watch until there is no Victor anymore and then I snuff

out the flames. All that's left of him is a smear of ash, and a pile of blackened bones across the tile.

It's more than he deserved.

I exit the kitchen to where Nora should lay on the ground. But she's not there. A trail of blood splatter tells me that she's left down the hall. I don't even consider going after her.

Even as I step into the bowels of the building, even as I return to our room and Nix reaches out and grabs my hand, cradles me to her chest as I cry—I wonder if Nora will ever break free from the experiment that gave us life. I wonder if I'll ever stop caring about her.

For now, I have Nix. I have my sisters.

And we have work to do.

EPILOGUE

Four weeks pass, and the basement labs finally start to feel like home. I'm not sure where Nora went after my final moments with Victor. Nix says that she saw her limping off into the surgical theater. And after that, she was gone.

Nix and I spend our days working on Lily, our nights drinking tea and feeling alive—really alive—for the first time.

The Victorian lives on above us. It smolders and peels and weeps the way it did before—but in the basement labs we are home.

I wait for Nora to return, for her to bring the people from the Beta facility to storm the place looking for us, but she doesn't—they don't. Within the labs we're safe, even if it's only temporary. I know I'll have to leave here eventually, make sure that they don't continue with the Silvie series, make sure that they pay for what they've done. At night, I lie awake and fantasize about all the ways that I'll destroy them—flames licking the inside of my skull until Layla begs me to make it stop.

But there is no stopping it, there is no stopping me.

Nix and I stand together in one of the smaller examination rooms, pale gray walls and shelves lined with jarred organs.

Unused backup drives, and a catalogue of livers and lungs, their purposes unknown.

Layla insists that the only thing she developed were the drives. There were other projects, other scientists heading different teams, but she neglected them in favor of the Silvie series, and from what she shows me, I can only assume that to be true.

The rooms where the first fire originated are sealed off, by whom she doesn't know. They were boarded up long before Nora and I appeared in the front yard. Sometimes at night, Nix and I swear we hear footsteps coming from below, not above, but Layla promises there's nothing beneath us—and from what I can see from her recollection of the past—there shouldn't be. Unless, of course, she's lying.

Lily lays propped up on the white linen of a hospital bed, the mattress and bedding taken from one of the other basement rooms.

"What should we try this time?" Nix asks, her voice tired. Sometimes we'll get Lily's eyelashes to flutter or her limbs to flail, but we haven't gotten any closer to her regaining consciousness.

Layla insists that it's possible, but nothing we try works; no dose of medicine or intravenous fluid can wake her up.

"What if we tried a higher flow of electric current?" I ask, smoothing back Lily's hair. There are two thin panels attached to her chest directly above her scar.

"Depends on if we can figure out the proper voltage," Nix says.

I tilt my head to the side and listen. "Layla says six hundred volts."

Nix nods.

We shock Lily. One. Two. Three tries. Her fingers twitch but then she goes still again.

I retreat into my head and Layla surfaces. She flexes my

fingers; the way she always does every time we switch. When she controls our body, I'm still present, I float, watch, listen, feel. We've gotten much better at the transition, but it's an art form that we're still working to perfect.

The same way we're working to wake Lily up.

"Layla?" Nix asks.

She nods my head. "I want to try one more thing, and it's not that I don't trust Silvie, I just have more experience with these sorts of things."

You have steadier hands, I tell her.

She chuckles.

"Layla?" Nix asks.

"Silvie says I have steadier hands than she does... even though we share the same body."

You have better control over them.

"I suppose that's true," she whispers, knowing that control is a sore subject between us, and she should be thankful I allow her to surface at all.

"Your demeanor is different than hers though," Nix observes. "You always seem so much taller when you take over."

"She is a short little thing, isn't she?" Layla teases as she sticks more electric panels to the side of Lily's neck.

Guess that makes you short now too. I kick out inside our body and Layla laughs again. No matter how many times I warn her that this arrangement isn't permanent, that the only thing making me okay with any of this is how she's helping me revive my sister—she still tries to make me like her. She still jokes around, attempts to be friends.

But we both know that I'm only keeping her around for one purpose.

She sends another jolt of electricity through Lily and her body convulses then falls silent.

Nix paces back and forth.

"Give it time," Layla says.

"We have been giving it time."

We wait but Lily doesn't move, and Nix lets out a sigh. "We will try again tomorrow. We will find a way eventually."

Layla sinks back into my head, and I surface. I run a finger across Lily's scar. A jolt of electric current jumps between us and I pull my hand away. A circular burn mark the size of a marble smooths the swirl of my fingerprint away. Pink and waxy. Another scar for my collection.

I stare at it dumbfounded until Lily reaches out and her fingers clamp around my wrist.

"What..." I lean in and from within her chest comes the familiar sound. The soft thump, thump, thump of a heartbeat sung in groups of three.

"Nix... Layla..." I murmur.

Lily releases my wrist and stirs, her eyebrows furrowing. She grabs at the white sheets, pulling at the corners of the bedding as her eyes flicker open.

"Seventeen," she says, her gray eyes locking with mine.

She's alive.

ACKNOWLEDGMENTS

This book wouldn't exist without the support of countless humans over the course of many years.

Infinite thanks to my editor, Finch, for helping shape *Whispers* into what it is today. Your enthusiasm, attention to detail, and genuine love for this story mean more than I could ever express.

Megan Barnard, thanks for your endless support. Whether it's venting over Zoom, or celebrating publishing wins (big and small), I'm lucky to have you in my corner.

Karra Barron, I'm so grateful for our friendship. Thank you for all the bookish adventures, wagyu beef dinners, and hours spent spilling the publishing tea.

Sarah Graziano, you've been here for this story (and me) since the first, truly terrible version. Thank you for always hyping me up, and putting my characters on a t-shirt!

Melissa Guida-Richards, you're not only a stellar critique partner, but a wonderful friend who isn't afraid to call me out when I'm being ridiculous. I appreciate it more than you know.

Special shoutout to my husband, Will, for never giving up on me—and more importantly, not letting me give up on myself. I love you, I love you, I love you.

Thanks to my parents for always believing in me. You're the reason I write.

Thanks to everyone who's read and given feedback on this book over the years, even if we don't speak anymore. I'll never forget what you've done for this story.

And finally, thanks to all my family, friends, teachers, and critique groups old and new—anyone who's ever told me that I could. I finally did. And I couldn't have done it without you.

ABOUT THE AUTHOR

Danielle Renino writes horror and speculative fiction. When she's not writing she can be found exploring abandoned buildings, eating her way around Boston, or checking for monsters under her bed. Find her online at daniellerenino.com or @daniellerenino on Instagram, TikTok, and Twitter.

CPSIA information can be obtained
at www.ICGtesting.com
Printed in the USA
LVHW110716221122
733623LV00005B/762